AN OFFER OF MARRIAGE

Sarah stretched her toes nearer to the small fire and clutched her wineglass harder. "Will you stop lecturing if I admit I was feeling a trifle of panic before I heard Roland's call?"

Relaxing, Sherringham chuckled. "You are a delight, Sarah. Marry me."

Sarah instantly stilled. She had forgotten her fear that he would ask her to wed him, that his gentlemanly instincts would demand she do so to save her reputation. She sighed. "You do me great honor, my lord—"

"Bosh. I won't listen to that nonsense. Sarah, I want—"

"You want to save my reputation and would sacrifice yourself. I don't need anyone's sacrifice, my lord."

"That too is nonsense," he said . . . but he was talking to her back as she walked, her steps a quick tattoo against the wooden floorboards, toward the door.

"Oh yes," she muttered as she continued across the room, "you are the perfect gentleman, are you not? But I wouldn't wed at my father's behest and I will not wed for such a reason as this, either!"

Books by Jeanne Savery

The Widow and the Rake
A Reformed Rake
A Christmas Treasure
A Lady's Deception
Cupid's Challenge
Lady Stephanie
A Timeless Love
A Lady's Lesson
Lord Galveston and the Ghost
A Lady's Proposal
The Widowed Miss Mordaunt
A Love for Lydia
Taming Lord Renwick
Lady Serena's Surrender
The Christmas Gift
The Perfect Husband
A Perfect Match
Smuggler's Heart
Miss Seldon's Suitors
An Independent Lady
The Family Matchmaker
The Reluctant Rake
An Acceptable Arrangement
My Lady Housekeeper

Published by Zebra Books

MY LADY HOUSEKEEPER

Jeanne Savery

ZEBRA BOOKS
KENSINGTON PUBLISHING CORP.
http://www.kensingtonbooks.com

With many thanks to

Richard Tyacke, MFH
Atherstone Hunt
Warwickshire and Leicestershire

who gave generously of time and knowledge
concerning a world of which I knew little.

Prologue

"*It is not possible.*"

The late Lord Staunton's solicitor's brows arched up his dome-like forehead. At the same time he stared down his long narrow nose. "Not possible?"

Lady Sarah literally shook with temper but her voice was low and controlled, each word distinct, precise. "He cannot command me from the grave."

A thin smile tipped the corners of the solicitor's lips. "I think, Lady Sarah, you will find he *can*. For one year you have the use of this house and your bills will be paid. In that year you will choose yourself a husband. If you do not, then, *until you do,* you will have no more than your current pin money on which to support yourself." The solicitor continued his lecture in irritatingly patronizing tones. "That, you understand, includes finding a roof over your head and any servants you wish to hire. You will discover that five hundred pounds, although a generous allowance, is not a great deal when you must buy food for yourself and your servants and all else that is needed for daily survival. You would be wise to oblige his lordship in this. Finding a suitable husband will be far more difficult once your period of grace has ended."

"You repeat yourself." With effort Sarah brought herself under control. "What I do not understand is how he can forbid me the use of my fortune. He is dead."

The solicitor nodded, candlelight gleaming from his bald pate. "Exactly, my lady. We are reading his will."

"Mr. McAfferty, it is unlikely I am unaware of *that*." Sarah felt the debilitating rage rising again and again fought it down. This was important. Unfortunately she only partially succeeded and her voice was icy as she continued. "What I wish explained is how he can forbid me the use of *what is my own*."

"But, my lady, it is not."

"It was left to me by my grandmother. It is mine."

"No, no." The solicitor, who had frowned, now beamed, enlightened, it seemed. "Your father could not allow *that*. He saw that the money was left in trust for you. The trust continues. It will be turned over, as is proper, to the man you marry."

Sarah gritted her teeth. The sound was loud in the silence. She forced her breathing to slow, ordered her pulses to still their erratic pounding, and her mind to clear. "Mr. McAfferty, you *know* I am capable of dealing with my own affairs."

He nodded. His bland expression gave away nothing of his thoughts. That he was forced to agree did not imply he *approved*. It was unheard of that a lady, even the eccentric daughter of the late Lord Staunton, could manage her own affairs as well as any man—and, if he were to be completely honest about this particular lady, better than some.

Lady Sarah's ice-coated tones intruded on his thoughts. "Am I to understand," she said, "that you are now *my* solicitor?"

His gaze sharpened and his nod was less firm. Another thing he knew was that her ladyship was capable of finding herself a new solicitor if she did not approve her current man. If she were to do so—the loss to his income was not to be thought on.

"Then—" She pointed a finger directly at him. "—as your first duty in *my* employ, *assuming you wish to remain in my employ—*"

Yes. Just as Mr. McAfferty feared.

"—I order you to discover a means of—" Lady Sarah's voice rose. "—*setting aside this abomination of a will.*" As long as she was making demands, another came to mind. "*I would also,*" she added, "*be done with the indignity of a trust.*"

"My lady—impossible!" Color spotted the man's high cheekbones.

"Mr. McAfferty—" Lady Sarah's voice took on a dangerously silky note. "—do not tell me the will is unbreakable. Any will may be broken if one is determined."

Lady Sarah rose to her feet and stalked from the room. Her heavy silk skirts trailed behind, emulating a black cloud swept along by the wind, roiling and trembling and heavy with imminent storm.

Chapter 1

Sarah recalled that day fifteen months earlier when she had ordered Mr. McAfferty to discover a means of breaking her father's will. He had not done so.

Yet.

Nor had he set aside the trust, but she'd no real expectation he'd manage that. He did not approve, of course. Sarah tipped her head, frowning. *Does that mean he'll not do his best? Should I hire a new solicitor? One who has no loyalties to a man who has been under ground for well over a year?*

Sarah recalled the last occasion she had reason to speak with Mr. McAfferty. He had explained, in detail, all he'd done to date and appeared sincerely distressed when admitting his efforts had not answered. That they had *not* meant she'd no means of supporting herself in a manner to which she was accustomed by birth and indulgence.

Lady Sarah sent a disparaging glance around the sitting room of the housekeeper's quarters in what was, before his death, her father's Leicestershire hunting box. She had thought to find some comfort and security when she'd hidden herself away in the lodge—but it appeared that was a chimera, mere wishful thinking . . .

The past is done, she told herself. *Put it behind you.*

Again Sarah glanced around. The rooms looked much as they had when she had last seen them. A bit dingier perhaps than when she had spent hours before this very hearth. When only a child she'd often occupied herself sorting buttons, winding threads, doing all those things that returned a well-tumbled sewing box to order.

"Where, do you suppose, has Mrs. Gladden's sewing box gone?" she asked nobody in particular.

Mrs. Lamb, the hunting box's current housekeeper and cook, cleared her throat. "I have it, my lady."

Sarah turned on her heel. "You, Mrs. Lamb?"

The woman nodded. "Mr. Gladden gave it to me."

"*Mister* Gladden?" Sarah cast an impish look toward the plump woman, a teasing look that suggested there had been something between the old man and the new housekeeper.

Mrs. Lamb's eyes rolled in exasperation—exasperation revealed as well in the way she rolled her hands in her apron. "My lady, do we have time for such twaddle?"

Sarah smiled. The twisted self-deriding smile was not one of her better efforts. "I am behaving badly, am I not?"

"*Very.*"

Sarah chuckled.

Mrs. Lamb could see no humor in the situation. She lifted her wrapped hands, dropped them, and appeared very near to tears. "Oh, why is his lordship coming so early in the year? It is barely September!" Her voice took on something very near a wail. "Why could he not wait for November when the regular hunt starts?"

"You forget enthusiasts enjoy the cubbing. They come for the pairing, youngster to old hound. They watch the young hounds learn road discipline, study them as they learn their trade in the coverts," said Sarah. Feeling a pang of regret that, this year, she dared not join in, she bit her lip before continuing her inspection of the tiny apartment.

Sarah put all thought of foxes, fox hounds, and hunting from her mind. Foxhunters were her immediate problem. "My only thought," she said pointing a long slender finger toward the door to the hall, "is that I should like a bolt attached to the inside—"

The housekeeper opened her mouth.

"—and why, you would ask?"

Mrs. Lamb closed her mouth.

"I'll not have some carousing beast stagger this way, thinking to demand something of the *housekeeper*." Lady Sarah's mouth set at a wry angle. She crossed her arms and tapped her foot. "All I need," she added, "is for a man to barge in upon my privacy when I am not prepared for him." She picked up the gray wig that, earlier, she had dropped into a chair and glared at it.

Mrs. Lamb, the lodge's real caretaker, wore an expression of deep concern. "My lady, you should go away."

"I've explained that I've nowhere to go." Sarah turned a look of reproach on the woman she had come to like and respect. Mrs. Lamb was a softhearted woman for whom Sarah had developed a very real affection. "Perhaps you'd have me hire a room in Bath or in Wells where I might encourage the shabby genteel to call for tea? Actually *admit* that I have become shabby-genteel myself?" Her expression chilled. "I think not."

It was *exactly* the sort of thing, Mrs. Lamb thought. *Since Lady Sarah refuses to find a man she can bear to marry, she should take rooms somewhere. Her ladyship must add a hired companion to such a ménage, of course.* Mrs. Lamb did not speak her thoughts aloud. It was useless to continue an argument she knew she'd lose. *Except I must,* she thought. *I must try once more to make Lady Sarah see sense.*

"My lady, you have not thought." Mrs. Lamb's voice lowered. "All those men!" she finished in hushed tones.

"Yes. Men. Playing the games men play . . ." Sarah frowned at a sudden thought. "Mrs. Lamb, you will send the maids home today as soon as they finish their work. Hire extra footmen. When the huntsmen go out for the morning training runs, the maids may return and do those things the footmen will not do."

Sarah sighed softly, envying the men the opportunity to ride with the wind, to fly over hedges, take gates with hearts soaring . . . but it was no use repining. Even when her father lived he'd allowed her to ride Swallow in the hunt only on those rare occasions when he'd felt especially mellow.

"I wish I'd thought of that." Mrs. Lamb interrupted Lady Sarah's thoughts, the *housekeeper's* mind occupied by maids rather than mares. "In the past, when men came for the hunt, I tried to keep an eye on the girls, but it is difficult. This will solve that particular problem nicely." Mrs. Lamb heard the dull thud of footsteps coming along the drugget-covered hall and opened the door.

"Have you it all?" she asked the young footman who entered first.

"We cleaned out her ladyship's room, Mrs. Lamb." He looked around and, rather diffidently, added, "Do you think there is space here for everything?"

"I did not realize I'd so much," said Lady Sarah, embarrassed by the trio of men carrying most of her possessions. Two maids, clutching her more intimate garments to their bosoms, followed the men. She plucked at the skirts of gowns hanging over one footman's arm. "Mrs. Lamb, I cannot wear these sprigged muslins or the habits or even the walking-out gowns while the house party remains in residence. We will pack those away in trunks. What remains . . . ?"

Sarah spent the remainder of the morning sorting, retaining only those few gowns, the last of her mourning gowns, which she thought might be found in a housekeeper's rooms.

Someone with a good eye might wonder at the quality, but, she decided, *housekeepers tend to be invisible. It is unlikely anyone will notice.*

The packed trunks were carried up to the attics before Sarah tried on her disguise. She was standing before a mirror tying a cap over the gray wig Mrs. Lamb had unearthed from among things kept for charades and amateur theatricals, when suddenly the housekeeper bustled through the door with barely a pause for a single knock.

"The Earl of Sherringham has just this minute pulled up to the front door," she said, panting every so slightly, her hand held to her heart as if to hold it within her chest.

"Botheration." Sarah turned, her hands tangled in the cap's ribbons. "We are not ready."

"He wasn't supposed to arrive until tomorrow." The housekeeper very nearly wailed her words. "Drat the man. Is it not just like the creature that he says one thing and does another and then expects all to go on as if he had not thrown one's planning to the four winds?"

"Men have no conception of how dreadfully upsetting it is to our schedules when they arrive beforetime."

"There is worse," added Mrs. Lamb. She lowered her voice, a touch of horror coloring it. "You *must* go, my lady. He has brought a . . . a doxy."

Sarah felt her cheeks warm and fought down embarrassment. "Surely he is not the first to do so since you became housekeeper here."

"It is the first time *Sherringham* has done so. Not that he has been here for years and years, but I thought . . ." Mrs. Lamb swallowed. "Oh well, it makes no matter what I thought, does it?" She eyed Lady Sarah's stubborn look and sighed. "If you insist upon remaining, then you must welcome him, my lady, and I must go to the kitchen. His lordship will expect a decent dinner set before him no matter that we did not expect him to arrive for it."

"He can be disabused of *that* expectation," said Lady Sarah tartly.

Mrs. Lamb shook her head, a worried look creasing her brow. "No, no, my lady. If you will pretend to be housekeeper, then you must behave as one."

"I may not scold his lordship?" asked Sarah, pretending innocence.

"Of course you must not . . . oh. You are jesting. I think you must refrain from that as well," scolded Mrs. Lamb who had become very well acquainted with her ladyship in the few months since Lady Sarah's unexpected arrival on Blackberry Hill's doorstep. She was no longer in awe of her ladyship, in fact, she had discovered in herself strong maternal feelings for the lass, feelings she exhibited far more frequently than she felt suitable.

Lady Sarah had not chided her for it. In fact, not having had a mother since early childhood, she secretly liked it.

"Very well," said Sarah in response to the scold. She checked her cap in the mirror, smoothed down the lappets that hung to either side, and pushed a wave into a prominent position across her forehead. She fingered the keys hanging from her belt and then drew in a big breath. She turned. "Will I do?"

"Your skin looks too young for gray hair," objected Mrs. Lamb. There was a deepening of the worry lines that appeared the moment the letter was read announcing that Lord Sherringham had rented the box for the season. Since then the expression had not disappeared, merely fading slightly or growing worse as her thoughts decreed. "You haven't a single wrinkle."

"My greatest blessing," said her ladyship, tongue in cheek, "is that my skin has not aged as has my hair.

Where will I find his lordship?" she added before Mrs. Lamb could scold still again.

"In the great room, my lady."

It was Sarah's turn to frown. "Now I must scold you," she said. "You must cease your use of my title. I am not 'my lady' while this charade goes on. You dare not even *think* of me in that way. None of you may."

Mrs. Lamb sighed, her plump bosom lifting and falling. "This will never work, my—" She cast a panicky look toward Lady Sarah. "—hmm, Mrs. Walker."

"Emily Walker, widow. *Emily*, Mrs. Lamb. I always liked the name Emily," said Sarah. "Now. I am off to welcome his fine lordship to Blackberry Hill Cottage."

Lady Sarah left the housekeeper's rooms and moved up the short dark hallway connecting the kitchen to the front of the house. The Cottage was old-fashioned in several ways, the most obvious that the huge entry hall was also the main living area. The kitchen and such facilities were to the rear of the house. The large rooms to either side of the entry hall housed a billiards table in one direction and a card room in the other. Other, smaller, rooms opened from the side rooms. From the great room, broad steps of an open staircase led upward, dividing at a landing part way up, and continuing to the upper stories where family suites and guest bedrooms filled all space except the attics. The entrance to the kitchen and servants' quarters was hidden behind the staircase.

Sarah opened the door—and hesitated. Could she do this? Dared she?

She peered into the great room—and ducked back, her hand going to her heart. A tall broad shouldered man faced the room, his boot heel resting on the polished rock of the raised hearth behind him. He was a man she had thought never to see again.

He went into the army . . . Has he sold out?

It occurred to Sarah that the only reason an officer sold out was if badly wounded; if he could no longer fight. Her heart, which, at sight of him, thumped erratically for reasons of its own, now pounded with fear for him. Sarah peered again and again quickly ducked out of sight. Her heart slowed once she had assured herself he was not only healthy, but had all his limbs.

Her mind began functioning again. Even if he were who she thought he was, even if he had returned to England for some reason unknown to her, that was no cause for thinking he would remember her or recognize her. It was only her foolish heart and undisciplined intellect that gave any importance to his sudden and unexpected appearance. Sarah breathed deeply, squared her shoulders and stepped around the corner.

"Sir!" she said as she glanced around the room. "I was told Lord Sherringham had arrived. I, sir, am the housekeeper, er, Emily, um—" Flustered, more upset than she cared to admit, she tripped over her adopted name. "— *Mrs.* Walker." Sarah felt her face flame.

The man had turned to the fire in order to prod an ill-placed log with the toe of his boot. At the sound of her voice, he turned back. "Ah." A frown appeared, marring the strong even features. "Mrs. Walker? *I* am Sherringham."

"But . . . !" Sarah's eyes widened. *How can it be?* she wondered.

The Lord Sherringham she knew had been perfectly healthy and looked to live to a hundred when she'd seen the man six or seven months previously. Even if he had succumbed, from one thing or another, he had two sons. Beyond his direct heirs, there was a brother, a bachelor brother, was there not?

Sarah's mind whirled between suppressing personal,

utterly unwarranted, feelings for the man she'd deliberately idealized into perfection itself and her knowledge of Lord Sherringham's family. She felt as if she were the child she'd once seen within a circle of young bullies, pushed from one to the other to still another with no stop, turning and twisting, fearful . . . She bit her lip and did her best to order her mind.

Sherringham smiled a crooked smile. "You expected someone older, perhaps?" he asked. "Nevertheless I *am* Sherringham." He bowed slightly. "Lawrence Worth William Rathburn—"

As if I did not know, she thought.

"—seventh Earl of Sherringham."

He smiled the sweet smile she remembered and a deep frown cut lines into her forehead.

"I am certain you wish to scold me," he continued, "for arriving a day early, but *I* was informed too late to inform *you* that a cousin means to arrive today. He is a man I've never met so I felt he should not enter a roof of mine, even a leased roof, unwelcomed by me."

He waited a moment, but not long enough for Sarah to find and make an appropriate response.

"A footman informed us that our rooms will be available soon and, as to our dinner, please do not concern yourself. Bread and cheese and an apple will do very well. Perhaps a slice of ham if such is available . . . ?" He frowned. "Mrs. Walker, are you feeling quite the thing?"

He took a step toward her and Sarah backed away. "My . . . lord," she said. Preoccupied with the thoughts that, despite her best efforts, still whipped around her mind like wasps trapped in a bottle, she forgot herself and used her normal melodious tones. "Please. You must excuse me . . ." She turned and disappeared back under the stairs. Then, remembering, she ducked back, her spine stiffened by anger. "A simple but adequate dinner will be ready at the usual time," she snapped. "We will *not* be reduced to bread and cheese—even if we could manage the addition of an apple for a sweet course."

"*We?* Did that sound as royal a 'we' to you as it did to me?" asked Lord Sherringham after Sarah closed the door with a hint of a slam. "But perhaps," he mused, "she meant the household staff as a whole. Julie, what do you make of the woman?"

"Panicky as a rabbit," said the woman who rose from the chair facing a fire doing its poor best to warm the large room. She had watched the scene in the mottled mirror hanging above the mantel. "But my guess is that that is not," she continued in a voice surprisingly low and throaty for her petite size, "her *usual* character."

"You have that right," said Lawrence, his frown deepening. "The sharp tongue at the end might be the lady's, but not the goggling eyes of the tongue-tied, almost-cringing, wallflower sort of creature with whom we were first presented."

Julie chuckled, a musical sound that, as always, drew a smile from Lord Sherringham. "Wallflower?" she repeated. "You refer to her in a manner appropriate to a woman of your world," she teased, "rather than that of a servant."

"So I did. And as a much younger woman . . ." Sherringham's brows formed shallow check marks above his eyes when he raised them slightly and simultaneously frowned. Anyone with a guilty conscience might think it a faintly devilish look and, since almost everyone feels guilty about *something,* his odd brows had earned him the cognomen "Devil" Rathburn. He tipped his head. "Now why, I wonder, did I do that?"

An unusually perspicacious woman, Julie remained silent, knowing a rhetorical question when she heard one. The silence was broken when a footman padded down the stairs, catching her attention. She held out her hand to Sherringham. "My dear, I think our rooms are ready. If you've no objection, I will retire to mine until time for this dinner we are promised." She smiled a rather impish smile, her mouth forming an intriguing vee shape. "You insulted Mrs. Walker when you suggested she could not provide a decent meal, however unexpected your arrival."

"I will attempt amends—Yes?" he continued when the footman cleared his throat.

"My lord," said the young man and belatedly remembered to bow. "Your valet has seen to your possessions. He informed me he has unpacked for you." He turned a curious look toward Julie. "For her too." He drew in a breath and, bowing, added, "I will, if you've no objections, show you to your rooms now." His face reddened as he again looked toward Julie who was dressed fashionably but with that little bit more verve expected of a lady engaged in her particular occupation. With difficulty, he recovered his equanimity at finding himself in the presence of a famous—infamous?—courtesan. "If you wish it, Miss?" he asked, staring at her boldly.

She sighed. "*Mrs.* Green. And you are?"

"My name's Joseph—" He cast her a quizzing look from under lowered brows. "—*Mrs.* Green."

Julie turned a rueful look toward Lord Sherringham who frowned one of his darkest frowns. "Larry," she said softly, drawing his attention. "If you will escort me above stairs . . . ?"

Sherringham's devilish look grew still more pronounced. "You will be treated with respect in this house, Julie, or I'll have someone's ears." He glared at the footman.

The footman turned red all over again.

"Do you understand?" asked his lordship, his voice full of menace.

"Yes sir," muttered Joseph, his hands behind his back and his head ducked low.

"In that case, you may show us up," said his lordship and offered his arm to Julie.

"But I tell you that man cannot possibly be Sherringham." Sarah stalked from one end of the kitchen to the other.

"Lady Sarah, will you calm down?" ordered Mrs. Lamb. She wiped her floury hands on a towel. "Of course it is the earl. He explained himself, did he not?"

Sarah swung around to face Mrs. Lamb. "The Earl of Sherringham is not yet sixty. He has *two* sons. The elder is in the army on Wellington's staff. I do not know him well, but I'd recognize him. He had much the look of the old earl. The other was just down from Oxford when I departed London and raising the sort of riot and rumpus a green lad recently freed from tutors and books will raise. *And* Lord Sherringham has a younger brother. A bachelor and something of a recluse. He dislikes society, but I've met him once or twice and would know *him* as well."

Mrs. Lamb frowned. "It has been several months since you arrived here, my lady . . ."

Over five—which sometimes feel like five years . . .

Lady Sarah paused in her pacing, reminded herself she had made a logical choice for her future, the only possible choice, and drew in a deep settling breath to steady herself. Then she resumed her perambulations.

"That is so, but, only five. At the very least, the old earl, his direct heirs, and his brother stood between this man and the title. For all I know there were others. Do you believe them all dead? The earl, his sons, his brother, and those others who *might* have been *next* in line?"

"You are *certain* this cannot be his lordship?"

Sarah paused again, tipping her head to one side. She considered. "Certain?" She sighed. "I don't suppose anything is certain in this world." Certainly her life had taken an unexpected turn. She stared into the fire and considered further. "But," she said at the end of her cogitations, "it is a mere five months and a bit." She drew in a deep breath, turned, and spoke directly to Mrs. Lamb. "For my peace of mind will you set Alfie to discovering what he can from his lordship's grooms? At least, I presume Sherringham's hunters have arrived and are attended by his own grooms? Perhaps *our* groom could pretend to have met *my* Lord Sherringham and want to know how this one came to his honors?"

"Alfred likely has met his lordship. The one you remember, I mean." Mrs. Lamb pursed her lips. "*And* it is likely he'll have all the news before he comes in for his supper *without* our setting him to do anything at all."

"Yes," Sarah agreed nodding. "Alfred will know." She frowned, thinking of the old groom's advanced years. "He will be all right, will he not? It will not be too much, overseeing the stables?"

"For most of the year the work is nothing much at all—merely the old cob kept for the gig that takes me into the village and to church. And now your three horses, of course, the ones you brought north with you. Only during the season and only when his lordship was in residence was there any real work—and even then Alfred did little more than check that the lads kept up to the mark."

"Very good . . . if you are sure he'll not overdo?"

Mrs. Lamb nodded.

"So . . . Alfred will find out all there is to know." Sarah bit her lip. "If it is true this man has inherited unexpectedly, then he'll very likely think me a goosecap if not a slowtop for the way I behaved in the great room." She grimaced. "I'll be up in my room." Sarah shook her head, exasperated with her heedlessness. "That is, I'll be in my *new* rooms if you need me."

Mrs. Lamb watched Lady Sarah's shoulders slump. The young woman wandered into the hall off which the housekeeper's rooms lay and the housekeeper shook her head. "Such nonsense," she scolded. "Lady Sarah shouldn't ought to be here. There must have been somewhere where she could take herself for the hunting season . . ."

But Mrs. Lamb could think of no one Lady Sarah dared trust to that degree. No one who would keep the secret of her whereabouts once she'd secretly left her father's London townhouse.

No one knew, which Lady Sarah insisted was how it had to be. Not even her solicitor knew. Before absconding alone in the middle of the night and in disguise, she had sent him a message telling him not to be a complete jingle-brain, wasting his time as he had so far done, but *to get on with finding a means of voiding her father's will.*

"But, oh—" Mrs. Lamb wrung her hands. "—I do wish she'd come to her senses and go back to the world in which she belongs!"

With that Mrs. Lamb turned back to her kitchen worktable and instantly scolded the elderly kitchen maid who had been set to cleaning and chopping turnips. "Knock-in-the-cradle," muttered Mrs. Lamb in an exasperated but kindly tone. Gently, she wiped a bit of spittle from the elderly drudge's chin and got a vacant smile for her effort.

She set out the ingredients for a trifle, including the remains of a pound cake and the good sherry. A shepherd's pie, slices from the ham, a couple of birds from those she'd put on a spit earlier for the household's supper, good bread from that morning's baking, and home-made bramble jam. Then the trifle for dessert . . . It was not a fancy supper, but a far cry from bread and cheese!

Sarah stood in the middle of her tiny sitting room and stared at nothing at all, her mind full of images from the season when she'd last seen Lawrence Rathburn, then a mere mister. At party after party he leaned against a pillar or, if in the park, against a tree or, outside at a country house, against a balcony railing or a statue's plinth . . . from whatever position he chose, he watched her.

Time after time she had looked up to see him watching her, but, unlike the dozen men who courted her, he never once approached her. Not for so much as an introduction, let alone a dance or a flirtation or merely a conversation.

He intrigued her from the first time she'd noticed him. Tall and dark. Those odd eyebrows . . . When, throughout two whole seasons and into the third, he remained apart from her, he grew to be something of an obsession with her. He was, after all, the only man who appeared interested in her—or more likely her money—who did not attempt to woo her.

It made him unique.

It also made him the only man she dared allow into her dreams. Gradually, almost without realizing it, she endowed the square-jawed, wild-haired man with those characteristics a man must have if she were to allow herself to fall into love with him. He would be honest to a fault. Truthful. Trustworthy. He would care deeply for children. He would enjoy a quiet evening reading by his own fireside—but ride like the wind when mounted on the stallion he favored. He would drive like a nonpareil and shoot like a nonesuch . . .

Then, later, when an inheritance allowed the *real* man
to buy himself a commission, joining England's Penin-
sular troops, she added bravery and conscientiousness to
her dream man. He would *not,* however, be foolishly
reckless, a seeker after glory.

But, *most importantly,* the man of whom she dreamed
would care for her—*not* for her inheritance or her position in the *ton* or that she was healthy and could produce
his progeny without succumbing to the megrims or any of
the other trite reasons for which tonnish men married.

Foolish wench, she scolded. *How could I have been so stupid as to fall in love with a make-believe man?*

Because that is what she had done. Part of her knowing she was pretending, part not pretending at all, she
had searched the casualty lists after every battle, fearing
to see his name. She added him to her prayers, asking he
be kept safe. And she dreamt about her dream man, re-
fusing to so much as think of wedding any other.

Especially, she would have none of the men her father
thrust her way. She refused each and every one and each
time she did he bellowed. She would, he insisted, be
wed. To *someone.*

She could not recall the original battle with her father
concerning her future—just one more man who
thought she would do. She did remember her later decision that she would marry no one who did not come
up to the standards she set for a husband. Very occasionally she allowed herself to admit, if only for a
moment, that her standards were absurdly high. Equally
rarely she admitted her stubbornness. So long as her father insisted, she would refuse. Adamantly.

Sarah's mouth firmed as she recalled her father's will
and why she fled London, why she'd come to Blackberry
Hill where she'd thought to find sanctuary. She would

not be dictated to when he lived—and she would not be dictated to by a man dead and in his grave.

And why, she wondered, fuming, *does Mr. McAfferty not find a way of setting aside that abominable will?*

It did not cross Sarah's usually logical mind that the poor man had no way of informing her—assuming he managed the trick.

Chapter 2

Lawrence, Lord Sherringham, looked up from where he sat next to his fire in the master bedroom. His valet sniffed a second time. "What is it Merit?"

"How long do you mean to remain in this benighted place?"

Lord Lawrence chuckled. "I warned you you would not like it. You are too toplofty, too much the city animal," he said to the valet he had inherited along with the title.

"You *do* like it?" asked Merit, startled from his usual nose-in-the-air stance.

Lawrence looked around the beamed, low-ceilinged, half-paneled room. He smiled and nodded. "Yes, I believe I do. I like the old-fashioned high bed. I like the cozy feel, the worn but comfortable chairs. I especially like it that there is no noise of iron-shod wheels against cobblestones, of hawkers screeching their wares by day and watchmen calling out the hours at night. This is very much the sort of place I like."

Merit shook his head stubbornly. "Should be in London for the little season. Should be choosing yourself a wife."

Larry noticed a sly look accompany the latter suggestion. A muscle jumped in his cheek. "I'll wed when I get around to it," he said in a tone that closed that discussion.

In actual fact, it was a subject to which he'd given more than a little thought. He knew the title required he produce sons so he was surprised to discover the strength of his reluctance to take a wife. The cause was not difficult to find, however. Not when the bright star he watched in the seasons before he bought his commission remained such a vivid picture in his mind . . . and heart.

Lady Sarah Staunton had been very different from the other young women brought to London to find themselves husbands. In fact, she made it obvious she did *not* look for one, did not *want* one, and, to his knowledge, rejected one *very* good parti, two who were more than acceptable, and at least three fortune hunters—none of whom made the least attempt to hide their disappointment. He suspected there were others, men who did not advertise their failure to gain the lady's hand.

Since, at the time, he would have been classified as a fortune hunter, his pride would not allow him to approach her. On the other hand, he could not bring himself to avoid her and had watched from afar whenever they attended the same gathering. When he bought his commission, he hoarded memories of her, memories that kept him sane while enduring the horrors of war.

His life changed when he inherited the earldom. Once the folderol to taking up his new honors was completed and he was confirmed as Sherringham, it occurred to him he had become as eligible as any man gracing the *ton*. It also occurred to him that the woman he loved was unlikely to have remained unwed—at twenty-five or twenty-six, which she must now be, it was unlikely in the extreme.

Sherringham was surprised to discover she had never married and was more astonished to discover she had disappeared from the *ton* one year to the day after her father's demise.

Simply vanished.

Even her solicitor, whom he approached for information, could tell him nothing. Or—which was more likely—*would* not.

Perhaps, he thought, *it is the mystery that makes it impossible to forget her?*

A tap at the connecting door caught his attention. "Merit? Answer that and then make yourself scarce."

Julie strolled into his bedroom as unconcernedly as if it were a drawing room. But then she would, would she not? Lawrence laughed silently at his own faint embarrassment that she found him in dishabille, his cravat thrown across the end of the bed and his coat hanging over the rack built for it, part of a specially designed stand. Too, his sleeves were rolled up revealing muscular arms and the ties of his shirt hung down his chest. His fingers went to the slit and tangled in the dark hair revealed there.

He swallowed embarrassment which was out of place. It was not, after all, the first time this woman had seen him this way—or for that matter wearing nothing at all. But that was long ago . . .

"Julie," he said, standing. "How may I help you?"

"I found something as I finished unpacking. I think you should see it." She held out a slim volume tied at the edge by ribbons.

Lawrence's hand, automatically reaching for it, stilled. "It looks like someone's journal . . . ?"

"Yes." When one of his brows made that odd lopsided vee shape, she smiled. Her hand, however, remained steadily extended. "And yes," she added, "you are correct to suspect I peeked. *That* is why I believe you should see it."

Slowly he reached for it. Still more slowly he tugged at one of the ribbons. The bow fell open and he dug at the knot. It loosened and he looked up, meeting Julie's eyes. "This must be a private journal. We should *not* read it."

"I truly think you *should.*"

He sighed, hesitated, but then, quickly, opened the cover to the first page. Both his brows rose in his most extreme devil-look. "*Lady Sarah, Her Book?*" he read.

"That would be Lord Stauntons's missing daughter, would it not?"

Lawrence looked up and met Julie's innocent gaze. "You read this?"

He thrust it back at her and, to prevent it dropping to the floor, she took it. She shrugged. "You willfully forget who and what I am, Larry. I feel no shame in prying."

"I sometimes wonder why I even like you."

"Because I make you laugh. Because I remind you of when we were both much younger and far more foolish. Because you can be honest with me and know I'll not betray you."

"Knowing you will read another's personal journal does not jibe with believing you'd be true to me."

"Hmm . . ." Lines crinkled the skin at the corner of her eyes, revealing she was older than she cared to admit. "Would you like to phrase that a trifle differently, my dear?"

Lawrence frowned. Then, realizing he'd suggested that Julie, a courtesan, would love him and only him, he barked a laugh. "Believe that you'll not rat on me?" he rephrased his comment, mimicking her pretended innocence.

"You need never fear I'll give away your secrets, Larry," she said and, for once, there was nothing but utter seriousness in her face. "You made me what I am today—and I do not mean that you ruined me, because you did not.

You did, however, recognize that I am intelligent. You taught me to speak properly, to read, and chose books for me you thought would make me more the woman a man would pay good money to possess. We succeeded in those efforts, Larry, and I owe you more than I can ever repay."

He grimaced. "I saw an intelligent woman wasting herself and could not bear it."

"But you knew I could be nothing . . . how shall I put this?" Her brows twisted in self-derision. "Nothing prim and proper. That I could not drudge away in the sort of position in which a poor but *decent* woman is allowed to earn a living, or—" Her voice grew excessively dry. "—become a drudge in quite another way as some working man's wife."

"We did have good times, did we not?" he asked, feeling a trifle nostalgic.

"We could have good times again," she said and walked up to him, putting her arms around his waist and smiling up into his face.

Very gently he set her a little away from him, holding her elbows. "We are beyond that, Julie. You are my *friend*. Don't tempt me to do what I feel is wrong."

She heaved a sigh. Her lips compressed and something that might be sadness made her eyelids droop. Then she laughed. And if it sounded a trifle forced, neither of them allowed the other to know they'd heard the false note. "Then, my lad," she scolded to hide other emotions, "if you'll not smooth out that particular tweak to your conscience, I think you should set aside *another* of your blessed principles." She stepped back.

Lawrence, forgetting where the discussion began, frowned in earnest.

"I truly think you'd better dip into the journal." She held it out. "You'll be surprised."

He put his hands behind his back to avoid temptation.

"We will wrap it up and forward it to her solicitor. Very likely she has no notion where it is."

"She'll not thank you for it!" said Julie sharply.

"Why?"

"If you will read no more," she said, more than a trifle exasperated, "then read the last page."

They held each other's gazes for a long moment. Then, his hands less steady than he liked, Lawrence took it and flipped through something over half the book to where the writing stopped.

"The first date on the page," he said, "is some months ago." Reluctantly he read out the lines. "*Today I arrived safely at Blackberry Hill. How I dared make such a journey, even attired as a man, I do not know.* She came here?" His face hardened. "Blast McAfferty. Did he have to rent this place as well as the others? Where can she have gone?"

Having no answer, Julie made no response. Besides, she knew none was expected.

He looked down at the book. There was a space and then, the ink a different shade and the pen a trifle wider at the nib, there was one more entry, the date less than three weeks previously. Again he read aloud.

"I have made my decision. I am comfortable as things are. Father's stubbornness will not chase me from this, my final lair. Mrs. Lamb will help. So will the other servants. No one will guess I reside anywhere near the Cottage."

Lawrence looked up. "My god," he breathed. "She is hiding near here?"

Julie nodded. "Hiding, but why?"

"Father's stubbornness," he repeated softly and stared off into space, thinking. "There were rumors that Lord Staunton wanted her wed, that he didn't much care to whom, but that she must be married. It was also said she refused to oblige him."

"Is it possible for a dead man to control such things in another's life?"

Lawrence's eyes narrowed. "Difficult, but not impossible. Lady Sarah is, by all accounts, a very wealthy woman, but," he said slowly, thinking as he spoke, "it is possible her fortune is tied up in such a way she cannot benefit from it—unless she weds."

"Poor dear."

"If she is near here, then *where*, exactly?" He frowned. "Do you suppose there is a cottage somewhere on the grounds?"

Julie opened her mouth—and shut it again. If that very odd housekeeper was a disguised Lady Sarah, then it would be a very good thing if none of the men taking part in this party realized it. And that included Larry who, she knew, once had feelings for the woman. Julie thought that last thought over again and turned quickly, unable to control a muscle that jumped in the side of her jaw.

Is it mere selfishness on my part that I don't wish Larry aware of her ladyship's identity? Or is it that I feel sorry for her and want to help her?

Julie thought about that too.

Or is it, perhaps, a bit of both?

She sighed softly, knowing her motives for protecting Lady Sarah's secret were mixed and only partially altruistic. Assuming she'd guessed the secret.

"When does your cousin arrive?" she asked, changing the subject. She turned in time to see Sherringham set the journal on his bedside table and resolved to pick it up. Men were too trusting. If Larry left it there, his valet would tidy it away—and justify looking into it by the rationalization that he must in order to discover where to put it.

"My cousin . . ." he repeated.

It was obvious to the watching woman that he tore his thoughts from Lady Sarah with difficulty.

His mind on this new topic, he paced. "A man I don't even know," he said, "and he wrote that he will join me here and the date. He hadn't even the tact to hint and await an invitation. I could not allow an utter stranger to arrive and I not be here to receive him."

Tiny lines at the corners of Julie's eyes deepened with concern. "Perhaps that is what he wanted. Perhaps he needed time to look about and discover how the land lay before you could see him do so."

"You make him sound sly and . . . and . . . oh, I don't know what."

Julie laughed at Sherringham's expression of mild outrage. "You mean I am a suspicious soul and—" She sobered abruptly. "—find it a trifle odd that *you* find yourself in such an exalted position?"

A muscle jumped in Lawrence's jaw. "Don't, Julie. Fate plays strange games with our lives. I did not ask for this honor and I've a great deal to learn before I am comfortable in the role. There is no question that my relatives died in inauspicious but unsuspicious ways."

"Four of them? In less than three months?"

Lawrence nodded, but his mouth tightened.

"Larry—" She walked with studied grace to his side and placed her fingertips on his arm. "—will you indulge a foolish female's whim and promise me you will take care that you too do not die in an . . . what did you say . . . an inauspicious unsuspicious manner?"

His lips twisted into a suppressed smile. "I am always careful, Julie. How do you think I survived battle?"

Her fingers dug into his arm. "Promise."

He frowned. "If it means so very much to you, then I promise."

"See that it is a promise you keep," she said tartly and, whipping up the journal, she turned in a swirl of skirts and stalked from the room.

Lawrence, still frowning, watched her go. "Julie has never been one for fancy or the fantastic," he muttered. "In fact, a woman more rooted in the real world would be hard to find." Then he shrugged. He'd given her his promise and, although he thought it nonsense, *wanted* to think it nonsense, he *would* keep an eye peeled for trouble.

For reasons he refused to contemplate, Sherringham realized he was quite ridiculously uneasy.

Chapter 3

The boy stood awkwardly just within the great room, the double doors leading to the curving front drive open behind him. Lawrence, pausing on the landing, studied the lad. The autumn sun streamed in, gilding riotous golden curls, making rosier a clear pink skin, and silhouetting the half-grown coltish look of him. The lad's age was far less than Lawrence had expected.

In fact, thought Lawrence a trifle ruefully, *I think I expected some oily character, steeped in slyness, and perhaps a trifle dangerous.*

Despite what he had said to Julie, there was *some* question about the death of the heir just prior to Lawrence himself. The accident to that man had occurred as Lieutenant Rathburn, as he was then, countermarched over hot Spanish plains while Wellington, recently made an earl, searched for just the right position from which to face the much larger French army.

If he had not been so far away, Sherringham suspected he might have found himself under suspicion of murdering the man. At least, the questions asked upon his return to England left him just a trifle curious about his own future and *more* than a trifle curious about the lad now before him. He'd discussed those suspicions with no one, not even Julie.

The last thing he had expected was a mere boy edging toward manhood.

"Good afternoon," said Lawrence softly.

The boy turned quickly, looking around, and then up. He smiled. And what a smile it was. It seemed to light him up from the inside out.

"I am Lawrence Rathburn, Lord Sherringham. You," said Lawrence, "are my cousin Caldwood?"

The boy opened his mouth, shut it, performed a credible bow, and then, grinning the grin of a lad who is unsure of his social skills but not overly upset by it, he nodded. "Roland Caldwood. A terrible name, Roland, but it has been in the family forever." The lad sobered as Lawrence strolled down the remaining steps. "Cousin, I want you to know I'd not be here if it were not for my mother. I am strong and healthy. I can take care of myself, but . . ." The insecurity that had not bothered him earlier was now revealed in his search for appropriate words.

"But your mother cannot," was Lawrence's interpretation of Roland's hesitation. "You are aware that until my solicitor checks on your claim to be my heir I can do nothing for you?"

The lad nodded. "Oh yes. That was clear from his letter. Oh. Mother said I was to remember to thank you for this invitation," he added as if just recalling it.

Lawrence wondered where his mother got the impression an invitation had been issued. "We have no reason to disbelieve your claim, Roland. It is merely that it must be checked before anything is done to proclaim you, legally, my heir presumptive. In the meantime there is no reason we should not get to know one another."

Roland nodded. "Yes." He grinned again. "I was *very* glad to receive the invitation, you know. It isn't pleasant at home just now."

"No?" *Receive* an invitation? The lad seemed sincere in that and Lawrence put aside the question for later thought. "In what way has it been unpleasant?" he asked, willing, in fact *wanting*, to draw the boy out.

"An uncle has lived with my mother ever since my father died—trying to put things right, you know. It was a good idea when I was away from home. At school, you know. Because I was too young and he was company for Mother. But now I am home and—" The boy's expression took on a rather bleak look. "—well, *I* think it is time he began teaching me to take over my responsibilities for what is left of the estate and he insists I am too young. I am turned seventeen, you know—"

Lawrence had thought sixteen. At best.

"—and, well, we fight about it. Mama does not like it."

"Trying to put things right?" asked Lawrence, his tone one of sympathy. He blessed his years as an officer who often found it necessary to listen to recruits expound on everything from homesickness to losses at cards to—in rare cases—a young wet-behind-the-ears not-even-shaving-yet boy admit to being afraid of going into battle, afraid of making a fool of himself. Or worse.

This boy nodded. "My father, you know," he said confidingly. "Brought an abbey to a nutshell as the saying goes. My uncle managed to hold on to a bit of it when things were settled—one or two farms and the home farm and the house with the demesne around it—but there were still debts, you know."

"Gambling debts?" asked Lawrence, the sympathy still in evidence.

"Not entirely. Some, I guess. Well, yes, at the end, especially, he gambled, trying to win enough to cover expenses?" The lad frowned. Then he sighed. "Father spent money like—like water under a millwheel, my mother says. He'd had our old home torn down and a huge ugly structure built to replace it. I don't like it much, but my mother seems to. And then, of course, he had to furnish it, you know. And only the best would do."

Lawrence felt his eyes narrow and forced himself to relax. Unless the debts were gambling debts that one's honor demanded one meet immediately, there was no good reason for selling off land. In fact the law was quite clear that one could not be forced to sell land.

"Mother is chomping at the bit," Roland continued. "She thinks she has been good far too long and wants, desperately, to have another season. Before it is too late, my uncle says, and then he laughs. I don't like it when he laughs like that," Roland finished, a frown marring his smooth young brow. "It isn't a nice laugh."

"Perhaps he is teasing your mother about her age? That he thinks she may be getting too old to find a new husband?"

Roland waved his hand. "Oh, as to that, she's had offers. She says she doesn't want a husband. She wants to dance and wear pretty dresses and not have to turn my old coats or—" Suddenly Roland turned bright red. "—or anything. Sorry," he mumbled. "I don't know why I rambled on like that."

Lawrence chuckled. "Because I led you to it, of course. The best way to learn about someone is to get them talking about themselves. Well, enough of that." *Quite* enough for the moment. There was already a great deal about which to think. "I'll lay a wager you are hungry." He took the lad by the shoulder and led him toward the back of the room, under the stairs, into the dim hall, and on into the kitchen.

"Mrs. Lamb?" Sherringham's eyes widened. "I remember you!"

The woman looked up from the bread she was

kneading into a smooth elastic ball. She smiled. "Sir?"
A soft pink filled her cheeks. "My lord, I *should* say."

Sherringham ignored her embarrassment, pushing
forward his young cousin. "I'd like you to meet Roland
Caldwood. He is my heir presumptive and will be here
for several weeks. I think you will find he is at that age
when a boy is impossible to fill up, so I thought I should
bring him to visit you so he'll know whom to ask when
he wishes a bite in between meals." Sherringham smiled
at the cook and then at Roland. "I'll leave you two now
and set my valet to putting away your bits and pieces.
Mrs. Lamb will ask a footman to show you up to your
room when you are ready."

Sherringham nodded and left the kitchen, a frown
deepening the lines across his forehead, his eyebrows
forming those devilish check marks. He stalked unsee-
ingly into the dimly lit hall leading to the great hall. As
he reached a door off it, it opened and the housekeeper
very nearly ran into him.

She scowled and then, looking conscious, dipped a
curtsey. "Sir!"

"Mrs. Walker? Sorry," he said, glancing at her. His
frown deepened still more but he walked on without
stopping to wonder why.

"Were you looking for me?" she called after him before realizing how silly it was to ask such a question of his
receding back.

He turned. She was a silhouette against the light from
the kitchen beyond but again he felt uneasy about . . .
something. "You will find a young relative of mine in the
kitchen," he said. "I took him there to introduce him to
Mrs. Lamb whom he will wish to know as well as he knew
his nurse in bygone years. At least, I seem to remember
the importance of Cook in my life when about that age."
He smiled, nodded, and continued on his way.

Lady Sarah stood stock-still for a long moment after he was gone, his smile hovering in her mind's eye. "He does not change," she muttered to herself, a wistful wishful emotion filling her until she reminded herself he had brought a woman with him—something she could not approve. Not at all.

But how nice that he thought the lad might want feeding . . .

It was more than half a dozen years since she'd first noticed Lawrence Rathburn propping up walls and columns, watching her, his arms crossed over his chest. When he had not become another suitor for her hand, she tried but could learn little about him—little beyond the indisputable fact that, since he was not wealthy, he would be totally unacceptable to her father.

As time passed and she no longer feared his making advances, she wove fanciful tales about him, making him the embodiment of her ideal. At first she had pretended to be deeply in love with her dream man. In the end, often, she was unable to remember that the man she loved did not exist—except in her mind.

My feelings, she told herself again, *are utterly ridiculous. I don't know him.*

Lady Sarah reminded herself the *real* man was full of imperfections by visualizing a hussy on his arm. Her perfect man would *not* bring a whore to keep him company of an evening when he returned from the hunt. Definitely not. The new Lord Sherringham *had.* Therefore he was *not* acceptable to her. Was he?

She wondered why she questioned it.

Of course he is unacceptable. Why, she thought a trifle bitterly, *does he have to have so much the look of the man I wish would fall in love with me, the man I could love?*

That she had herself chosen him for the role was irrelevant and, instead of allowing logic to interfere with her sour mood, she went on into the kitchen, as she'd intended before Lord Sherringham bumped into her.

Roland Caldwood stood with his back to her, munching on a chunk of bread and alternating that with a bite from the cheese in his other hand. He nodded at something Mrs. Lamb said, swallowed, and replied, "Yes, it is a nice little house but perhaps a trifle small? It was the dower house and *old*, you know? Inconvenient, my mother says, with no amenities? The main house, which Mother would prefer, is let on a long lease." His shoulders slumped. "I am not happy about that but my uncle thought it best, given the state in which my father left things."

"Debts?" asked Mrs. Lamb in sympathetic tones. She continued peeling apples and slicing them, not looking at the boy, but letting him know she listened by nodding now and again.

"Mostly he spent a great deal trying to be someone he wasn't—or so my uncle says. He gambled. Some. Well, lots. But only at the end. And not, I think, so much as my uncle says. I was not so young I noticed nothing at all, you know," said Roland. He frowned. "*Mother* says it is in the blood, but she is against *all* gambling. I hope it is not in the blood. I don't wish to gamble. Not beyond my means, you know. My uncle says I will and that is why he must guard my behavior. He wasn't happy, my coming here to stay with an out and outer like my cousin. And the house party, you know." His voice dropped. "Do they really behave in such very lewd and immoral ways as my uncle insists?" he asked.

He blushed when Mrs. Lamb raised her head to stare at him and then, after a moment, nod a little nod.

"I won't join in," he said virtuously—and then sighed softly. "Can't. No horses and no proper riding gear and no money for cards . . . Or wenches," he added as an afterthought, blushing once again.

But you could hear a deep sadness in him and Sarah's heart went out to the boy.

"My uncle is such a fusspot," continued Roland, putting aside his downcast mood in the easy way of youth. "Every expenditure must be watched, he says. He disliked giving me money for vails but Mother insisted. She says he should have put things right by now and that it is *his* fault we must pinch every penny twice. It's been *somewhat* better recently. I mean, this last year or so, you know. I'm home and there are no school fees, you understand? And, recently, he's gone off for as much as a month at a time and we managed quite well without him. I do think we would go on ever so much better by ourselves, but Mother says he is doing what he can to improve things for us and we must accept that he knows best—but for all she says we must listen to him and obey him, she was angry about his last trip. I heard her arguing with him when he returned. He was in London, you know? She could not understand why he'd not taken her with him."

"Perhaps he stayed, himself, in a low inn which he thought improper for a lady," suggested Mrs. Lamb.

"That is exactly what he said—but Mother felt he could have managed a decent hotel, just a small out of the way place, for the two of them. She could not have patronized the good mantuamakers, of course, but she *could* have seen the current fashions and contrived something more up to date once she was home again. And she loves the theater, you know. She'd have seen a play or two, perhaps."

"I'm certain she'd have enjoyed that," said Mrs. Lamb.

The boy sighed. "It is so very boring, listening to her repine, which she does, you know. I do hope Lord Sherringham will see fit to give me an allowance. I'd use it to see Mother had a bit of fun in her life. Perhaps not London, which is very expensive, but Bath? Or Wells? Or even Harrowgate, although *that* is not what she wishes, being far too near to Doncaster and rather old-fashioned. Harrowgate would not feel like going away, you know?" Roland's eyes narrowed and he took on a faintly belligerent tone when he continued. "I'd not let Uncle take every penny to put into the farms, although——" An odd little frown creased the boy's brow. "——I cannot, for the life of me, see what it is he's doing to improve them . . ."

Mrs. Lamb's head came up sharply at that and her mouth opened. She saw Sarah shake her head and closed it. Instead of the question she'd had in mind, she asked, "Would you like something else to eat? An apple perhaps?" The cook hefted one and, when the boy—who had somehow managed to finish his bread and cheese while talking—nodded, she tossed it to him. He caught it one-handed and grinned.

Mrs. Lamb smiled in return. "My . . . housekeeper is waiting to speak to me." She nodded and Roland turned. "Do let me introduce you to Mrs. Walker before you go exploring. If you ask him nicely, perhaps our Alfred, out in the stables, will find a horse you may ride while here. Perhaps one of his lordship's?"

Roland straightened at that notion and, after acknowledging Lady Sarah, politely but not effusively, as was proper to a mere housekeeper, he went out the door nearest the stables.

"Why did you wish me to hold my tongue when the boy made that comment about his uncle's work?" asked Mrs. Lamb.

"If there have been underhanded dealings, I think the lad should not be made suspicious. *More* suspicious, that is. He does not seem the sort who will approach such a situation appropriately. He is more likely to go off half-cocked and cause problems that a more mature soul could avoid."

"So?"

"So I wonder," said Sarah slowly, "if you might not draw him out, find out more detail. If we conclude his uncle is cheating him of his inheritance, then I will write my solicitor and have him look into it. He can turn whatever information he discovers over to Lord Sherringham who can do with it what he will."

Mrs. Lamb did not remind Sarah that she had, rather heatedly, expressed a desire to never again communicate with anyone in London—including her solicitor. Instead, she asked, "And why should his lordship do anything at all?"

Sarah frowned. "Why *do* I think it?"

She didn't wish to admit she knew Sherringham, that she had had—still had—a tendre for the man she pretended him to be. But did she have any *good* reason for thinking the *real* man would help Roland?

"I don't know," she admitted. "But if Mr. McAfferty finds proof of wrongdoing and his fine lordship is not interested in helping, then McAfferty will know what to do next." That settled to her satisfaction, Sarah nodded and returned to her rooms where she looked around, straightened a picture that hung crooked on the wall, touched a crack in the wall next to the hearth, looked around herself again—

—and sighed lustily.

It occurred to Sarah that if she did not find some means of occupying herself, the next months, the cubbing season followed by the four-times-a-week meets of the Quorn—*which she could not join because she was in hiding*—were going to be more difficult, even, than she'd feared.

* * *

A day or so later, Julie wandered down the stairs and into the great room. It had crossed her mind that, while Larry and the other men would be busy with their hunting and their gambling, with eating and drinking and whoring, that she would find herself bored to tears. She wondered what one did with oneself when there was no theater, no shopping, no mantuamakers, no lending libraries, nothing, in fact, to occupy her in her normal fashion.

She crossed the room to one of the two fireplaces and scowled at the smoky fire. When shoving a log farther back did not improve things, she went to the door under the steps at the rear of the great room and opened it. A dark hall faced her and she hesitated. Should she intrude on the servant's territory? But how else was she to find help with the fire when there was no bellpull?

Determined she would not be forced to sit in a smoke filled room when there must be a means of avoiding it, she entered the hall. As she did so the housekeeper's door opened and lamplight spilled into the darkness. Silhouetted in the opening was the housekeeper. Was she Lady Sarah? Or was it Mrs. Walker, truly a gray-headed, widowed, housekeeper-caretaker at the lodge?

The housekeeper started toward Julie who remained perfectly still. A soft humming of a song that had been popular several years earlier reached Julie's ears. It was a very good contralto voice and, feeling in a funning mood, she sang the words in her light soprano.

"Emily" ceased humming abruptly. "Did you want something?" she asked, peering.

Julie nodded and then, realizing movement would be unseen in the dimness, added, "The fire. Out there . . ."

"In the great room. Is it smoking?" Lady Sarah-Emily repressed an urge to swear. "The wind must be in the east. It always smokes when the wind is from that direction."

"Is there nothing to be done about it?"

Lady Sarah hesitated. She had never, herself, spent a great deal of time in the great room. There was a parlor off the billiards room, a smallish room, cozy. It warmed up nicely in bad weather and was well lit for any occupation in which one wished to indulge. Lady Sarah's usual occupation had been reading and she had brought a small library with her—rather than extra, unneeded, clothing.

Three trunks were all that fit into her carriage. With her mare tied behind and her tall frame disguised in male attire, she'd driven herself north. It was an experience she wished never to repeat. Driving so far was, in itself, tiring. There was also the need to avoid regular inns, which resulted in the necessity of caring for the horses herself, finding grazing and water, harnessing and unharnessing. . . .

When she arrived, half exhausted, at the hunting box, her difficulties were not over. She could not instantly rest but must first convince a horrified Mrs. Lamb of the need for secrecy, that no one must know of her arrival . . . No. Never again would she attempt such an adventure.

"Is there," repeated Julie, this time more sharply, "nothing to be done?"

Lady Sarah, drawn from her thoughts, very nearly snapped. At the last moment she caught her tongue between her teeth and restrained herself. "There is a room off the billiards room you might prefer," she said in the harsher tones she'd adopted for her disguise. The harshness, this time, could not be laid to the fact she must not give away her identity, but was, in part, that she must give over her personal refuge to this woman with whom, in a normal way, she'd never have speech.

Then, curious about the woman Lord Sherringham chose to fill his evening hours, Sarah cast aside normal usage. "Allow me to show you the way," she said and moved forward unhurriedly.

Sarah and Julie crossed the great room and entered the billiards room, off which were two more doors. Sarah pointed. "The one nearer the outside wall was the baron's. He used it as an office when he resided here during the hunting season. The other is more of a sitting room. I think you'll be comfortable. If you agree it will do I'll send a footman with wood and kindling and he'll start a fire for you."

"The chimney does not smoke?" asked Julie lightly. She started for the indicated door but, when the housekeeper did not follow, turned. She raised one brow and tipped her head, a question in her eyes. "If you would join me for a few moments . . . ?"

Only half-reluctant, Sarah followed. She stopped just inside the door and cast a longing look around the nicely appointed apartment, a look Julie did not miss.

"Yes," said Julie softly. "This will do very well—if I can keep it secret from the others."

"The others?" asked Sarah.

Julie chuckled. "That was exceedingly rude of me, was it not? The others?" She grimaced. "The women the other men are certain to bring. It is out of place for *me* to look down on them, but I find them boring and dislike spending a great deal of time with them. They have no conversation beyond their gowns, hair, jewels, and, worst of all, their men."

"You do?" Sarah was surprised into voicing her thought and, thereby, revealing her prejudices. Realizing that, if she insulted Mrs. Green, she would discover nothing about her, she flushed. It had become—for reasons she did not understand, did not *want* to understand—important that she do so.

But the woman did not appear to have been insulted. "I have been educated beyond my station," explained Julie easily, smiling, her expression asking Sarah to join in the joke. "My taste in reading has startled or, on occasion, upset my gentlemen friends." She paused. "Of course, it is my taste in literature and history which drew certain other men into my orbit, and those, I admit, are the men I prefer."

"Educated."

Julie nodded. "For instance, has Mary Wollstonecraft's *Political Justice* come your way? Most men disapproved that one!"

Sarah had brought a copy with her and, unthinkingly, glanced toward the bookcase half hidden behind a well-padded chair. Julie instantly went there, but the corner was too dark to read titles and she returned for a lamp. She lit it, having no problem with the old-fashioned tinderbox that, on occasion, defeated Sarah.

Sarah, biting her lip, watched Julie return to the bookcase. She clenched her hands, possessive about her books but curious about Mrs. Green's response to the eclectic collection. She felt exceedingly ambivalent about the notion that such a woman, *a whore*, might have read many of the same books she herself had read, that they had so much in common.

That they had *anything* in common was contrary to everything she'd been taught.

There were oohs and ahhs and, once, a muttered: "I've not seen this one…" and other such sounds coming from behind the chair where Julie was crouched. "Oh how wonderful. Here is *Sense and Sensibility*!" She stood up, her eyes sparkling. "I have never read a book I liked better. Do you know it?"

Sarah nodded, bemused.

Excited, clutching the book to her bosom, Julie approached. "Do you recall the scene where Mrs. Jennings twits Miss Steele?"

Sarah nodded again.

"Did you not laugh and laugh?"

"I did. I do. Every time I reread the book."

Julie did not so much as raise an eyebrow at the housekeeper's softer tones. She was very nearly certain this was the missing Lady Sarah. Instead of showing suspicion, she asked about another scene and what Sarah thought was the author's reason for including it. Before long they were seated across from each other before the empty grate and passing the book back and forth as they searched out passages pertinent to the lively discussion.

The conversation continued for some time. Only when Lord Sherringham raised his voice to a level entirely beyond what one would expect in a gentleman's residence did it penetrate to their attention.

Eyes widening, they stared at each other. Then, simultaneously raising hands to their mouths, both giggled. Only then did Lady Sarah realize she had been intimately involved for far longer than she would ever have dreamed possible with a woman to whom she should never have spoken.

During her former existence in tonnish circles, she would not, *could* not, have done so. Guilt filled Sarah, but then she admitted, to herself, how much she'd enjoyed the discussion. She concluded that perhaps her former life had been a trifle *too* restrictive in that she would not have been allowed such an interesting and satisfying association.

Perhaps, she thought with inward humor, *there are compensations for lowering my place in the world?*

Even as the thoughts raced through Lady Sarah's

mind, she rose to her feet. "I believe your presence is required elsewhere. I will order a footman to build a fire here each cool morning," she finished in a formal manner, her voice returning to that required by her disguise.

"Yes." Julie too rose. "Why," she continued just a trifle diffidently, "do you not remain here while I see what Larry wants? Then, when we are out of the way, you may continue on wherever you wish to go?"

"You do not want him to know we were conversing?" asked Sarah, her back stiffening.

Julie blinked. "It is more that I thought *you* would not wish it known."

It was said in such simple straightforward tones that Sarah blinked as well, quite as surprised as Julie had been. She half laughed, the laugh cut off sharply. And then she shook her head. Her chin rose. "I am not one to ignore another when I find I like their company. If you can manage to put up with a . . . a *housekeeper,* then I do not see why I should not admit a . . . a . . ." Sarah, flustered, could not, for the life of her find a word with which to finish the sentence.

"I prefer the word courtesan," said Julie, her voice dry as dust."

"A *courtesan* to my coterie of friends," said Sarah firmly.

Julie nodded, her head turning when her name was called still again and this time with something approaching concern. "I must go. Will you be insulted if I tell you that you are the most interesting women I have met in a very long time?"

"Not at all—assuming I may return the compliment?" asked Sarah, her eyes twinkling. "Shall we go?" She bent her elbow invitingly and the two women, arm in arm, swept from the room, through the card room and into the great room.

"Really, Larry, must you shout down the house?" chided Julie.

Lord Lawrence blinked. He looked from one to the other. "Mrs. Walker?" he asked, eying the intimacy between the two women.

"Mrs. Walker has been showing me around." Julie released Sarah and strolled toward Sherringham. "Larry, my adored one," she cooed in tones very unlike her usual contralto, "will you indulge me a trifle . . . ? Just a very little?" Julie touched his chest with one finger.

Embarrassed, the suddenly wary man grabbed her hand and cleared his throat, his eyes flicking toward the housekeeper who kept an interested eye on the proceedings. "I never accede to wishes until I know whether or not I should," he said in somewhat pompous tones.

"It is a very little thing," coaxed Julie, her eyes brimming with mirth.

Minx, he thought, and cast another wary glance toward Mrs. Walker. *Julie knows she embarrasses me.* The realization half amused and half angered him. "If it is a very little thing," he asked, "then why do you not tell me what it is?"

"Oh very well, but you should, you know, accede to my every request and not *require* knowing beforehand!" When his scowl deepened, she chuckled. "Devil," she said softly and touched his brow. His eyes closed in a give-me-patience sort of way and Julie ceased teasing him. "There is," she said in her normal voice, "a little room. Back there—" she pointed. "—that I would make my own. One that no one may enter that I have not invited to do so."

"A private bower?" asked Lawrence.

He relaxed. Julie, who nodded in response to the question, and Sarah, too, wondered what he had thought might be asked of him.

"I don't know if I *can* enforce such a rule, Julie," he mused. "Perhaps," he continued, "to begin with, you should not make a big thing of it? Only if you find you are invaded more than you like?"

"To be *invaded at all* will be too much, but—" She heaved a dramatic sigh. "—I do see the problem. I will try hard to make it a very boring place and then perhaps no one will wish to enter it."

"I knew you'd find a means to your ends." Lawrence looked up and found the dark blue eyes of the house-keeper still on them. Finding himself caught by the deep sapphire gleam, he frowned—and then hid a grin when it was the housekeeper's turn to look flustered.

Muttering, Lady Sarah excused herself and stalked across the room to disappear behind the stairs. Out of sight she opened the door and closed it and, reprehensibly, eavesdropped. Embarrassing as the self-knowledge was, Sarah desperately needed to know why Lord Lawrence had wanted Julie's presence.

"Lawrence," scolded Julie. "You must not embarrass my new friend, because I have a premonition that she is the only thing here that will keep me sane. She likes to read, you see." When she went on it was in tones of pretend outrage. "You forgot to warn me, Larry, old boy, that there would be nothing for me to do here!"

"The problem of what you would do with yourself had not crossed my mind. There is riding, of course . . ."

She shook her head.

"Oh, lordy," he said, his tone rueful." I forgot you do not ride."

"I have never had the opportunity to learn," said Julie. She hid the sudden lowering feeling he was next going to suggest she would now have the time.

He did. ". . . an enjoyable pastime, Julie. You *should* learn."

She thought of how tall a horse was, how small she was in comparison. "I have no habit," she objected.

"Perhaps Mrs. Walker can find you an old one. Something stored away."

"It would not fit," objected Julie.

"It could be made to fit," contradicted Lord Sherringham.

"You'll not have time to teach me once your guests arrive and Lord Cannington, at least, is due tomorrow."

"There is a very nice old man in the stables who has, I suspect, taught a great many youngsters to ride. He will enjoy a new student."

"I am not a youngster."

Lawrence eyed her for a long moment and then shouted with laughter. "Julie, *you are afraid.*"

She pouted. "And if I am? Such great stupid beasts! I would fall off and hurt myself, maybe kill myself, and then you would be sorry."

"A nursery threat! I'd not thought it of you." When she didn't smile, he added, "Julie, it isn't like that. Not when you are a novice. One learns on a placid beast and goes very easily until one is sure of oneself. One *walks* the horse. One does not *gallop* it or leap over fences."

"Does the horse know that?"

He chuckled as she'd meant him to do. "A good one does," he said. "We will ask about a habit."

She sighed. "Larry . . ."

"Hush. You said you needed occupation. This will be an excellent means of filling some of your time. We will think of others."

Lady Sarah, hearing that last, felt heat climb her neck and into her face—even though his tone had not been suggestive in the slightest. *Think of other ways indeed,* she thought crossly, as she carefully opened the door and then, equally quietly, closed it behind her.

"Well," she muttered, "you wanted to know why he called for her, did you not? So now you know . . ."

Chapter 4

Lady Sarah fumed as she visualized the two in bed, their limbs intertwined. They would kiss and they would . . . she could not think what else they would do and forced herself to put the whole notion from her mind. She would think of other things, for instance, that—

She let herself into her rooms as she searched her mind for a topic that would obliterate the one that upset her.

—that she had enjoyed a long conversation with a trollop! *No.* Mrs. Green preferred the term courtesan. *With a courtesan.*

Would not her father have had fits at the notion? Sarah smiled at the thought and then, recalling that Mrs. Lamb had asked her about menus earlier, before Julie came complaining about the smoking chimney, she picked up notes she had made and went, belatedly, to the kitchens where, virtuously, she discussed the coming week's meals with the hunting lodge's real housekeeper.

Lawrence, tired of arguing, told Julie she would enjoy learning and that he meant to go immediately to the stables and discuss her lessons with the old groom. Speaking in the tone of voice men use to convince one a subject is closed, he added, ". . . and if there isn't a horse suitable for such work, I will ride into Melton Mowbray and purchase one."

With that Sherringham stalked from the great room.

Blackberry Hill now housed two fuming women. Julie had rather gotten out of the habit of dealing with a man she could not cajole or manipulate into doing her will. She had forgotten how self-assured this particular man was, how stubborn he could be.

Since she was glaring toward where he'd disappeared, the unexpected sound of Roland's voice, coming from near the still smoking fireplace, made her blink. Startled, she turned on her heel.

"*Are* you afraid?" he asked again.

Julie closed her eyes, regained her equilibrium, and opened them. "You were listening to a private conversation."

The top of Roland's head to just below his eyes appeared, along with fingers curled over the top of the high backed chair. He straightened, revealing himself to his shoulders, obviously kneeling on the seat of the chair that hid him.

"I know I should not," he said. "I thought perhaps I would not intrude on Lord Sherringham, you know, when it was you he wished to see and when I realized I should not listen it seemed too difficult to explain that I was here. *Are* you fearful of horses? I know a girl who kicks and screams whenever forced near a horse. Her horse senses fear and then the *horse* is afraid. I have tried to explain to her, but she won't listen," he finished, sounding aggrieved.

"I can understand her problem perfectly," said Julie, her voice dry.

"If you get to know your mount first, then perhaps you will not fear it." Roland brightened, having found a way to help. "We will take apples to the stable and old Alfie will tell us which animal and I will introduce the two of you."

"Old Alfie?"

"Yes. He's nice. He says I may ride the cob any time I want. He said he will ask Lord Lawrence about his hunters. You know. Discover if maybe, when his lordship needs one of his extra mounts exercised, he'll let *me* do it?" As he spoke he squirmed out of the chair and approached Julie. "Alfie was groom and then head groom to Lord Staunton. His lordship brought Alfie here when he got too old. When *Alfie* got old, I mean, not his lordship. Now he works for Lady Sarah, of course. Alfie does," he added, clarifying that it was not her ladyship's father he'd meant. "Alfie taught Lady Sarah to ride and she, you know, is said to be a bruising rider. I had a friend who once saw her. She goes like the wind, he said, and might be a part of her horse like those odd creatures in Greek mythology about whom I had to read when in school."

"Centaurs?"

"You know about them?" A look of surprise widened his eyes. Then the boy's face twisted with a look of confusion. "Except . . . were there *lady* centaurs?" he asked.

"There must have been. Otherwise how could there ever have been new little centaurs?" asked a teasing voice.

Julie turned and smiled a welcome. "Mrs. Walker. You have met Lord Sherringham's cousin, Roland Caldwood?"

"Yes. Earlier. In the kitchen. Roland, Cook has just removed fairy cakes from the oven," she added.

Roland licked his lips. "Do you think," he asked in worried tones, "she made a few extra?"

"I know she did," said Sarah, her eyes laughing. Roland politely, if a trifle hurriedly, excused himself. Sarah turned to Julie. "Lord Sherringham asked that I find you a habit so that you might begin riding lessons. Will you come this way so that we may choose one?"

Julie bit her lip but then, remembering this might— probably was—Lady Sarah, she could not bring herself to admit before such an excellent horsewoman her own stupid fears. Meekly, she followed up into the attics.

Instead of going to the far storage room and an armoire Mrs. Lamb said was stuffed with ancient clothing, Sarah turned into the small room in which her own things were kept. She had decided that it was foolish to own perfectly modern habits and pretend they did not exist. Julie might as well choose from the older ones, the colored ones she'd worn before her father died—*not* the black one she would wear herself if she dared to take out her mare while the party remained in residence.

The first trunk's hinges were stiff and it was an effort to put back the lid. But when she accomplished it Julie immediately knelt and, with a delicate touch, fingered the rich silks and lush woolens, the fine cottons and the delicate lace.

"Why are such lovely things hidden away?" Julie asked before she recalled that it might be Lady Sarah kneeling at her side, in which case the stored clothing was hers.

Sarah hesitated. "Their owner has no use for them. She is in mourning," she said shortly. She had forgotten she should give Julie no hints to her identity. Julie was far too intelligent, too quick, to need *more* than a hint.

Julie was disappointed. For half a moment she'd thought Sarah might confide . . . but then told herself she was a fool. Lady Sarah Staunton would never confide in a whore. Even a whore who called herself a courtesan.

As the thoughts ran through Julie's mind, Sarah lifted an item or two. "The habits aren't here."

Hoping they were lost, Julie asked, "But will she not, whoever she is, object to my using her things?"

"I would not show you if it were not permitted. By the time she can wear them again, they will be out of style," said Sarah with only a touch of bitterness. "Since the habits are not in this trunk we will try that one." She knelt by the second trunk. Its lid rose more easily and she found what she wanted. She looked from the contents to Julie and bit her lip. "I don't know . . ."

"Have you changed your mind?" Julie decided that only the truth would solve this particular problem. "I will not object. I am not convinced I *wish* to learn to ride."

Sarah straightened. She blinked. "Not *wish* to learn?" The tone, if not the words, asked, *how could one not wish it?*

"Not everyone is enamored of horseflesh," Julie muttered, flushing. "Oh, if you must have it, I am afraid of the beasts. Great stupid creatures! In London I've a gentle mare and a cabriolet and I have grown fairly skillful at driving myself when there is not too much traffic, but to sit up high on the back of one? No. I will fall off."

"Nonsense. Even if you tried you could not fall. Your knee holds you steady. You sit as firmly on the saddle as you do in a rocking chair. My dear Mrs. Green, *Julie,*" she amended, "I assure you, you will very soon wonder why you ever thought you would not like it."

Julie shook her head but knew there would be no arguing with this earnest woman for the same reasons she could not convince Larry. Both were idiotically enamored of the beasts and could not conceive how others might find them fearsome.

She turned back to the habits. There was a gorgeous black on top, but Sarah was already laying that aside. Under it were a green one, a muted red, and a reddish brown. Sarah's hands hesitated on the red but then lifted out the brown. "I believe this one is a trifle looser about the top. I think it will fit you. . . ."

But there was a hint of doubt in her tone and Julie drew in a deep breath, increasing the size of that which was under discussion. She glanced down at herself and then at Lady Sarah who still frowned.

With any luck, thought Julie, eying Sarah's slender body, *I'll not fit into the thing and then I can postpone, perhaps indefinitely, the lessons Lawrence has decreed.* "Very well. I will take it to my room and try it on."

Sarah nodded. "We will see what must be done to make it presentable. Beyond shortening it, I mean."

Julie had not meant for Sarah to come, but could see no way out of it and hoped the fit of the habit was so far from presentable it would be impossible to make it so. Unfortunately, it was not so very bad and Sarah was soon on her knees at Julie's feet putting pins around the hem.

Lawrence opened the door between the bedrooms and stopped short, staring at the scene. Something bothered him. It seemed wrong that the housekeeper knelt at the feet of a courtesan. Why he felt that way he could not say. And, because it was an absurd thought, he set it aside.

"I see you have found a habit," he said, forcing a grin.

"You also see," said Julie, "that it is *more* than a trifle tight." She tugged at the jacket lapels.

He laughed. Very gently he moved her hands. Carefully he drew the edges together. "If the buttons are moved it will do."

Julie sighed. "I am sure it will not."

"Because you do not want lessons?"

"Yes," she said. The word burst from her and she scowled at him. "Devil, my dear, I do not *wish* to learn to ride."

"You will forget that nonsense as soon as you have

begun your first lesson. Come, Julie," he coaxed, "I know you are not a coward."

"Am I not?" she looked thoughtful. "Are you certain?"

Sarah, at her feet, snorted softly at Julie's tone, which was meant to draw laughter—although not from her.

"I am quite certain," said Lawrence who did *not* laugh. "You remember how we met? That was not the behavior of a coward."

Sarah looked up in time to see a mottling flush climb Julie's neck and face. She tipped her head. "I hear a story," she murmured just loudly enough to be heard.

Sherringham glanced down. He'd forgotten the housekeeper was pinning up the skirt. "Yes. A story," he admitted. "I was beset by a mob of urchins in an alley into which I should not have wandered. The noise drew Julie to her window. She saw that I failed to fend them off and came to my rescue, wielding a broom with great verve and more strength than one would expect from someone her size."

"What he is *not* telling you is that he could not bring himself to hurt the little horrors," said Julie sounding disgusted. "*They* had no such qualms. One of them had a sort of cudgel. If the lad had been the least little bit taller he could have reached Larry's head and the end of the story would have been a great deal different."

Sherringham shrugged. "A few black and blue marks. I was to break a child's arm to prevent them?"

"You are too softhearted for your own good," scolded Julie. Then her impish grin appeared. "For *my* good, however . . . !"

Sarah recalled Julie's story about learning to read and write. She cast a speculative glance toward his lordship and then, quickly, brought her eyes back to her work. She put more pins into the merino twill and had to move and, soon, move again. She grimaced. The work was not comfortable. She feared her knees would be quite red when she finished.

She forgot her hurts by speculating about Lord Sherringham. Perhaps one characteristic with which she had endowed her ideal was a part of his true character? He certainly seemed to have understood his young cousin's needs, taking him, first thing, to the kitchen to meet Mrs. Lamb. And now she knew he had accepted what must have been a bad bruising rather than hurt a child wielding a cudgel. It sounded as if he cared for children, that he would not harm them if he could avoid it, so her requirement that he like the young was met in the real man if nothing else matched her ideal.

But it was a mystery, was it not? That he could be sensitive in that way, but so insensitive that he brought a doxy with him to her lodge? Surely that had never before happened. Her father would not allow such goings-on under his roof. Would he? And then Sarah recalled occasions when, much to her disappointment, he refused to bring her with him, leaving her with relatives while *he* hunted. She had always thought it most unfair.

Did his guests bring such women on those occasions? A further thought slipped under her guard, causing consternation. *Did my father?*

For the first time ever she wondered about his lordship's private self, the side of him he would have kept carefully hidden from her. Sarah inserted the last pin and, with difficulty, she pushed herself up.

Sherringham put a hand under her arm, helping her. The contact startled her and she looked up, meeting his eyes. His gaze sharpened. She felt frozen under that stare and could not look away. He blinked, relaxed, and, grimacing ever so slightly, turned away. Sarah exhaled and only then realized she'd held her breath.

Julie, stepping out of the skirt, hadn't noticed. "I have the horrid feeling that Larry is correct—"

Sarah very nearly stopped her from undressing. *Sherringham was watching.* And then the absurdity of warning a lightskirts that her lover was in attendance almost made her laugh.

Or cry.

Sarah wasn't certain which.

"—that moving the buttons will be sufficient to make the top nearly adequately large for me."

Julie looked down at the short jacket that was covered halfway down the front by a jabot that spilled lace-edged frills from a band at the throat. Below the jacket she was covered by silken drawers, lace trimmed, with white silk stockings between them and her slippers. Sarah felt herself blush for Julie who seemed utterly unconscious of her state of dress. Or undress!

"Please, Mrs. Walker—" As she spoke, Julie shrugged out of the jacket. "—take all the time you need to complete this task. I am in no hurry to have the costume returned to me since that will mean the dread day is upon me. A week? *Two* perhaps?"

The droll tones caught Sarah's attention, drawing it away from wondering if she herself would dare to wear such delicate drawers. With nearly equal drollness, Sarah replied, "Oh, at least two. I cannot see finishing in less."

Since Lady Sarah was incapable of finishing it at all, the use of her needle not an art she'd mastered, it had not occurred to her that Mrs. Green would expect it of her. That she did was clear. And, as housekeeper, Sarah could hardly deny the woman's request. Nor did she have any excuse for lingering.

No excuse, in fact, for interfering in anything Sherringham had in mind for the two of them once they were alone. Sarah accepted the jacket, bundled up the skirt and, her face flaming, marched from the room.

"Now why did she suddenly look as if she had caught the two of us in a most indelicate situation?" asked Julie.

"Perhaps it occurred to her that it was for that I came," mused Sherringham, his brows forming those little check marks above his eyes as he frowned. "Not that it is her business what we do, and, of course that is *not* what I had in mind, so . . ." Which brought the reason to the fore. He drew in a breath and let it out. ". . . Julie, have you come to a conclusion concerning the boy?"

"Roland?" She threw a dress over her head and turned back so that Lord Sherringham could fasten it. "He hasn't been here all that long and I have had little time to get to know him."

"Do so—" With no particular thought to what he did, his fingers busied themselves with tapes and buttons. "—and give me your opinion, will you?"

"Have you not reached your own conclusions?"

"I have—but in this particular case I am uncertain if I trust myself."

She smiled. "You have absolved him of all guilt, is that not so?"

Lawrence nodded. "He is just a boy like any boy. Better than some, actually. Julie, when I was in the army, I knew so many his age. I had to deal with all sorts. I would swear Roland is just what he seems."

"You fear your instincts might be at fault?"

"Four men died one after the other in the three months before I came into my honors. Despite what I told you earlier, I have some trouble accepting that in each and every case it was mere fate."

She nodded. "I suspect I have greater fears for you than you have for yourself. Who is in line after the boy?"

Lawrence cast her a startled look. "You mean the succession?"

She nodded.

"I haven't a notion." He paused, thinking, and then added, "It is an excellent question." He frowned. "On the other hand," he continued after another moment's thought, "could anyone rationally expect six men to expire—"

"Five men and a boy."

"—so that he might inherit?"

"Who suggested such a person is rational?"

"Ah." He bit his lip, his brows more devilish looking than ever. "I think I will write my solicitor."

"I think you should."

He stood there, thinking.

"Now, perhaps?" she added.

The teasing tone brought him to attention. "Now? Ah. You wish to finish dressing and would prefer that I depart while you do so?"

"Yes."

He grinned at the hint of pique in her tone. "Julie, sometimes you surprise me. You stood there in your shift completely unmoved and now, decently covered, you find my presence, while you do your hair, embarrassing?"

He put his arm around her shoulders, placed a brotherly kiss on her forehead, and, releasing her, returned to his room. He shut the door with just a bit of a snap and Julie, allowing humor to erase her irritation, suspected the sound meant, "*women—I'll never understand them.*" Julie went to her dressing table and reached for the cosmetics she used with such care now that age was beginning to show itself . . .

* * *

The next several days saw the arrival of the three men Lawrence had invited to his party. Each brought a woman. Mrs. Lamb accepted this but Sarah, outraged, found the courage to ask if, when her father lived, he held such parties.

"Yes, of course," said Mrs. Lamb. She chuckled at Sarah's shock. "Surely you did not think your father a monk?"

"I did not think at all." Sarah bit her lip. Then she sighed. "I suppose I should have done."

Sarah wandered around the kitchen, picking up the salt bowl and setting it down where she picked up Mrs. Lamb's rolling pin. She put that on a ledge and plucked an apple from the bowl set there for Roland's benefit. She took a bite, chewed it as she wandered toward the other end of the long low-ceilinged room, put the half eaten fruit down on the mantel and picked up a porcelain shepherdess with a chip out of her skirts. She fingered the small flaw as she moved back to where Mrs. Lamb, her rolling pin retrieved, rolled out pastry for a meat pie.

When Sarah reached for the rolling pin as the cook laid it to one side, Mrs. Lamb took it back. "*Oh no you don't.* You aren't running off with that. Not again, you aren't."

Sarah blinked. She picked up the statuette and frowned at it, looking at the mantel where she knew it should be. "How did this get here?"

Mrs. Lamb shook her head. "My dear Lady Sarah, you *are* blue-deviled, are you not?" When Sarah merely stared, she added, "*You* put it there." Sarah frowned and the cook shook her head still again. "My lady," she said softly, "everyone is gone on that pick-nick. Doubtless, they'll not return until late. Perhaps you should take the opportunity to put on a habit and gallop off your fidgets."

"*And* take myself out of your way at the same time?" asked Sarah as the notion wormed a way into and through her moodiness. The idea found favor and her mood lightened. She grinned, her eyes shining.

Exercise, thought Sarah. *That is exactly what I need.* But then she wondered if she dared. *But, oh, to gallop again, to feel the wind against my face . . .*

"Go on with you now," urged Mrs. Lamb, smiling. The smile turned to a worried look. "But," she warned, "you come home betimes so that you will not be caught where you ought not be."

"I'll do that." Sarah hurried from the kitchen. She lifted her skirts and nearly ran up the back stairs all the way to the attics where she pulled the black habit from its resting place and carried it downstairs, wrinkling her nose at the strong scent of lavender.

Sarah wondered if Mrs. Lamb was anywhere near finished with the habit for Julie. She asked as she went back through the kitchen after changing for her ride.

"It is so far around the bottom and, with the maids here for such a brief time each day, I've so much else to do I've little time to put into it." She glanced up and, her smile fading, she stilled. "Lady Sarah, your *wig.*"

Sarah frowned. "You yourself said there was no one about."

"But there might be when you return." Mrs. Lamb lifted a finger and pointed toward the stables. "Besides, there are strange grooms out there." A look of horror crossed her plump features. "Those grooms! That settles it. You must wear it."

"It is so uncomfortable."

"Better safe than sorry," quoted the cook, frowning. When the younger woman hesitated, she spoke again, her tone coaxing rather than scolding. "Lady Sarah, do think of the consequences if you are caught in this escapade."

Sarah wavered. Abandoning the hated wig had been such a relief. Unfortunately Mrs. Lamb was correct. She heaved a great sigh and, obediently, returned to her rooms to don the wig and replace her hat, before, once again heading for the stables.

Chapter 5

Swallow, Lady Sarah's mare, flowed over a three-bar gate. It had not been a difficult jump, and it had felt so good, flying through the air, landing with a gentle thud, and trotting off down the lane. There wasn't the excitement of the chase, which she would not have dared join even if the house were not as full as it could hold with strangers, but it was still wonderfully freeing to ride again.

That she could not have hunted depressed her, but, as they walked along the lane, her mood lightened. She wanted to sing—so she did, her warm contralto soaring. Swallow's ears twitched and laid back so she stopped, chuckling that her mare was such an unappreciative audience.

She urged the mare to a canter. A mile or so on, she entered a sunken lane. A little distance along that she approached the only place where one could see over the high banks. The lane had worn so deep from centuries of use that her knees were at the level of the surrounding ground. Thick brush and trees grew along most of the way, interfering with the view everywhere but just ahead.

As she reached the thinner growth she heard pounding hooves, the sound drawing her eyes to the left. A rider, riding hard, leaned over his horse's neck. He approached at a fast pace. She wondered if he knew about the lane. Beginning to fear he did not, she rose in her stirrup and shouted, waving her hat.

"Sunken lane! Beware!"

The rider looked up. Consternation marred Lord Sherringham's strong features. An excellent horseman, he gathered his gelding and they jumped. The horse nearly made it—but not quite. His rear legs scrambled against the far edge, slid down, scrabbled some more, and, with great effort, he heaved himself and his rider up onto level ground.

Lawrence instantly dismounted and checked the animal.

"Damn and blast," he muttered, finding a scrape. He looked up, met Lady Sarah's gaze, and drew in a deep breath. "Thank you. I should be glad it is merely a scrape and not a broken leg. Or worse."

"Your broken head, for instance?" she asked.

His mouth thinned. "I suppose there is, for a horse, no worse than a broken leg. Mrs. Walker is it?" he asked, suddenly recognizing her. Consternation widened his gaze. "You ride?"

Sarah thought quickly. "I am a distant relation to Lord Staunton. When Lady Sarah was young, after her mother died, I was companion to her for a time. When *she* learned to ride so did *I*. Lord Staunton left it in his will that I was to be mounted for the rest of my life, for which I am thankful. I enjoy it very much, you see."

Sarah spoke with great earnestness, something she always did when she told a tarradiddle, but Lord Lawrence was not to know that. She, remembering something an out and outer had once told her, spoke accusingly. "I'd not be out but I thought that *you* were attending a pick-nick party." Sarah allowed one brow to arch.

"I *was*," he said, flushing slightly.

Ha! she thought *That caught his attention so perhaps "a good offense is a good defense" might sometimes be true?*

"I find," he continued reluctantly, "that, except for Cannington, the men I knew before I entered the army are . . . have not . . ." He sighed softly and raised his eyes to meet hers. "I guess what I should say is that I have changed and they have not?"

"They bore you?" she asked, sympathy in her tone.

"Bore me?" He looked away. "I suppose that is part of it. Sometimes. It is more that what once seemed hilarious now seems mere childishness. *Roland* appears to find their antics comical."

Sarah nodded. When she had graced a London season, she had often found examples of his friends' humor rather trying. She glanced at his horse. "Can you ride him or must you walk back to the stables?"

"If I go slowly, I think I can ride." He mounted and walked the animal a few paces. "He isn't limping is he?" he asked.

"He doesn't appear to favor the leg," Sarah replied.

"I interrupted your ride. I will leave you to it if you will—" Sherringham suddenly looked embarrassed. "—point me in the right direction? I don't," he admitted, looking chagrined, "have the least notion where I've gotten to."

Sarah laughed freely for the first time in ages. Lawrence looked startled and Sarah broke off, blinking. "What is it?"

"I suppose it is that you are related to her. Do you know you sound exactly like Lady Sarah when you laugh in that fashion?"

Sarah looked conscious. "I suppose it comes from our long acquaintance."

"The relationship is also apparent in the shape and color of your eyes." He tipped his head. "Do *you* know where she is?"

Alarm filled her. "What . . . what do you mean?"

"You *must* know she has disappeared. Even her solicitor has no knowledge of where she has gone. It occurs to me that if the two of you were close *you* might have been informed?"

"And if I do know?" The earnestness returned. "Should I break a trust by telling anyone?"

He pursed his lips, looking into the distance and then sighed. "No, of course not. If you could tell me she is safe and comfortable, I would appreciate it," he added, again looking directly at her.

"She is safe and reasonably comfortable," said Sarah softly. She was surprised he seemed to care. *The man,* she thought crossly, *is a confusing mass of contradictions. Is he or is he not my dream man?*

"Thank you."

How, she wondered, confused, *could a man who keeps a mistress be so interested in a stranger's whereabouts?*

It occurred to her that perhaps, for men, the one thing had nothing to do with the other. The notion did not please her so she pushed the new evidence concerning his character to the back of her mind.

"I should return to the house myself," she said with a glance toward the sun. "We may ride together." She pointed her crop back the way she had come.

"Is there anywhere I can come down into the lane without scrambling down the bank?" he asked.

He remembered his mount's scraped leg! This thought *did* please. But putting that out of mind as well, she nodded. "Around that curve is a gate. I'll meet you there."

Lord Sherringham looked along the edge of the field from his higher vantage point, saw the gate, and set off.

Soon they were riding slowly along the lane. "Will not your party wonder where you've gone?" asked Sarah when the silence seemed too loud.

"I told Julie I could bear it no longer."

"And Mrs. Green said?"

"She asked if she must continue to bear it or if she too could sneak away."

"And your reply?" asked Sarah.

"Unfortunately Julie drove the carriage in which our other female guests rode and, quite obviously, they were not ready to leave what they considered the first pleasurable high jinks to occur since their arrival."

"So poor Mrs. Green must suffer?"

"I have had a notion," he said and flashed a grin her way. "I will send Alfred with a gig to retrieve her and a note to Canny—Lord Cannington—that *he* must drive the carriage home."

"An excellent solution. Alfie will feel like a king with Mrs. Green up beside him. Tonight, he will preen and pose at the inn, boring all his cronies with how he had the privilege of driving a regular high flyer all the way from the castle ruins back to the Cottage."

"I will tell Julie. She will laugh."

Sarah wondered if Mrs. Green *would* laugh—or if she would be *touched* that the old man found pleasure in driving a lovely woman. But that was not a question she could ask and she searched for another topic of conversation. "You were in the army, were you not?" She knew he was.

A muscle tightened in his jaw. "Yes."

She glanced at him, the bitten-off word startling her. "You do not wish to speak of it. I am sorry for reminding you, but," she persisted, "I wondered if you had much to do with Wellesley—Lord Wellington, that is," she corrected, recalling he had recently been made an earl. "I much admire the gentleman."

He glanced at her but Sarah was staring over her horse's head into the distance. "You do not feel he spends far too much time running away from the enemy?" asked Sherringham sarcastically.

"It is my understanding," she said, "that our army is considerably smaller than the one the enemy has in Spain. If that is true, then I think I would be equally cautious as to exactly when and where I face them."

He cast her a look of surprise. "Excellent woman!" he said. "I don't suppose you would care to explain that to the politicians who insist he should chase down Nappy's troops and beat them to flinders whenever and wherever he can? And, *most* importantly, as *soon* as he can?"

Sarah chuckled. "Do you think they would listen?"

"They will not listen to experts, but perhaps your delightful self would manage the thing in a more tactful manner?"

Sarah sent a quick glance his way. Was he flirting with her? How could he? Her gray hair alone should protect her from any flirtation.

Ah, if only he were!

The ache she felt along with the thought startled Lady Sarah. She forgot herself to the extent she loosened her reins—and instantly had her hands full when her mare responded accordingly. When back in control, she found Lord Sherringham poised to interfere.

"What was it?" he asked. "Until she attempted to bolt, I had thought your mare particularly well behaved," he added.

"She is. It was my fault, my lack of attention." As an explanation it was inadequate. Hoping to divert him from wondering at it, she pointed her crop across an intervening pasture. "See those trees beyond the crest of that hill?" she asked.

"Hmm."

"I want a run before I return, but you will find the stables just beyond that grove." She backed her mare away from him, turned, and raced across the meadow. At the far side was a hedge. She and her mare rose over it gracefully.

"Well done," Lord Sherringham exclaimed. He rode on, thinking aloud. "How she rides! If she were not so obviously matronly, I would assume her ten, maybe twenty years younger."

And then he walked his horse on to the stables where he had a long talk with his head groom about the scrape on his horse's leg after which he asked Alfie to drive the gig to the ruins in order to bring Julie home.

". . . I will write a note for Lord Cannington while you harness up," he said.

Once she was out of sight, Sarah pulled the mare to a walk. A frown creased her brow and Mrs. Lamb, if she'd seen it, might have thought the expression very nearly suited the gray wig.

Why, even for a moment, wondered Sarah, *did I wish he were flirting with me? He is a womanizer. He brought a party of gambling and carousing men to my father's hunting box. They drink too much. They are loud and not particularly polite. They demand service far into the night and then one or another will awaken early and demand service too soon in the morning. They are thoughtless and a trifle cruel and surely I cannot like a man who likes such things?*

She recalled that Alfie, describing the scene, said Lord Sherringham interfered when one of his guests was about to beat his groom.

So, if he interfered, as Alfie said he did, then he does not *approve such behavior?*

On the other hand, she knew for a certainty that Lord Sherringham had over-indulged in heavy drinking more than once since his party arrived. She had seen him in the morning, bleary-eyed and grim looking, his *head*, at least, unready to rise and meet the day.

But he did rise, she reminded herself, *however out of frame he was. He promised Roland he would teach him the way of a water jump and he got up and dressed and went out despite his late night. He endured the lad's prattle when his head must have felt like a drum throbbing.*

Then she recalled the first night all the guests had arrived. Someone suggested a game of hide-and-seek. Women squealed and men roared with wicked laughter keeping her awake far past her bedtime. Did Lord Sherringham enjoy such wild pastimes? She sighed, remembering her own participation in similar entertainments at house parties. Why should she be shocked that his lordship played them here?

Because, she told herself virtuously, *playing with members of the muslin company is not the same as playing with ladies.*

And then she berated herself for thinking the two classes of women so different as she'd always believed. Was not Julie more the real lady in *her* ways than some of the women she knew among the *ton?* And were there not ladies of the *ton* who comported themselves as freely—if with more discretion—as did the whores? Her thoughts continued in circles until, angry with herself for her inability to come to any conclusion, she looked up and glanced around herself.

"Where," she asked herself "have I come to?"

She flushed when she realized how far beyond Blackberry Hill property she was. Instantly she turned—but it was too late.

"Lady Sarah," called a woman from behind a low hedge.

Feeling distinctly guilty, Sarah ignored her.

"Lady Sarah!"

Sarah pulled Swallow up. She turned. "Are you speaking to me?" she asked, using her rough voice.

"Oh dear," said the little old lady, looking confused. "I was so certain you were . . . well, someone else."

Sarah was lucky it was Mistress Petrony, who was a trifle shortsighted. Sarah liked the woman's chirpy personality and was sorry to have had to ignore her. She nodded, waved goodbye, and turned to go on her way, hoping she would run into no one else who knew her well.

Realizing she should have been home much earlier, Sarah kicked her heel into her mare's side and cut across country. The mare put her heart into the run and they soon approached the stables from the rear. Sarah heard shouts of laughter—male chortles and female giggles mixed. The pick-nick party had returned before her.

Mrs. Lamb will scold, she thought. *Why did I not go home with Lord Sherringham when I had the opportunity?*

Not that she wondered for long, her mind returning to the debate it had had with her emotions. "He is a womanizer and light-minded and that is not what I want in a man," she told the mare. The mare's ears twitched and the animal shook her head, rattling the bit and reins. "You disagree, but, foolish as the notion may be, I want what I have always wanted. A man who will love me."

Lord Lawrence held out his wrist to his valet and glanced to where Julie sat in a chair, her knees pulled up and her arms hugging her legs in an exceedingly unladylike fashion. "You will laugh," he said.

"Will I?" she asked. "Then tell me. I could do with a good laugh."

"I actually had the suspicion that Mrs. Walker might be Lady Sarah in disguise."

"Did you?" asked Julie.

"Her eyes. She has the same vividly blue eyes as Lady Sarah."

"Does she?" Julie had, prior to this trip into the country, seen Lady Sarah only in the park and at a distance so had not previously seen the eyes in question.

"She explained it."

"Explained it, did she?"

"Mrs. Walker is a distant cousin," said Lawrence, holding out his other wrist. "She was Lady Sarah's companion when Lady Sarah was young and Staunton not only gave her this house for a home—as housekeeper and caretaker—but he left funds to keep her mounted on good horses for so long as she wishes to ride."

"Interesting," said Julie. She debated whether it might be true. There was the quality of the gowns in the trunks and of the black dresses Mrs. Walker wore with such grace. And that wig . . .

It is a wig, is it not? she asked herself.

Julie decided, again, she'd not point out this possibility to Lawrence. While the house party continued it was better if Mrs. Walker remained Mrs. Walker. What the lady did once the party ended—well that was up to the lady, was it not?

"I will admit to disappointment," said Lawrence, his chin lifted, while his valet wound a starched cravat around his neck.

"Now, my lord. *Gently,*" ordered the valet, critically watching while Lawrence lowered his chin. "Very good milord," he added, pleased their first effort was successful. He picked up an overly large sapphire pin and tucked the fingers of his other hand beneath the folds, preparing to place it.

Lawrence grasped his wrist. "No. We've discussed this before."

"But my lord!"

"*No.* No jewels. Where is the pin with the regimental insignia?"

"It is not the fashion, my lord," said the valet stubbornly.

"To Hades with fashion."

Sternly, the valet caught Lawrence's gaze . . . but it was his gaze that faltered, dropped. Obviously unhappy, he returned to the dressing table and dug through a wooden box with an intricate design of different colored and highly polished woods inset into it.

"It is not here," said the valet.

Lawrence's head snapped up. "Not?"

"Not."

"Nonsense. It must be."

"It is not. Will you allow me to use the emerald? It is a much more modest jewel . . ."

"You did not leave it behind, did you?"

"You wore it the day before yesterday, did you not?" asked Julie.

Lawrence remembered he had. "Yes . . . and came to bed quite late."

"You told me you did not need me, milord," said the valet, faint accusation in his tone. "I should have been here."

"No, no. It is nonsense that you remain up when I foolishly stay below stairs hours beyond any reasonable man's bedtime," said Lawrence ruefully. "Still, what did I do with it?"

While his coat was fitted to his shoulders he searched his mind. "I remember loosening my cravat. Canny removed his and his coat. He threw his things over the arm of a chair. Then," mused Lawrence, trying to recall, "I undid *my* coat. Did I remove it?" He frowned. "I think not . . ."

"But did you remove your cravat?" asked Julie.

"No," he said slowly and went on more firmly. "No, I did not. I remember pulling it from around my neck when I returned to this room. The pin must have flown from the material. Merit, I detest asking such things of you, but will you search for it? It may very well have been flung anywhere. Into the drapery. Into a corner. Behind the bed. I don't know. But I like that pin. I do not wish to lose it."

Merit bowed, hiding a hint of a grimace. *But, unlike the last, this Lord Sherringham rarely requests anything out of the way.* Therefore, he would not object to this one odd request when his lordship was not, in the usual way, a difficult taskmaster.

"Are you ready?" Sherringham asked Julie.

Julie did not bother to hide her grimace. "As ready as I may be," she said and lifted her eyes to the ceiling as she drew in a deep breath and let it out in a bit of a huff.

He chuckled. "I should never have asked you to come here. It is very much *not* your proper milieu."

Julie sobered. "Never say you cannot ask anything of me, Larry. I would do anything for you, up to and including giving my life for you."

"We will hope it never comes to that," he said lightly—but he was deeply touched.

Chapter 6

Each day the men—or, at the least, Lord Cannington, the most enthusiastic—rose early and rode off into the cool morning damp, the sun barely above the horizon. Somewhere, wherever it was that the huntsman meant to exercise the hounds, they would meet up with the kennel men who had the youngsters in charge. By six-thirty the paired hounds would have arrived at the first covert and would be straining at the leashes.

Sarah fumed as she climbed the stairs. She envied the men the freedom to ride out into the low-lying scent-laden mist. She envied them the hours among like-minded men—and the two or three women who flouted convention in order to join in. Something *she* would do if she could.

Sarah wanted, desperately, to feel the wind in her face while following the pack, or even to merely study the young hounds' behavior, forced into obedience by the chain attached to their collars and that of the older dog paired with them, as they trotted along the road to the next copse, kept by that means to the business at hand.

Today the men hadn't far to go since, this particular morning, the Cottesmore hunt, the nearest of several in the region, was gathering at Blackberry Hill Cottage. Such meets were a break in the monotony for the servants, perhaps, but required a great deal of extra work from footmen and kitchen staff and of course the stablemen.

Sarah, hurrying and only a little out of breath, reached the attic and found a window from which she could watch but not be seen by neighbors who had known her from childhood.

What a glorious sight, she thought as she stared down on the milling horses, the excited dogs, the men and the few women who were brave enough—or eccentric enough— to join in. How she envied them.

This particular morning Lord Sherringham and his guests were all out. For a long moment her eyes rested on his lordship. *How well he sits his horse,* she thought. That a man know horses, and horsemanship had been one of her requirements. Why, she wondered, did Sherringham have to be so very near her ideal and yet so far off?

Forcing mind and eyes away from his lordship, her glance fell on the bobbing feather of one of two women who, side by side, just then trotted up. She felt her blue eyes turning green with envy. How she longed to join them. They were to have a good long run with exciting jumps and a full morning in the fresh air while she must hide herself away . . .

Sighing, Sarah glanced around the busy yard. Julie stood to one side, speaking to those who spoke to her and ignoring those who looked through her. Sarah wondered how she could bear it, the snubbing she received from more than one person who hadn't a notion how lucky he was merely to eat regularly—and who was very likely less well read and boring as well!

Sarah bit her lip as it occurred to her she would, herself, not long ago, have felt forced to ignore Lord Sherringham's *chère amie* as these female riders did. She eyed the women, bound by little but their mutual love of the hunt, eccentrics who participated in the face of the disapproval of other women and most men, who believed it a man's sport.

Sarah leaned forward as everyone mounted up, the whippers-in collecting the hounds and bringing them to attention. Her brows arched when she realized the pack was led toward a covert on her land. Excitement gripped her and she wondered if a fox would break in a direction where she could see him, could watch the pack in pursuit.

She waited, almost as restless as were the horses and riders also awaiting word the fox was sighted. She released the catch on the window and shoved. It stuck and she glanced toward the copse in which the dogs worked. Putting both hands on the frame she shoved hard and, with a crack, it swung open. The sound drew no eyes and her held breath released. She breathed again and, her heart thudding, she strained to hear the dogs' voices, waited for that change in tone that indicated a hound had raised the quarry.

A movement off to the left caught her eye and she giggled. Sly old Mr. Fox was quietly sneaking away along the edge of a gully that hid him from the riders watching the woods and listening, as she did, to the hounds.

I should, she thought, *point out the escaping fox.*

Almost as if he heard her, the fox crouched, swinging his head up toward her, his tongue hanging out in that humorous fashion unique to the animal. It was as if he looked at her and said, "Ye'll not be so rude as to give me away, will ye now, m'lovey?" and she found she couldn't, didn't want to. Silently she wished the fox good luck—for today.

Only when Reynard was out of sight did she piously remind herself—having just remembered it—that she could not have warned anyone of the fox's escape in any case. She dared not call attention to herself!

Not too much later the hounds were called to order and leashed. The hunt moved off in quite another direction from that taken by the fox. Filled with hot uncomfortable jealousy, Sarah watched the riders and dogs trail up and over a hill and disappear.

Closing the window, Sarah stood staring into the distance for a time and then, feeling particularly morose, took herself slowly down the stairs. In her blue-deviled state she forgot that she should take the back stairs and found herself in the great room where three of the doxies played at spillikins on the long table used for dining. Bickering, testy with each other, one swearing the other had moved a stick while removing another, the second swearing she had not, they were, quite obviously, bored to tears. She wondered how Julie had escaped them.

"*You,*" one called as Sarah started for the door under the stairs.

Sarah put her chin up and took another step. Then she recalled she was pretending to be the housekeeper and that she must keep to the role whether she wished to or not. Mere housekeepers hadn't the choice of ignoring a guest living under the same roof. Even guests such as these.

"You spoke?" she said.

"Tell us how we may entertain ourselves," demanded the redheaded wench, the brashest of the three.

Sarah wanted, even more, to snub the rude woman, but it was not, after all, an entirely unreasonable request, even if voiced in sour tones. After a moment's thought, Sarah said, "Charades."

Another girl, a thin-faced blond with surprisingly fine skin, wrinkled her nose. "No fun when we don't have our men here," she whined.

"No, no," said Sarah. "I was thinking you might bring down the boxes of oddments saved for charades and sort through them, make them ready for all of you to play later?"

The girls looked at each other. One shrugged. Another sighed. The third pushed back from the table at which they played, and said, "Why not? We've nothing better to do."

"Show us," said the redhead, again making a rude demand of the order.

Sarah felt her spine stiffen. Enough, after all, was enough.

"*Now*," added the woman who was not such a slowtop she did not notice.

Sarah's chin rose. "I will send in Joseph to help you, Miss Murphy. He will show you where the boxes are kept and bring down those you wish to use." She turned on her heel and went under the stairs to the door to the servants' quarters, ignoring the woman's outraged "*Here, now*" and cutting off the rest of whatever demand the doxy might make by shutting the door with a bit of a slam.

She met Roland in the hall. "Were you looking for me?" she asked, bringing her temper under control.

"Not especially." The lad sighed.

"Bored, are you?"

He nodded and turned to trail her as she continued into the kitchen. Sarah sent Joseph into the great room with orders to see that the girls did *not* get into things they were to stay out of when he brought down the boxes of costumes and props for charades.

"And how am I to make them stay out of things they shouldn't get into?" asked Joseph. "I caught *one* of them coming from Lord Sherringham's room only the other day. She just laughed when I said she shouldn't ought to be there."

"From his *room*? Which one?"

"The Murphy."

"Miss Murphy? Why was she there?"

"I don't know," said Joseph. "But I'll say this. She looked like a cat who got into the cream, *she* did."

Joseph and the doxies were still in the attics when Sarah heard a commotion in the stable yard. She went to the back door and opened it—and paled, her hand going to the doorjamb for support. She straightened. "Have you sent for the doctor?" she called to the men carrying the gate toward her.

"I am here," said the local man morosely. His nose was red and his eyes bleary even that early in the day and Sarah looked doubtful. "J'st a broken leg, dearie," said the man, slurring his words.

Sarah met Lord Cannington's eyes, a worried look. Cannington shrugged, but he too seemed concerned.

Mrs. Lamb, wiping her hands on a towel as she came, was suddenly barring the door. "You get away from here," she said, shooing the doctor with the flip of the towel as if he were a chicken. "Get on with you now. Alfie will see to his lordship better'n you and you know it."

"His lordship'll need bleedin'," said the doctor, scowling mightily.

"He'll not then. For a broken leg? You take yourself back to the hunt, you old tosspot." Mrs. Lamb put herself between the doctor and the men carefully edging the gate into the kitchen. "Go," she said, turning on him and pointing.

Sarah joined her. "We can see to this problem, so thank you but you may go," she said in a more kindly tone as she dug in her pocket. She had found a half crown that morning when moving furniture back into place, dropped by someone when at cards and very likely should be returned. This was more important and she held it out to the doctor who looked at it, his eyes blinking rapidly as he attempted to see clearly. "You take this for your trouble," she said. He grabbed it with a hot moist hand and she turned Mrs. Lamb, pushing her inside and closing the door behind them.

Sarah went instantly to the table on which Lord Sherringham had been laid. "He is unconscious?" she asked sharply.

"Better Devil stays that way until the leg is set," said Cannington.

Devil? Sarah blinked. Hadn't she heard him called that before? She made a note to ask Julie how he'd acquired such a wicked nickname.

"Doesn't seem to be much else wrong. Just the bump on the head and the leg." Cannington looked up. He sounded apologetic when he continued. "Sorry about the doctor. Just the thing to do, you know? Ask if there's a doctor available?"

"You couldn't know the local man is impossible," she said in absent tones, her fingers very gently probing the back of Lord Sherringham's head.

Julie burst into the kitchen as Sarah cut another stitch at the side of Sherringham's boot, white of face, her eyes huge and scared. "Larry!"

"Devil's fine, Julie," said Cannington. "He'll be just fine." He caught her before she could bump the table in her desire to get near. "Here now. A broken leg! Won't be the first he's had," he added.

"And a bump on the head," said Sarah and caught Julie's eyes. Sarah held the other woman's gaze, her own stern, and slowly, Julie straightened. She swallowed. Hard. Sarah looked around.

"Mrs. Lamb?" Sarah's hands remained busy. "Has someone run for Alfie?"

"I did," said Roland, panting. He had just entered and

looked back out the door, waving the old man on. "Hurry, man," he called.

Alfred, muttering imprecations on all boys who thought the world would end if one didn't run around like a chicken without its head, stumped through the door and the boy closed it behind him as Mrs. Lamb told him to do.

". . . before you let in the whole outdoors," scolded the worried woman, going to drop more wood on the fire.

Sara ignored the byplay. She was wielding the sharpest of the kitchen knives along the seam of Sherringham's boot. She asked Julie—to give her something to do—to hold his leg steady while she worked. "I'll have this off in a minute, Alfred," she muttered when she realized he'd come up beside her.

The old man's gnarled hand closed over hers. He took the knife, making short work of the rest of the stitching. Tossing the boot to one side he began on the trousers. "I'll see to him," he said and added, "Off with you now . . . This is no place for the likes of you," he continued more briskly when Sarah didn't move. She still didn't move. He stopped what he was doing and turned on her. "Go. I'll not have the old man a'haunting me for letting you stay where you aren't wanted!"

Sarah cast a quick look toward Julie who tipped her head toward the door and then Sarah recalled Cannington's presence and looked at him. His lips were pursed slightly and there was a quizzical look about his eyes she didn't like. She turned on her heel and left.

"Alfie's oldest friend's daughter," she head Mrs. Lamb say in reply to a question from Lord Cannington.

Sarah told herself to be certain to thank Mrs. Lamb for her quick thinking, but she wondered if his lordship would allow the wool pulled over his wide-open eyes in such an easy fashion. Lord Cannington had, on *several* occasions, danced with Lady Sarah.

But that worry was for the future. Sarah fumed, wondering what was happening in the kitchen, whether Lord Sherringham had come to his senses, if Alfred was having any trouble with the leg . . .

She wanted to be there more than anything in the world. Instead, she climbed the stairs and entered the master bedroom—and stopped. Sitting in a chair near the bed was the most intelligent of the whores, discounting Julie.

"Miss Murphy," said Sarah as politely as she could. "Did you too come to turn down his lordship's bed?"

"Turn it down! More like I'll climb into it," said the redhead, laughing coarsely as she gave a toss to ringlets too bright to be real.

Chapter 7

Sarah stared, appalled at the woman's lewd admission and her self-satisfied smirk.

The whore tossed her wild red curls again, this time in defiance. "His lordship'll not be wanting that namby-pamby cotton-mouthed, long-in-the-tooth wench he brought along. Not for long. He'll want a *young* woman what'll give him excitement. Give him pleasure like he never had before."

Sarah felt her cheeks redden as she realized the woman was proud of what she considered skills. She fought embarrassment and curiosity and—wondering how she kept her voice steady—said, "You will have to wait. Lord Sherringham was brought in on a hurdle and I doubt he'll be wanting *excitement* for some time to come."

"On a hurdle." Miss Murphy's eyes narrowed. "What's that mean?"

"It means he broke a leg and took a knock to the head that'll give him an exquisite headache," said Sarah, already working on the bed. "Ah. Merit. You heard the news?"

"His Lordship's leg? Yes, ma'am. I'll do that," he added, laying down the nightshirt he held in his hands. "And you, miss," he said to the whore who stood in the way, "go along with you. You aren't wanted here and you shouldn't be here." His voice took on a fussy but scolding tone. "Lord

Cannington will toss you out on your ear if he learns what you've got up to."

Miss Murphy's lightly freckled skin turned bright red. "You old spindleshanks! You'd tell him, too, wouldn't you?"

"Only if you do not cease this nonsense and leave his lordship in peace," said Merit smoothly but with a touch of ice that made the words a threat.

"I'll be going then. But you're cheating his lordship of a right treat that you don't help me to him!"

"As to that, his lordship is more than capable of making his own decisions as he did when he chose Mrs. Green."

The bickering continued, the sound escalating until the door was flung open and Julie marched in. "You." She pointed her finger at the door. "Out."

Miss Murphy started to open her mouth but, meeting Julie's glare, closed it. Raising her nose into the air, she marched from the room. "You'll be sorry," muttered Miss Murphy as she passed Julie.

"I doubt it," was Julie's ironic reply. "Larry and I have known each other a very long time. We understand each other. You, you poor child, haven't got what he wants. Not at all."

Miss Murphy swung around, her fists tucked into her hips. "And what would *that* be?"

"Far more," said Julie, silkily, "than a romp in the hay. He wants to converse with his women. And you, my dear, wouldn't know where to begin or, if *he* did, what he was talking about."

Julie shut the door with a snap, Miss Murphy on the other side. And then she leaned against it. "You had better go as well," she said to Sarah, her tone much more polite. "I will tell you when you may visit him."

"Perhaps I could wait in your room?" said Sarah. *Blast Alfie!* Julie, it seemed, had guessed her identity. Assuming she had not done so before . . . ? But there was no time to think of that. She cast a pleading look toward Julie.

Julie hesitated. "Oh, very well. We'll put him to bed and then you can come in." Merit opened his mouth. Julie shook her head. "Do not say what you are thinking," she warned.

Merit frowned, looked from one woman to the other and heaved a sigh. "Women," he said, his tone pregnant with disgust.

"Just one more question and I'll go," said Sarah, fearing the valet had also guessed. "Did his lordship regain consciousness?"

"For a moment only. Then the pain of moving the bone into place knocked him out again," said Julie. "Go. I hear them coming."

Sarah went but left the connecting door ajar. She waited, desperate to know how he came through his ordeal, extended fingers tensed and trembling against her thighs.

Lord Sherringham was soon in bed, his broken leg propped at a comfortable angle. As she and the valet settled him, Julie organized his nursing. Merit, it was decided, would take the daytime and she would take the nights.

"You had better go do whatever you need to do, Merit, while Cannington and I are here. When you return I will nap so I'm ready for tonight."

Merit left reluctantly, but he admitted there were things he must do before he began sickbed duty.

When the door closed, Julie moved nearer Lord Sherringham's friend. "Canny," she said, something urgent in her voice.

"What is it?" Cannington stared at Lawrence, willing him to wake up.

"Tell me what happened. Exactly."

"Hmm? Oh. You mean his fall?" Cannington described the scene. ". . . charging after a young fox. More than half the field had gone over that hedge. Wasn't all that high, you know, although some went round by the gate. I followed Larry closely, but a little to the side. You know how one does."

Julie didn't but she nodded, wanting him to get on with it.

"Actually—" Cannington frowned slightly. "—I don't know what happened next. It was the first really good jump of the day, so I suppose it was bound to happen there."

"*What* happened?" demanded an exasperated Julie.

Sarah, listening, silently echoed that demand. She too wanted to know.

"What happened? Oh. The cinch broke." Cannington shrugged. "It happens."

Julie grabbed Cannington's arm. "Listen to me."

Cannington tipped his head toward her, gradually moving his gaze from his friend to her face.

Julie shook him. "Have I your attention, you great oaf?"

Cannington blinked and, finally conscious of how desperate Julie sounded, asked, "What is it?"

"Has it never occurred to you how unlikely it was for Larry to inherit the title?"

"Hmm?"

"*Four deaths in only three months.* Has it not crossed your mind it might be *five* before another has passed?"

It took half a moment for her suggestion to register. Cannington's head swung back to the bed. "You think it no accident?"

"*I'm* no rider. *I* haven't a notion, but you *should*. Check his saddle. The reins. The *horse,* for heaven's sake. Check everything. *Carefully.*"

Sarah, peering through the door, felt cold all the way to her center. Did Julie really believe that someone had tried to kill Sherringham? She watched a muscle jump in Cannington's jaw.

"*Very* carefully."

Cannington turned to Julie and gripped her arm. "Devil mustn't be left alone."

"Why do you think I mean to share the nursing with Merit? Merit's loyalties may be to the title rather than to Larry, but however that may be no one questions his loyalty. The two of us are to be trusted but I wonder about everyone else. Even *you.*"

Cannington's smile was without humor. "You never did like me all that much, did you?"

"No, but—" She drew in a deep breath and let it out. "—if you love him at all, *go check that equipment.* Discover if it was tampered with."

"I'm going." His hand on the door handle, he turned back, his features set in a far more serious mold than was his wont. "I *am* to be trusted. I owe Larry more than you can know. I'll share the nursing. You and Merit cannot do it all."

"I believe Mrs. Walker will help if someone must. There is no reason to believe *she* is in a plot to do him in."

"She could be bribed . . . ?"

Sarah bristled at the accusation but controlled herself and refrained from storming in to confront the man for suggesting such a thing. He, after all, merely smiled thinly at Julie's slightly different insult.

"I think not," said Julie. "Mrs. Walker is not capable of such treachery—"

Sarah felt warmth fill her at Julie's trust.

"—and if someone *were* to approach her for such a purpose she'd be outraged. If she did not give the poor soul a piece of her mind right then and there, she would come directly to Larry and tell him what happened."

"There's something odd about the woman. I cannot be so trusting until we know more about her. We will not argue about it now since I must go at once—before that saddle is fixed or disappears."

He left the room and Julie waited a moment before calling, softly, "You can come in now."

Sarah hesitated but then pushed open the door. "You knew I listened."

"I would have done. I assume you are as sensible."

Sarah sighed. If Julie knew she listened, then there was no reason to believe Julie trusted her more than she did Lord Cannington. "You cannot know it of a certainty, but you are correct that I would not harm Lord Sherringham."

"I *do* know." Julie hesitated but decided it was not the moment to reveal she was now certain of the sham housekeeper's real identity.

"You truly believe him in danger?"

"Yes."

Fear seeped into her bones as Sarah looked at the still figure. "He should awaken."

Julie agreed. The two stood by the bed.

"I might be able to find smelling salts," said Sarah doubtfully.

"Or vinegar. Sometimes that tart odor works as well."

"Or perhaps we should wait and allow him to wake naturally?"

The door burst open and the two women turned spreading their arms as if that would protect the figure lying so deathly still behind them.

Roland had a wild look about him. "Lord Sherringham. He is . . . they said . . . he's *dead?*"

"No! Merely a broken leg and a bang to the head," said Sarah. It didn't seem to soothe the boy. "Surely he has suffered worse in the past. He was a soldier, you know," she added, moving toward the panicky looking youth.

"Let me see him," begged Roland, peering around her.

"Later, Roland. Allow the poor man a bit of time to regain his composure," she said and forced a smile. It felt false, but seemed to calm the lad.

He chuckled weakly and some of the tension drained from him. "You would say I am behaving badly?"

"I believe it barely possible that one might come to that conclusion."

He didn't laugh again, even at the wry look that went with her teasing. He didn't even smile. "I would *hate* it if anything were to happen to Lord Sherringham," said the lad fiercely. "I *like* him. He has been . . . you know. Been like a *brother* to me. Or, you know, like I think a brother should be?"

"He will be again. When he has healed." Sarah put her hand on Roland's arm and, although she did not wish to leave the room, she led him to the door. "Now do come along," she said, pushing him out. "We will see if Mrs. Lamb has readied a luncheon for those of us who are not chasing after that poor fox."

"*Poor fox!*"

That, as Sarah intended, distracted Roland.

"What nonsense to call vermin a poor creature!" Roland, his fears eased or set aside, and his ever-present appetite roused, continued to object strongly concerning what he assumed to be her attitude as he trailed after Sarah who led him downstairs.

"I am very glad she took him away," said Lord Sherringham from the bed.

Julie swung around at the weak sound and went, immediately, to his side.

"I do not think my head would allow me to deal patiently with the boy right now." His eyes smiled. "What happened?" he asked after a moment and moved. He let out a muffled squawk.

"Don't! You've a broken leg."

He frowned. "Broken leg . . ." His eyes opened wide and then closed. "Ah!"

"You've remembered."

He nodded and then, obviously, wished he'd not. "Yes." His hand reached for her wrist, grasping it more tightly than she'd have thought possible. "Julie, there was something wrong with the saddle. It shifted in an odd way and then something snapped. It wasn't at all like a frayed cinch. I've experienced that. Quite a different thing altogether."

"I sent Canny to check it."

He opened one eye and stared at her. He closed it and nodded . . . and again regretted it. "Drat this head."

"You must have bumped it pretty hard. You've been unconscious for quite awhile—except for a moment before Alfred set your leg."

"Tied to my bed," said Lawrence after a moment. "That isn't good."

"You'll not be left alone. Merit and I mean to share the nursing. One of us will be here at all times."

"I want to talk to Canny as soon as he comes in."

"Of course." She crossed her fingers. If Larry fell back to sleep she would not awaken him.

After a moment he again opened that eye. "Julie, if you say 'I told you so' I'll have your neck."

"Would I do that?" she asked, smiling, her brows arched. She sobered. "Besides, I don't have to, do I?"

He grimaced. Then grimaced again when even that caused pain. "I have done nothing," he groused. "Why do I feel like I've been through a full scale battle?"

"Maybe you have. Sleep is good for you. Go to sleep."

Much to Julie's surprise that was exactly what he did.

Cannington was more perturbed than he allowed his friend's groom to see—but he didn't fool Alfred who followed him from the tack room.

"That didn't get that way natural-like," said the old man in severe tones.

"I agree," said Cannington, a muscle jumping in his jaw.

"I'll send a message to Lord Kenwicker."

"Who? Why?"

"Our magistrate. If someone deliberately did this for his lordship, then it should be invest-ee-gated." Alfie's chin rose to a belligerent angle. "Old Lord Staunton would have my gizzard if I did less."

"Staunton is dead—"

"More's the pity," muttered Alfred.

"—and Lord Sherringham would not approve."

Alfred's eyes narrowed.

"Don't look at me that way. I'm sending away the guests. No one will get to Larry while I'm around," said Cannington, a grim look settling in around his eyes. He thought for a moment. "First off, have you seen any strangers around and about where they should not be?"

Alfred nodded. He held up his hand, turning down fingers as he spoke. "Half a dozen grooms. Their masters. Doxies. We don't need those lightskirts here. Not—" Alfred caught himself, recalling he was forbidden to use

Sarah's name. "—with Lord Staunton underground and unable to keep an eye on things." He pushed down still another finger as he drew in a breath. "Then there are those silly prancing dollies what call themselves valets—"

Cannington winced, thinking of his own valet who definitely pranced but was, nevertheless, an excellent man with starch and hot iron—an important skill when modern fashions decreed a great deal of starch and a great deal of pressing.

"—*and* the new footmen and—" Alfred scratched his nose. "Guess maybe that's all, right here close anyway," he finished.

Cannington was reluctantly suspicious about several possibilities. Nevertheless, he repeated his original question, elaborating on it a trifle. "Those are members of the household. I meant someone new to the area who is not of our party."

Alfred looked at him as if he were a knock-in-the-cradle. "'Course there are. It is the cubbing. 'Tain't like when the hunting season starts, when the whole shire's as full as it can hold with strangers, but, like you, some do come to see how the youngsters are shaping."

Cannington sighed. "Unfortunately true."

"Lord Kenwicker would check on everyone," continued Alfred still more belligerently. "He'd find out if there really is a stranger around, one '*tisn't* wanted."

Cannington's eyes narrowed and he stared into the distance. Perhaps he should . . . He shook his head. "Larry will come to his senses soon if he has not already done so. I'll see what he has to say. My guess is that he'll not want our suspicions bruited about the area for the gossips to catch hold of and make mountains from."

"Might do a power of good if they did—Scare the bastard away," added Alfred when Cannington tipped his head questioningly.

"And then, someday, when it was no longer expected, he'd come back for another try?"

Alfie's bottom lip pushed against his upper, relaxed. "Didn't think of that, did I? Better catch the bastard now."

"Very much better. Keep your suspicions to yourself, Alfred, and your tongue between your teeth. *And* an eye to those extra grooms. One might have been bribed and might try something else, I suppose."

"I'll keep an eye peeled. No fear I'll not."

Cannington nodded, but thought of how bleary those old eyes were and how easily the old man might nod off at just the wrong moment. He decided to have a word with Larry's head groom.

The one-armed man Larry had hired for his head groom was a soldier wounded in Larry's last battle. He had nursed the man while at sea and, when he saw the conditions in the over-crowded military hospital in Dover, had taken the man to his own home and cared for him there.

Jeremy Wright would give his other *arm for Larry,* thought Cannington. He'd have that little talk just as soon as he could do so with no one the wiser.

Inside, Sarah fumed. She wanted, desperately, to care for Lord Sherringham herself. She wanted to see that he did not develop a fever, that his head was bathed with lavender water—which, even if he objected to it, would make him feel better. She wanted to fix him a posset and see he drank it since she was certain he'd insist he did not want it.

She could do none of that. Besides, it was all nonsense for nothing more serious than a broken leg and a bump on the head. At least she hoped the bump would prove no danger to his lordship.

Sarah was coming through the hall toward the kitchen when the kitchen door opened. The opening seemed overly full of the over-sized Lord Cannington.

"My lord," she murmured. "What did you discover?"

His eyes narrowed.

Sarah sighed. "I was in Mrs. Green's room and listened to your discussion. Now, please, what did you find?" She waited. "Or must I ask Alfred?" she added when he didn't respond.

He scowled. "Alfred would tell you, would he not? Even though he agreed we must not discuss this with anyone?"

"He would tell *me*," she said quietly.

Putting aside until a less worrying moment renewed suspicions concerning the housekeeper's identity, Cannington sobered. "It was as Julie feared. Someone tampered with his saddle. It was deftly done, but if you look closely, you can tell."

"I will have Alfred hire local men to guard us at night. The villain will be scared away."

Cannington shook his head. "No. Do that and—" Patiently, his lordship repeated his argument with Alfred. "—we cannot know when the scoundrel will return to try again. We must catch the bas—er—*dastard*. Now."

Sarah felt the power of that, but her heart wanted Lord Sherringham safe. She bit her lip. Finally she straightened her shoulders and swallowed. "What *do* you mean to do?"

"It isn't at all polite to remain in a house—enjoying oneself, you know—when the host cannot play his part. With Larry tied to his bed, the house party must break up."

"You will suggest it?"

"When everyone returns which—" He pulled his watch from the fob pocket and studied it. "—should be soon. Before I went to the stables I asked a footman to tell the women they must pack. Ah! I'd better give word to the valets as well."

"Do you think the women will obey such an order?"

"Unless they wish to leave everything behind when my friends drag them away they will," he said, "because," he added, his tone grim, "they'll leave this house before night falls."

There was a silent "or else" attached to that last and Sarah came very near laughing at how grim Cannington looked. "I will be content to see them go," she responded, gently.

He glanced at her and his cheeks reddened. "Should I send away Mrs. Green and Miss Murphy as well?" he asked a trifle diffidently.

"Lord Sherringham needs Mrs. Green, but, as to Miss Murphy, *you* must be the judge." Sarah debated saying more and couldn't resist. "As things are she must be aware that, assuming she consents to stay, she will be bored to tears." It was as near as Sarah could come to agreeing that he should tell her to go. She did not like the woman—brassy, ambitious, greedy—*and*, she thought, with an eye on Lord Sherringham.

Hoping, perhaps, for a change of protector? Whatever the woman's plans, Sarah hoped she would go with the rest.

Chapter 8

Miss Murphy left Blackberry Hill eventually and Sarah breathed a sigh of relief. Not that the woman was happy about leaving. Or that she immediately arrived at the decision to go. Instead, the woman schemed. Her first plan involved an almost hilarious attempt to make up to Lord Sherringham's valet. Julie, who was in her room with the door ajar, described the scene to Sarah.

"I peeked," said Julie. "She was dressed in her finest night rail, a sheer material that showed off her rouged nipples—"

Julie's eyes flew to meet Sarah's, chagrined that she'd mentioned such a thing to an innocent. Sarah returned her look with such a bland innocence that Julie, thinking that Sarah had not understood her, was reassured.

"—but Merit was magnificent," she continued. "You would not have known he thought her dressed in anything but the most proper of day dresses. Icily unperturbed, he refused her proffered mug of Mrs. Lamb's good homebrew and, when she would not take her foot from the door, opened it a trifle more and—" Julie's eyes sparkled with remembered glee. "—slammed it on her great big ugly toes!"

Sarah didn't laugh. "I would," she said slowly, "like to know if she poured out that ale or if she drank it herself."

Julie sobered instantly. "Drugged?"

"Poisoned?"

The two women stared at each other. Chills ran up and back down both straight spines. Julie swallowed. "It never crossed my mind that she had more in mind than to get next to Larry."

"Very likely that *is* what she wanted. But it is impossible to look at anything even the least little bit out of the way and not see plots and dangers," said Sarah.

Both women sighed with relief when, after her third failure to enter Sherringham's room, Miss Murphy demanded that Cannington take her into Melton Mowbray. As she waited for the carriage, she poured over poor Cannington's head a stream of steaming vituperation. Sarah had never heard many of the words and phrases. When she asked for clarification of some of the more vivid, Julie refused to explain. Even when Sarah pouted, Julie refused.

Sarah's concern for Sherringham interfered with her sleep. Two more disturbed nights and her eyes had a sunken look about them, and were surrounded by dark circles. When she did not attend to it, her body fell into weary lines, an unladylike posture that would have had her last and sternest governess hunting for the backboard.

In the middle of still another night, realizing she was wide awake, she rose and dressed. Thinking Julie might like company, she made a pot of tea and, putting some of Mrs. Lamb's good biscuits on a rose patterned plate, arranged a tray. She carried it upstairs.

"How is he?" asked Sarah, speaking in whispers so she would not waken the sleeping man.

"He'll not rouse," replied Julie in a soft but otherwise normal voice. "I gave him a mild dose of laudanum. As to how he is, his head still aches more than I like and there is pain in the leg if he moves it unadvisedly. But that last is normal." Julie shrugged. "He goes on about as you'd expect," she added, glancing toward the high bed across the room. Then, speaking in a disarmingly mild tone, she asked, "Why have you disguised yourself and hidden away as you've done?"

Sarah was staring at the bed but, at Julie's question, she turned so suddenly tea spilled from the spout of the teapot onto the embroidered tray doily. For a moment she stared, unsure she had heard what she knew she'd heard. Very carefully she set down her burden and straightened. "How did you guess?"

"A dozen different clues. That very first day your voice gave you away. You were surprised to see Larry and forgot to roughen it. Then he recognized your eyes. You explained that to *his* satisfaction, but it seemed an odd sort of explanation to *me*. I could see Lord Staunton leaving your pretend character an annuity perhaps, but that he'd say she was to be kept in good horseflesh?" Julie shook her head. "Not the man I knew."

Julie's eyes flew to meet Sarah's, a touch of horror in her gaze.

Sarah grimaced. "I only recently realized my father did not live a monkish life. I don't know how I came to be so naïve that I thought he had." Rather diffidently, she said, "I am surprised, however, to discover that you . . . ?"

Julie shook her head. "Not me, but I am friends with a woman he favored with his patronage the last years of his life." Julie grinned, looking up from the tea she poured since Sarah forgot she'd been about to fill their cups. "Will you be angry to learn he left *her* an annuity?"

Sarah's brows climbed up her forehead. "*Cousin* Aurelia?"

"Aurelia, yes, but—" Julie's brows emulated Sarah's. "—*cousin?*"

"The only annuity I didn't understand was that one—

and that is *exactly* what I asked. I had never heard of a cousin named Aurelia, you see, but Mr. McAfferty insisted all was in order." Sarah sighed. "How could I have been so blind?"

"At first you were too young and then immersed in the social world. Besides, why *would* you think of such things? Were you not taught *not* to think of them?"

Sarah tipped her head. "I suppose I was. Julie, may I ask how . . . what led to . . ." Sarah stopped. She sighed. "Forgive me. It is not a question I should ask."

They glanced toward the bed when Lord Sherringham moved restlessly. He settled and they returned to their discussion.

Julie asked for clarification. "How I became what I am?"

Sarah grimaced. She leaned forward to hide her embarrassment and picked up the teapot, pouring the tea. Then, holding the pot still, she raised her eyes. "I admit I am curious."

Julie shrugged. "What else was there for me? I came from a ramshackle family—if, indeed, it could be called a *family*. We lived by our wits near India Docks. My father—at least I called him Father—worked when he could get work, and did . . . other things when he could not. My mother, well—" A muscle near her ear rippled. "—The less said the better. She found me my first customer, Sarah."

Sarah could see the memory was not pleasant.

"We ate well for some time after that first experience," continued Julie, a hard note entering her voice. Then she shook herself. "That was a long time ago. Thanks to Larry, my life took a turn for the better. I have retired, Sarah. Men such as your father were generous."

Sarah refrained from glancing, again, toward Sherringham. "Do you . . . see your family?"

Julie, who did not guess that Sarah wondered about the term *retirement* and what was meant by it, shook her head. "There is little if anything left of it. Two brothers took the long trip south—"

Sarah guessed Julie referred to the prison colony in Australia.

"—My dad was hanged and my mother died long ago. My sisters? I haven't a notion if they survived." She shrugged and continued without the least emotion. "If they lived I'd think they'd have found me—once I gained a certain notoriety—since they did not, I'd guess they too are dead."

"This is a hard side to you I'd not have guessed existed," said Sarah, eyeing Julie.

Julie laughed but there was no humor in it. "I'd be dead too if it were not for Larry. I'd give my life for that man. It has not always been easy, even after he showed me the way to bettering myself. But before that—" Again that hard look that made Julie look older. "—you do not want to know. Or if you do, I'm not talking about it because I'd rather forget it."

"It is over, Julie." They both swung around when Larry spoke. "You are not that woman. Why is Mrs. Walker here?"

"I brought tea for Mrs. Green," said Sarah quickly, wondering how much he'd heard.

"And then the late hour and the dark led to confidences?"

"I could not sleep," muttered Sarah. *Surely he hasn't been awake so long he heard my secret.*

"Nor can I. Julie doses me but still I sleep very little." He moved restlessly.

He couldn't have heard. He'd say something . . .

"I wish," he continued pettishly, "that there was some way of occupying myself. I hate just lying here."

The two women smiled conspirators' smiles of understanding.

"I don't suppose you play chess," suggested Sarah daringly.

"Do *you?* I mean, can you do more than make the pieces move in their proper ways?" he demanded, staring across the dimly lit room toward her.

"I wonder," mused Sarah just loudly enough he could not help but hear. "Do you suppose I should have any more to do with such a rudesby?"

Julie chuckled. "No. Definitely not. Or perhaps *yes?* Perhaps you should pick up this pot and pour the remainder of the tea over his head?"

Sherringham half laughed and half groaned. "I can think of a better use for the tea." Neither woman ceased to glare at him. "I'm thirsty," he added. When there was no response, he sighed. "I see I must apologize. No matter what your skill, Mrs. Walker, would you indulge me in a game of chess?" She didn't immediately respond. "Please?" he asked, his voice adopting a sweetly coaxing note that made her heart jump.

Sarah gave in to the charm as much as to his real need for occupation. "Julie, there was a chess set in your room. On the table in the far corner. Is it still there?"

"It is. I shall get it while you put pillows behind Larry's head so he can see the board. This I must see!"

The game began with Lord Sherringham expecting very little in the way of a challenge. An hour later he looked up and met Sarah's twinkling eyes. "I believe I can mate your king in three moves."

"I think you mistake yourself. I will escape that little trap and you will find yourself in check in four."

He glanced down at the board, studying it. Then he swore softly. He studied it further and then, sighing, tipped his king. "You are correct and, for myself, I see no escape." He yawned. Then he looked startled. "I think I may actually manage to go to sleep now," he said, surprised.

Sarah, stifling a yawn of her own, thought that, with any luck, she too might manage a nap before time to rise for the day. "I will leave you then. Julie, do you need anything before I take myself back to my rooms?"

"I have a book. Merit will return to duty in only an hour or so now." As she spoke, she removed pillows from behind Lawrence's head and settled him. She leaned toward him, but hesitated before bending further and kissing him. When she straightened she didn't dare turn to look at Sarah. Normally she would have kissed Larry quite naturally and she only just thought of Sarah's reaction to her behavior when it was too late to pretend it was anything but what it was. Then she thought it better to continue so that she not reveal her embarrassment by *not* kissing him.

Also, she thought later, *it indicates how comfortable I have become with a real lady.* She frowned, musing. *My mother would instantly form plans for using the acquaintance to her own advantage. I . . .*

For a moment something inside Julie froze.

. . . I, on the other hand, must do my best to get Sarah and Larry to see each other in a romantic light. Larry loved her once. And I think Sarah has more feeling for him than she wishes to reveal. Julie compressed her lips and blinked back something that might have been a mote in her eye—or might not. *They were made for each other if they will only admit it,* she told herself, stifling a moan of distress. *And, my unregretted progenitoress,* she continued, speaking to her dead mother, *that is not to my advantage however you cut the loaf.*

Julie repeated the oath she had sworn when Larry went to war. She'd keep it too. No matter how it hurt.

She had promised that, if he survived, she would do anything in her power to make him happy. Now that meant losing his friendship. Forever. Because, once he wed, Larry would no longer deal with a courtesan—no! Her skin prickling as the blood rushed from her head, Julie named herself what she was, a *whore*.

He'll have no dealings with a whore, even in innocent ways, lest he embarrass his wife.

Julie sighed softly, her tender mouth drooping. Losing him in her life would leave a hole impossible to fill—

—*but I'll do my best to dig that hole. And dig it as deep as ever it need be!*

Cannington entered the bedroom the next day on Sarah's heels. He had seen the housekeeper carrying Larry's breakfast tray up the stairs and followed her. Now he turned, picked up Miss Murphy—who was on his heels—and set her back into the hall.

"You go back to Melton the instant I'm ready to take you," he said and shut the door on the lightskirt's outrage.

There was a scowl on his craggy face when he turned back into the room. The woman had returned to Blackberry Hill the evening before and begged Cannington to take her back. It was too late to return her then but his lordship was determined he would be rid of her before the day ended.

"Don't laugh," Canny growled when he saw that Larry grinned at him from where he was propped up against a pile of pillows. "I told her when she came back that no one got into this room but Merit, Julie, and Mrs. Walker, but she will not believe me. What can a man do?"

At that Larry did laugh. "You can't have given her her congé with enough firmness, Canny. Ah! *I* know the problem! You did not have a proper gift to give her, proving you were truly done with her."

"She'll know it this time," growled Cannington.

Sarah felt her face flame and tucked her head down, pretending to rearrange the things on the breakfast tray. When she looked up, she saw that Lord Sherringham was looking at her with a slightly perplexed expression. "Should I apologize?" he asked softly.

Sarah felt still more deeply embarrassed. *Why,* she wondered, *can I think of Julie as my friend, but find it mortifying to listen to Lord Sherringham and Lord Cannington jest about the other one?*

"You do not answer," he said.

She sighed softly. "I don't know how it is. I like Mrs. Green excessively, but I cannot like that woman at all. I do not think of Mrs. Green as a . . . as . . . ."

"Come, friend," laughed Julie, who had not yet retired to her room. "We agreed on that a long time ago. The word for which you search is courtesan."

"Retired," added Larry quickly.

He got a sharp look from Cannington at that, but ignored it. "I think, Mrs. Walker," Sherringham continued, "that you have recognized the great difference between the two. Julie is a very special woman and would be that, whatever her place in this rigid and unforgiving world, but Miss Murphy . . ."

"Miss Murphy," said Cannington harshly, "is just what she appears to be and she makes no pretense that she is anything else."

Sarah glanced toward Julie and saw spots of color burn her cheekbones and turned to glare at Lord Cannington. Her hands firmly fisted and slightly raised, she demanded, "Apologize this instant. Mrs. Green, *Julie,* has no need to pretend anything. She is, as Lord Sherringham said, a very special woman. I will not have friends living under my roof insulted and if you cannot apologize properly, then you can pack your traps and be off along with all the rest!" As she spoke, Sarah stalked nearer Cannington until she was very nearly nose-to-nose with him. "You and that woman both!"

"Your roof, is it?" asked Cannington. His eyes narrowed, his gaze settling on her hair. Suddenly, before she could think to stop him, he pulled loose the ties to her cap and lifted wig and cap away from her head. "Yes," he said into the utter stillness. "*Your roof.*"

"Oh, my God," breathed Sherringham.

"Now you've done it," said Julie and there was no humor in her voice. She sighed, stepped forward, and turned an appalled Sarah into her arms, pressing the taller woman's head down so Sarah's forehead rested again her shoulder. "Canny, did you have to?"

"Damn," he said. Then quickly apologized for his language. "I didn't think, did I? I lost my temper. But, Lady Sarah, what the *devil*, er, *what* are you doing here and in such a disguise?"

"I live here," she mumbled. "I have lived here since I left London. Why Mr. McAfferty was so stupid as to rent this place, the only place left me as a refuge, I cannot understand."

"But why do you need a refuge?" asked a confused Canny, putting into words a question teasing everyone. "You are a very wealthy woman."

Sarah sighed. She removed herself from Julie's comforting arms and faced the men. "My father, in his great wisdom, tied up my fortune in such a way that I haven't enough to support myself decently. I lived here in comfort if not elegance until Mr. McAfferty's letter arrived, revealing Sherringham's plans for the hunting season. At first I thought I must rent rooms elsewhere, but that would have required the addition not only of rent but also a companion to my expenses." She shrugged. "Besides, I have a plan. I could not bear to set it aside."

"May we know your plan?" asked Lord Sherringham politely. Somewhere inside him a fight was going on between utter glee that she was here and abject horror at the dangers she'd run putting her plan into action—and by remaining when he and his party arrived.

"I am allowed the pin money I had before my father died. I will invest it each year except for the bit required to keep me. I—" She looked a trifle embarrassed. "—seem to have a knack for picking winning investments, you see. When I have enough invested that I may live decently on the income, I mean to rent a certain cottage near our old home where I have friends."

"You would abjure the *ton?*" asked Cannington, appalled that anyone could live anywhere but London—except for country house parties or when hunting or when off to various sporting events such as the races or pugilistic bouts. London was, to his mind, the only possible place to *live,* other places available merely as locales for amusements of one sort or another.

Sarah nodded. "I also had—*have*" she corrected herself, "hopes my solicitor will find a way of setting aside my father's despicable will, in which case my plans would change drastically."

"Your father died very nearly a year and a half ago?" asked Sherringham. He was only waiting until he knew everything she was willing to tell them before shooing the others from the room and doing what he had wanted to do for many a long year.

"Yes. I was *allowed*—"

The sneer that colored the word brought quickly repressed grins to the men's faces.

"—one year in which to find myself a husband, all my expenses paid. The fact I would be in deep mourning during that year must not have crossed my father's mind. Not that I would have looked for marriage in any case, but the will stated that if I was unwed at the end of that year there would be no more than my pin money until I changed that status—for the rest of my life if necessary . . ."

"Nothing unless you married?" interrupted Cannington, rubbing his chin. "I don't suppose," he added, when she nodded, "that you would consider marrying me?"

He said it with such obviously false hopefulness he brought chuckles from all of them. Even Lady Sarah.

Sarah curtsied. "You do me great honor, sir, but we would not suit."

"Ah well. I didn't think you would."

Sarah, embarrassed, looked around the room, saw that Lord Sherringham had not been given his breakfast tray, took one look at the congealed eggs and greasy bacon, and whisked it up. "Mrs. Green, if you'd be so kind as to open the door, I will return this to the kitchen and send up something edible."

"Lady Sarah, wait," said Lord Sherringham sharply. "Julie will take it down. Or perhaps Julie and Canny will take it down. I would like a word with you."

Sarah had hoped to avoid having words with Lord Sherringham but the tray was removed from her hands, Julie held the door for Lord Cannington, and both— they had seen Lawrence's jerked thumb ordering them to leave—disappeared through it.

Julie, before she shut it, winked at Sarah, smiling brightly as she disappeared, a smile that faded the instant she knew Sarah could not see her. Larry was about to propose to the woman he loved. The woman he had loved for years.

Very, very softly Julie sighed. *Hearts*, she told herself, *do not break.*

Chapter 9

"Well," said Sarah, backing toward the door, "now you know my secret. I'll just . . ."

"You will come here and listen to me." An imperious finger pointed at a spot near the bed.

Sarah blinked. It was a tone she'd not heard since her father died and, without thinking, she reacted as she always had. She tipped her chin, half closed her eyes, and, her mouth barely open, said, "I think not." Then, she was out the door before Lord Sherringham could open his mouth. With great difficulty, Sarah managed to halt a headlong rush toward the back stairs.

He cannot be left alone, she reminded herself.

She heard her name but ignored it. She wanted to disappear into nothing at all, but she couldn't, dared not leave him . . . Then, luckily, Merit appeared.

"Ah! You are just in time. Everyone must be elsewhere and his lordship must not remain by himself until he can protect himself."

With that righteous comment Sarah nodded and stepped to the side, allowing Merit—his arms full of freshly ironed linens—to move by. Sarah went immediately to her rooms. She crossed her parlor and entered her bedroom.

Reversing direction, she re-crossed the parlor, shoved the bolt into position, and turned on her heel, returning to the bedroom. Only then did she throw herself on her bed and gave in to the tears that had threatened to fall the moment she had been discovered.

Thoughts raged.

She was ruined as thoroughly as if she had galloped during the daily promenade in Hyde Park at the height of the season or had lifted her skirts and retied her garters during an Almack's Assembly.

"Blast Mrs. Lamb for being right," she snarled, rising up slightly and glaring at her pillow. She flopped back and used one fist to pound and pound it again.

Eventually Sarah controlled her temper. Rolling onto her back she stared at the ceiling. "Now what?" she asked herself.

Another long interval, this one filled with more rational thought—less heated emotion—and she asked, "But what has changed?"

"Nothing," she concluded. "I will still receive my pin money. I will continue to invest it. Eventually I will search out a comfortable cottage in some part of the country that has excellent riding, adequate if unexciting society, and I will live my life as I expected to live it. *Excepting that I must make new friends, nothing has changed.* Only my eventual home must be elsewhere than expected."

She frowned slightly. "Well, one other thing. I will have to change my name."

She grinned. It was weak as smiles go, but she did smile. "I believe I once admitted to liking the name Emily. A very good thing, is it not? Since I am likely to be Emily Walker from here on out?"

Sarah went to her washstand. She poured in water and wet her cloth. She glanced into the mirror as she picked up her soap and was appalled by what she saw. Temper was never kind to her looks. Temper and tears were disastrous.

"Oh dear," she muttered and ducked her face into the wet cloth.

It was nearly an hour later before she felt ready to leave her rooms. Mrs. Lamb was in the kitchens. "I am going riding," said Lady Sarah as she swept toward the door.

Unfortunately, her grand exit was spoiled when the door opened and Roland appeared. Disheveled, one eye swelling and beginning to blacken nicely, he looked as if he'd lost his last friend.

"Good heavens, lad," said Mrs. Lamb bustling over to join them. "Whatever have you done to yourself?"

Sarah, more familiar with the male of the species, asked, "What does the other fellow look like?"

It was the right thing to say. Roland grinned, then winced, his split lip hurting like the devil. "I think he'll have *two* black eyes."

"Good. Come along now. Mrs. Lamb has a sure cure for what ails you. Do you not, Mrs. Lamb?"

"Arnica," said Mrs. Lamb doubtfully. "And perhaps cold water?"

Lord Cannington walked into the kitchen just then. He took one look at Roland, changed course, and, taking the boy by the shoulder, led him to a chair. He gave orders that Mrs. Lamb scurried to obey—and Sarah, seeing her chance, escaped, heading directly for the stables and her ride.

Cannington watched her go and fumed. He wanted to find out why Lady Sarah, only daughter to the late Lord Staunton, would hide herself away like a fugitive from justice. It made no sense. She was an exceedingly wealthy woman, however the money was tied up. She had relatives and friends with whom she could live in comfort. And if marriage was required of her in order for her to benefit from her fortune, then it would be simple for

someone so wealthy, to say nothing of more than hand-
some, to find a husband with whom to enjoy it.

So why was she hiding?

As he worked on Roland's cuts and bruises, he continued to form questions in his mind but could find no
answers. Allowing his thoughts to go in circles helped
nothing. To distract himself, he said, "You haven't said
with whom you were fighting, Rolly."

Roland blushed rosily. "Don't like to say," he muttered.

"Someone with whom you should *not* have fought?"

"M'mother would say so," the lad growled out.

"Mothers can be the devil," agreed Cannington.
"Would I have found it dishonorable of you to fight this
person?"

Roland glanced up, winced as the arnica poultice was
pressed to a particularly livid bruise, and then shut his
eyes. "I don't know," he admitted.

"But you know the name of your opponent?"

Roland nodded, looking at his bloody knuckles. Part
of him felt satisfaction that he actually had reason to lose
his temper. Another part felt ashamed, certain he had,
somehow, misunderstood what had been asked of him,
that he had flown into alt for no reason. For half a moment he wondered if he should tell the whole to Lord
Sherringham's friend.

But no. Surely he had taken the wrong meaning! He
must have done. Because if he had *not*, then what was
proposed to him was nothing short of murder. Which, of
course, was impossible.

For the first time since he'd accidentally met up with
his uncle, Roland drew in a deep breath of relief.

I must remember to apologize when next I see him, he
thought, and raised his chin when Cannington pulled
his hair back in order to reach a scrape on the side of his
jaw.

* * *

Lady Sarah spent the next several days avoiding Lord Sherringham's room. Julie and Cannington, individually, informed her that Larry wished she would play chess with him, that no one else could give him a game. She was tempted, but she feared what he would say to her, what she had avoided hearing him say the day they had discovered her identity.

Then one afternoon she walked into Julie. Literally. Julie had paused and was stretching, one elbow bent so her hand could cover a yawn. She jumped when Sarah, almost hidden behind a large vase filled with grasses, evergreen branches, and oddly bent twigs, bumped into her.

"What an interesting . . . bouquet?" said Julie.

"Why are you not sleeping?" asked Sarah. "You look like you'd been dragged through a knothole backwards."

Julie grimaced. "Thank you for those kind words."

"What is it, Julie?" asked Sarah, setting aside the vase. She tipped her head. "You *should* be sleeping."

"I should, but I find it difficult to do more than doze during the day. You'd think, in my profession, I would have become used to it, but I find, now I've retired, that I much prefer waking early and going to bed early." She yawned again.

"But you've stayed up with Lord Sherringham each night. You must be exhausted."

Julie nodded. "Oh, it isn't so bad as all that," she said, contradicting the motion. "I would do anything for Larry. But for him—" She shrugged. "—I'd very likely be dead by now. Or diseased to the point I would wish I were dead." Her eyes flew to meet Sarah's. "Drat. I should not have said that. What is it about you that makes it seem possible to say anything that comes into my head?"

Sarah smiled. "I haven't a notion, but I am glad you feel free to do so." Her smile faded and she bit her lip. "You cannot go on this way . . ." She eyed Julie. "Does Lord Sherringham sleep at night?"

"Oftentimes not until well after midnight," responded Julie. "But, yes, he sleeps. Why?"

"Tonight I will lay down on your bed. When he falls asleep you come wake me. You can go to bed and I'll sit with him until it is time for Merit to come in."

"Would you? Sarah, I would appreciate it so much. You cannot know how tired I am."

"Is he such a terror?"

Julie laughed. "No more than any man reluctantly keeping to his bed! It isn't that. It is the worry. Someone tried to kill him. I'm sure of it. Worse, I believe they'll try again."

Sarah nodded. "I know," she said. "There is a tight place in my spine up near my shoulders that will not go away."

"He is not happy that you are avoiding him," said Julie, forcing herself to discuss it with Sarah.

Sarah's lips tightened and her chin rose. "I'll not have him proposing to me because he feels he has compromised me. Besides—" She lifted her chin a trifle higher. "—I do not *wish* to marry. Anyone. Ever. My father made it impossible for me to think of the married state with anything but aversion."

"Was he such a bad husband to your mother? I'd not have thought it." Julie added the disclaimer before Sarah could respond.

"It wasn't that. Or not that I know. I was not old enough when my mother died to know much of their relationship. It is that we fight . . . fought! He and I. He was forever ordering me about, or insisting I wed this peer or that lord or some well-connected mister. I would not do it then. I will not do it now. He will *not* control my life."

Julie chuckled. "Stubborn, are you not?"

Sarah grimaced. "As stubborn as he." She set her jaw, her eyes sparking. "*I'll not be ruled by him.*"

Julie nodded. "Men. They have got it in their heads that poor weak little women must be manipulated for their own good and patted on the head and told they are nice little infants and not to worry. Big strong men will take care of them."

Sarah chuckled. "Yes. It is time we women taught them otherwise." She picked up the vase, carrying it toward the game room where she meant to place it on a table in the corner farthest from the fireplace. Julie watched her disappear and then continued on to the kitchen where it was time to put together Larry's luncheon tray.

Normally Cannington would have done it—or watched while Mrs. Lamb did it, but he had been chafing at the bit and trying to hide it. Unsuccessfully. Larry urged him to go out with the hounds and, after a great deal of argument, he had done so.

As Julie placed everything just so on the tray, she thought of what Sarah had said about not being ruled by her father . . . but was she not even now? In an odd sort of way? Sarah still fought him, a battle she could not win. Not when the man was beyond knowing what she did and did not do. So, in that way, was *he* not winning?

"It is time she put all that nonsense behind her and decides what she wants for *herself*," muttered Julie.

"What was that, dearie?" asked Mrs. Lamb who had, despite herself, taken a liking to Julie. It shocked her to the core, the fact she liked a whore, but she did and she was not one to pretend what was not true.

"What? Oh. I was thinking of Lady Sarah. She claims she'll not be ruled by her father—but she still is, is she not? She will not wed because *he* insisted, while alive, that she *must* and then, again, in his will. Merely because he *ordered* it, she fights it. I wonder if she has thought of that . . . ?"

Mrs. Lamb pursed her lips. "I cannot say what she thinks or does not think. She does not confide in me." Mrs. Lamb felt a hint of jealousy that Lady Sarah *had* confided in Mrs. Green!

"I will think about it. Perhaps there is something I can do." Julie nodded, picked up the tray, and climbed the back stairs. She tapped on Larry's door and entered at the same time. The door hit something . . . or actually, someone. Roland stumbled away from the door, allowing it to open far enough she could completely enter—but she had spilled the soup and slopped the tea from the teapot spout and the tray was a mess. She swore softly.

"I'm sorry," said Roland, looking desperate. "I shouldn't have stopped just inside the door, but I didn't know if I'd be welcome—" He glanced from Lord Sherringham's blank expression to Merit's obviously disapproving one. "—so I'll just go away . . ."

"Why do you not ask Lord Cannington to discover when the two of you can talk to Lord Sherringham?" asked Julie. She looked down at the tray, avoiding Larry's very slight shake of the head and Merit's half-strangled negative. "I'm certain he can arrange something. I'll return to the kitchen for a fresh tray . . ."

"Forget it. I'm not hungry. If there is tea I'll have that," said Lawrence, with a hint of a snarl in his tone. "Roland, if you would make yourself useful, take the tray away. I'll talk to Canny since Julie thinks I should. You and I will talk later when Cannington can be here."

When the boy had gone, Merit cleared his throat. "I thought you were asleep, miss."

"Missus," contradicted Julie, automatically. "I can't sleep. If there is something you need to do, then you should do it now. I'll sit with Larry for an hour or so and nap once you return."

Sarah, her fears and concerns once again sending her out riding, drove her horse and herself along the tops, as her father called the upland country, until she was miles from Blackberry Hill Cottage. She had lost count of the hedges she jumped, the streams she had crossed, and wooded areas she passed around while climbing up into the wold and, as she pulled her horse into a walk, she realized she had lost track of something else. She hadn't a notion where she was.

"Stupid, stupid, stupid!"

Her mount sidled at the tone and she patted the mare's neck. "Not you, Swallow," she said. "How often did Father tell me not to ride blindly? Of course, in those days I was riding for the pure pleasure of the ride and not because I was doing my best to escape my thoughts." Sarah sighed.

She walked the mare until she cooled to the point where Sarah felt it safe for her to drink. Her horse waded into the shallow pond and dipped her head.

Sarah stared around. She was east of the cottage. At least, she'd gone east and north upon leaving the stable and she was almost certain she'd not circled around. That meant she must now go west. She tugged the reins and, after one more noisy slurp, the mare raised her head. Obedient to the rein, she turned. Sarah trotted across the high meadowland toward the low fence she'd last crossed, took it easily, and hoped that before long she'd see something she recognized.

Just how long she wondered *was I riding before I realized poor Swallow was sweating?*

Not until she herself had begun to droop ever so

slightly in the saddle, and that suggested it must have been some considerable distance. She remembered no houses or even a lane . . . When she'd gone another mile or two, a glance at the sun had her wondering if she were not in danger of finding herself stranded for the night. The days were still warm but the wold would be dangerously cold at night. Then it occurred to her she might have to go without her dinner and she discovered a more immediate problem. She was hungry.

Breakfast had been minimal—a slice of bread and cheese she'd snatched when no one was in the kitchen. She often skipped a midday meal and had done so today. And, if the sun were to be believed, it was now late afternoon. In old-fashioned households, it was dinnertime. She wished she could see such a household. She'd get directions—*after* they fed her.

Sarah's stomach growled and she giggled. In response, her mare tossed her head, jingling her harness. "Yes I know. Here I have been running from one problem and find myself in the midst of another. The first I cannot escape. It is within me. The second I brought upon myself, did I not?"

She came to a spring-fed rill leaping its way down the hillside and followed it. If nothing else it would lead her down from the uplands and perhaps guide her to a farm nestled in some corner of the shire, a place where she could get directions without too many questions asked.

Sarah grimaced. If it were not so late in the day she would ride farther west to where she would be sure to know the person she approached. Whoever she spoke to in this part of the shire would gossip about the lost lady who rode without so much as a groom to keep her company. She would be described and, since it was no longer needed, she was not wearing the wig that had kept her identity secret for so long.

Disgrace cannot, she supposed, *be made worse by piling indiscretion on top of it.*

The stream pooled. Sarah looked into the clear waters and saw fish swimming in the depths. Her mare took the opportunity to drink and Sarah looked around. Unfortunately there were no boulders of such a height she would be able to use one as a mounting block. Without such an aid, she dared not dismount so that she herself could drink.

And because she could not, thirst added torments to those she already experienced. Sarah was not stupid. The *days* were still pleasant, but the *nights* were more than a trifle chilly. She knew she was in danger of lung fever or some such thing if forced to endure the elements overnight. She had to discover a road, find someone to direct her . . . at the very least find a barn or shed to protect her.

An *occupied* roof over a houseful of *pleasant* people who would *feed* her would be best of all.

She clucked to Swallow and they set off around the pond to where a runlet of water poured toward the valley. Another rill joined it and another and soon it was a merry little stream. Sarah wished she could go more quickly, but the ground was rough and the hillside dangerous for a hoofed animal. The danger was not that it was so steep, but that it was rocky and irregular and one was forced to pick one's way. On top of that, the occasional patch of wooded ground meant she had to find a way around it and still head both west and downhill.

Finally she came upon a cart track. It was nothing more than two ruts, grass growing in the middle and along both edges, but it was the first sign she'd seen that she was not the only person left alive in the whole world. Sarah very nearly cried with the relief of coming upon it.

She could move a little faster now, still mostly down-hill with only an occasional upward climb, still headed toward where she hoped to find a dwelling or a real road leading somewhere . . . anywhere . . .

Chapter 10

Lord Sherringham's brows clashed together. "But, Mrs. Lamb, you are saying she has been gone hours." He struggled up onto the palms of his hands, upsetting the half finished game of chess resting beside him.

"I know," said a worried Mrs. Lamb. "Alfie came in asking if she meant to go somewhere in particular. When he found she'd simply gone for a ride, he admitted to being . . . concerned," she finished—the understatement of the year.

"Alfred is worried," said Lord Sherringham. He turned to Lord Cannington, their gazes meeting.

Thoughts concerning the threat to Sherringham and the various means by which his death could be achieved passed silently between the friends. Using Lady Sarah as a means to that end was only the worst that occurred to them.

If she had any knowledge of that danger, it would have upset Mrs. Lamb even more than Alfred had done. Because Alfred, who did know, had muttered all sorts of dire predictions, Mrs. Lamb had come straight upstairs to where Lord Sherringham and Lord Cannington played chess. Merit sat to one side, dozing. Mrs. Green, of course, would be asleep so she could sit with his lordship at night . . . although why he still needed an attendant all night every night when nothing was wrong with him but a mild concussion and a broken leg Mrs. Lamb could not for the life of her understand. No one explained it to her, of course, and she didn't think it her place to ask.

"Yes, sir," agreed Mrs. Lamb when she realized both men had turned to stare at her. "Perhaps she's been thrown or maybe the mare went lame, but something, he says, is wrong or she'd have returned by now."

Cannington rose to his feet. Sherringham lay in his bed, swearing violently. "Canny, *find her.*"

"I'll do my best," said his friend, sweeping a mock salute. He stalked from the room, shutting the door with a snap.

"Has she ever done such a thing before?" asked Lord Sherringham.

Mrs. Lamb shook her head. "She seemed a mite upset when she came through the kitchen . . ."

His lordship squirmed, trying to find a position that would give him some comfort. "I have to get up. I cannot lie here one moment longer. Merit!"

The valet woke with a start and, when Lawrence repeated his demand, the wispy-haired valet stood, his arms crossed and a glare in his eyes. "You'll stay there and like it until your head stops swimming whenever you try to stand!"

"Merit, come help me up or I'll let you go without a character! Now."

Merit sighed. "You know what happened when you tried before."

"That was yesterday."

"Very well, my lord."

While his man went to the corner where he had placed the crutches Mrs. Lamb had brought down from the attics, Sherringham pushed himself up to sit on the edge of the bed. He waved Merit aside when he'd have put a hand under his arm to help him to stand. For a moment, he wondered if he *could* do it. Gritting his teeth he eased himself down until his good leg touched the floor although he still leaned against the bed. He took one crutch, placed it, then the other . . .

His lordship stood. He stood very still for another long moment and he—and everyone else—held his breath. He breathed out.

"Yes, I feel weak," he said to those observing him with concern. "I admit it—but that's natural. I've lain on that bed for days and days. Far too many," he finished grimly.

If it had been possible, he'd have been up and about the very next day after his accident, but his head . . . Yes, it was already aching. Not a great deal, but enough to be irritating. He felt the beginnings of a sigh and squelched it. Feeling sorry for himself would not help Lady Sarah.

"Where can she have gotten to?" he wondered.

"She likes to ride along the tops," said Mrs. Lamb, her hands folded before her in her usual manner, but—which was not usual—clenched together tightly.

Sherringham stared. "The nights have grown cold."

Mrs. Lamb nodded. She bit her lip, making no attempt to hide her concern.

"I think you must heat water. Lots of water," suggested Sherringham. "If she comes in half frozen, she will like a warm bath. She'll be hungry, too."

Mrs. Lamb's expression didn't lighten but something inside did. Here was something useful to do which would help. She left the room at once.

"Sir?"

"I'm not dizzy," said Lawrence, his tone sharp. He realized it. "Sorry, Merit, but I'm worried about—" Did Merit know Lady Sarah's identity? In his concern he could not recall. "—Mrs. Walker."

"Lady Sarah," corrected Merit, his tone that of a man

relieved he no longer need pretend, "is an excellent rider. I will not believe she has taken a fall. I think," he said slowly, "that she left in a bit of a state, rode hard and farther than she meant, and that if anything is wrong it is that she is lost. And if she is lost, then she is a sensible woman. She will know she must come down off the wold in order to find guidance." Merit nodded firmly.

"An excellent analysis, Merit," said Lawrence. "Run out to the stables and repeat it to Canny. It is not impossible she is lying somewhere in the uplands unable to move, but someone needs to scour the roads as well, in the hope she has done exactly as you've suggested. Damn and blast this leg!" Lawrence, angry he too could not join the search party, swore long and fluently. And loudly enough that he brought Julie to the connecting door.

"Oh," she said. She yawned and stretched. "You are up." She looked around and, sharply, demanded, "Where is Merit?"

"I sent him to the stable with a message. Sarah is missing."

"Missing . . ." Julie's heart did a flip-flop and she didn't know if it were concern for Sarah or a forbidden hope her rival had disappeared for good. *Most likely,* she ruefully decided, *a bit of both.* "You are worried," she said.

"Sarah is missing and I am unable to ride. I am tied by this blasted leg like a useless piece of . . ." He blinked. "What did you just suggest?"

"Drive?" she repeated.

"Drive . . . ?" Slowly he grinned. "Julie, you are a genius." He swung around and headed for the door.

"Here! Wait a minute!"

He grinned over his shoulder. "Well? For *what* are you waiting?"

She cast him an amused look. "Perhaps you mean to dress first?"

Sherringham glanced down at his nightshirt and flushed. "Julie? Can you valet me?"

She grinned. "Did it in the past, didn't I? I guess I can do it again."

Dressing Lawrence was not easy but they managed. He settled against his bed, looking more than a trifle drawn, while she slipped slippers on his feet.

"I don't think this is a good idea," she said and frowned.

"Maybe not—" He clenched his jaw as he stood. "—but it's the only one to occur to us. Let's go."

The door opened. Roland stood there. "What is wrong?" he asked, his young forehead creased with lines. "Something is wrong but no one will tell me what it is."

"Mrs. Walker is missing," said Julie, kindly. "Run to the stables and harness a horse to the gig, please? Everyone else may already be out looking for Sar . . . Emily."

Roland nodded. "If that is all . . ."

He ran toward the back stairs and Lawrence frowned after him. "*If that is all?* What did he mean by that?"

"I haven't a notion," said Julie, her head in his armoire where she searched for his coat. She handed it to him and headed for her room. "I'll return in half a moment. I'll need a pelisse and a blanket for later."

Lawrence glanced down at the ruined trouser leg Julie had slit up the side and then, loosely, sewn the edges so they wouldn't flap about his splints. Struggling with crutches and coat left him wrung out, sweat beading his brow. He wondered if he could get as far as the stables . . .

His jaw clenched. Sarah was in danger. She must be found before nightfall and in Leicestershire, at this time of year, night fell early. If only it were high summer when it was light far into the evening . . . and warm!

He reached the stairs, looked down them and again wondered if he could manage.

"Sit down and scoot," ordered Julie.

"Since no one can see me make a fool of myself I will."

"So I'm no one, am I?" she asked, attempting a light note.

"You are my very special friend, Julie," he said. And then, in a tone she knew meant he meant *exactly* what he said, he added, "And you always will be."

Something inside Julie unwound. It had always been impossible that he marry her. Even *before* he was raised to the peerage. That event, of course, made it inconceivable that he take her to wife. But if he said she would always be his friend then it was true. He would always think of her as his friend.

Even when the day came when he no longer spent time with her.

She sighed again. Softly. That day *would* come. Larry was too honorable to take the chance his wife might be hurt. He'd not want word returning to the woman he married that he was consorting with a member of the demi monde. Not when the rest of the world would refuse to believe it was innocent.

She stifled still another sigh and prayed a little prayer that Lady Sarah would have him. He had talked through some of the long nights since Canny unmasked Lady Sarah. He loved Sarah. Had loved Sarah for years. If Sarah could return even a portion of that love, then he would be content. Above all—even while Julie hated with a passion the idea of his wedding another—she wished him content in his marriage.

Besides, she liked Lady Sarah. Despite herself, she liked Sarah.

Sherringham was forced to rest when he reached the bottom of the stairs. Sitting on nearly the last step, he bent over, his elbow on his knee and his head on his hands. "I'm weak as a cat," he muttered.

Sweat beaded his brow and Julie, seating herself beside him, found her handkerchief and wiped it away. "You'll return to normal in a day or two. Just take it easy. We'll get to the kitchen next and you can rest again."

He struggled to his feet. The crutches firmly under his arms, his mouth set in a grim line, he moved around the bottom of the stairs and under them, where he waited for Julie to open the door. "I hate this," he muttered.

"Of course you do. You've always been an independent soul and the notion you need help is anathema to you."

He grinned. "Where did you learn that word for something detested?"

She smiled. "You were not the only one to direct my reading, Larry," she said, her tone teasing. She opened the door to the kitchen and, immediately, he started across the flagged floor toward the back door. "Here now," she said sharply. "Sit down."

"I'll sit in the gig. You must drive, Julie. I don't think I've the strength for it."

"Something else you hate to admit?"

"Yes."

She sighed. He'd not be teased from his bad mood. When he did not pause, she hurried after him. For half a moment, she'd debated leaning against the door, forcing him to rest. It would not do. He'd set her aside and very likely hurt himself in the process. She opened it.

Outside the kitchen a surprise awaited them. The gig, harnessed to one of Sherringham's carriage horses, awaited them. "A groom helped me before setting off in the direction Lord Cannington told him to go," said Roland. "May I drive you?" he asked more than a trifle diffidently.

"Julie will drive, but saddle a horse—if any remain—and follow us."

Roland ran back toward the stables and Sherringham turned to the gig. He stared at it, his jaw set at a grim angle. Then, determined, he handed Julie the crutches, grasped the side and hopped his good foot up onto the iron step. He very nearly fell into the bottom of the gig and then turned onto his bottom. With Julie lifting his bad leg, he scooted back until he was sitting on the floor. A final struggle, and he got himself up onto the seat.

He stared down at Julie. "You're crying. Why?"

"*You.* You gallant *fool.* You don't have to do this."

"Yes, I do," he said softly.

There was a look in his eye, half determination and half desperation, which had her ducking her head and wiping away more tears.

"I cannot sit at home doing nothing, Julie. Not when Sarah is in difficulties."

She nodded. "I know."

Keeping her face turned away from him, she took her place and picked up the reins. "Which way?" she asked.

Larry frowned. "I'm thinking . . ."

She remained silent. Roland appeared and she shook her head when he'd have spoken. He came to her side of the gig. "Which way?" he asked softly.

"Shh."

"I saw her head up into the hills. She was going just a bit north but mostly toward the east."

"Larry, did you hear?"

Sherringham nodded. "It agrees with my best guess. If she went west or south she'd have ridden into more settled areas and I think she rode because she wanted to be alone . . ."

"I think so too." Julie lifted the reins, gave the horse the office to go, and, never really happy when dealing with horseflesh, even at once removed as when driving, she felt her shoulders tensing. She knew she'd be exhausted and sore when they returned, but she also knew that if she did not drive him, Larry would try to drive himself.

The road wound up the side of a long deep valley above the boggy bottom, crossing small streams here and there, going through wooded areas and passing the occasional cottage. Occasionally a track headed up into the hills and, at each, Roland took off, racing up them and, when he'd achieved some distance, called the name by which he knew Lady Sarah. When he heard no response, he would ride back to the road and catch up the two in the gig.

The sun dropped farther and farther toward the west and, as the heat gradually left the day, Julie was very glad for the blanket she'd brought.

"How far should we go?" she asked.

"I wish I'd some notion of when she left," muttered his lordship.

Julie turned to Roland and asked, "Can you guess at the time you saw Sar—Mrs. Walker ride off."

Roland asked, "About . . . two? Two-thirty?"

Sherringham calculated. "Another couple of miles, Julie." His mouth compressed and a bleak look entered his eyes. "Then we will turn back. Even upset she'd not gallop blindly over rough terrain. She has too much respect for horseflesh. There is another lane. Roland, we are losing the light. Be careful your horse doesn't stumble in a rut as you follow that track. I don't want to have to rescue you as well as La—Mrs. Walker."

Roland frowned ever so slightly as, once again, someone stumbled over the name. He looked from one to the other and decided it was none of his business. He reined around, turning up the track into the hills. At the top of the first rise, he shouted. For the first time he thought he heard a response. He hurried down into a small valley and up the other side. At the top, he again shouted.

"*Mrs. Walker.*"

This time he was certain. Excited, he set off—but without the care he should have taken and, within minutes, his horse not only stumbled, but slid and then came down on its side, trapping Roland's leg. Scrambling up, the horse dragged him a ways by the foot caught in the stirrup. The well-trained animal stopped, looked at him, and then dragged him a bit farther before stopping again.

Sarah saw what happened and moved forward, talking calmly to the anxious horse. She caught the bridle. "Are you hurt?" she asked, knowing that she'd never be able to remount if she had to get down.

"I . . . don't think so," said the lad. He moaned as he reached to free his leg from the stirrup but cut off the sound. When his foot dropped he was unable to bite back an exclamation of pain.

"You are hurt," said Sarah, looking down at him where he grasped his ankle.

"Yes, but if you hold my horse steady, I'll get back into the saddle."

Sarah admired the fortitude it took for Roland to pull himself upright and then up onto the horse's back.

Roland settled, found the stirrup for his good foot and looked at her. There was pain in his eyes, but a weak smile on his lips. "I just twisted it. I'll do," he insisted.

Sarah wondered if he would as, her hand on his bridle, she started up the hill. "Hold on. It is steep here and the horses may have to scramble."

They did. At the top she took a quick look at Roland and instantly moved nearer. "Here! You can't faint. I can't do anything for you if you fall off!"

Her sharp words got through the haze of pain and Roland gritted his teeth. "Some hero I am. Here I thought I'd rescue you and you end up rescuing me."

"Since I had begun to feel as if the population of the whole world had taken French leave, you cannot know how very glad I am to have you here. Can you continue?"

"Yes . . ." he said a trifle doubtfully.

The rest of the way to the road was less difficult terrain but it took them four times as long getting back down as Roland had required riding up.

Julie and Sherringham were waiting, debating what they should do about the fact Roland was so long about the business. When they saw two riders, Sherringham jumped to the conclusion that it was Sarah who was hurt, but Julie, less emotional, realized it was Roland weaving in the saddle.

"I thought you told the boy to watch where he rode. He looks as if he might fall at any moment."

His panic didn't fade until he too perceived that Sarah helped Roland rather than the other way around. "What has the young fool done?"

"We'll soon know."

While they waited, Julie, maneuvering carefully, turned the gig.

"Roland has hurt his ankle," were Sarah's first words. "It is paining him dreadfully. You came by road, so perhaps you know how far to the nearest cottage?"

Two hours later, Sarah, Julie, and Lawrence sat together in the small room Julie had appropriated for her own. They'd met grooms returning from their search and sent them with a well-sprung carriage and pillows—and motherly Mrs. Lamb—to retrieve Roland, whom they'd left at a farmhouse. No one spoke as they sat awaiting the other members of the search party.

"You frightened me to death," said Sherringham, finally.

"Nonsense. I went for a ride, that's all."

"Accidents happen."

"Yes. They do, do they not?" She glanced at his leg and smiled when he swore softly.

Sherringham drew in a deep breath. "Perhaps this—" He tapped his splint. "—is *why* I worried so about you—"

Julie, looking from one to the other, quietly left the room. Neither Lady Sarah nor his lordship noticed.

"—because I *know* accidents happen."

Sarah stretched her toes nearer to the small fire and clutched her wineglass harder. "Will you stop lecturing if I admit I was feeling a trifle of panic before I heard Roland's call?"

Relaxing, he chuckled. "You are a delight, Sarah. Marry me."

Sarah instantly stilled. She had forgotten her fear he would ask her to wed him, that his gentlemanly instincts would demand she do so to save her reputation. She sighed. "You do me great honor, my lord—"

"Bosh. I won't listen to that nonsense. Sarah, I want—"

"You want to save my reputation and would sacrifice yourself. I don't need anyone's sacrifice, my lord."

"That too is nonsense," he said . . . but he was talking to her back as she walked, her steps a quick tattoo against the wooden floorboards, toward the door. She shut it firmly against his demand she stay.

"Oh yes," she muttered as she continued across the larger room, "you are the perfect gentleman, are you not? But I wouldn't wed at my father's behest and I will not wed for such a reason as this, either."

"For what reason *will* you wed?" asked Julie, who had been unable to force herself beyond the billiards room. She stood on the far side of the table, a cue in her hand, the thick end resting on the floor.

"What?" Sarah looked up. "Oh. Well."

"You appear a trifle flustered, Sarah,"

"I suppose I am. Your friend just asked me to marry him. Pure nonsense, of course. He asks only because he believes he must." If there followed a very small sigh, even Sarah was unsure of it. Her chin rose a notch. "I made my plans before I left London and what has happened here need not change them."

"Hmmm." Julie fought back an ungenerous urge to be pleased. Larry *wished* to marry this woman. Therefore she must wish it for him.

Sarah frowned at the sound. "What do you mean by that?"

Ignoring the desire to leave well enough alone, Julie asked, "What I asked when you appeared. I wonder what *would* make you change your plans."

Julie's persistence irritated Sarah and her voice was a trifle sharp when she said, "I refuse to wed for any of the reasons a tonnish woman is supposed to wed. Since I refuse, there is no use discussing it."

"So . . . what less than tonnish reason might you have?"

Sarah glared. "Enough of this. Why don't you go to your *friend* and leave me alone?"

Julie's eyes narrowed for half a second. Then she nodded, a small cat smile playing around her mouth. "Yes, I think I will."

Sarah turned as Julie, her skirts swaying gracefully, passed by her. She watched the other woman enter the room where Sherringham sat, tired and with an aching head.

Sarah bit her lip. *Of all the stupid things to do,* she told herself, *sending Julie in there must have been one of the most stupid of my life.* And then she berated herself for acting dog-in-the-manger. She didn't want him. So why did she resent Julie's presence in his life?

"Because I do want him," she said, realizing it for the

first time. "I do. Him. *Not* that ridiculously *perfect* man. The one I made up. *That* man would have been boring. Boring, boring, boring!"

Muttering, berating herself, Sarah took herself to her rooms where, once again, she locked her door and wet her pillow—but this time not from anger—and then, rising, swore she would never cry again over something that could not be helped. She loved Lord Sherringham but he did not love her—and she would wed for nothing less.

Her plans were set. She would make for herself the life she had planned.

And she would never wed *anyone* simply because someone said she should. No matter what *anyone* said. Only for love. For love or nothing.

And here she would find no love.

Chapter 11

"Cousin," said Roland, softly, peering around the half open door. Then he blinked, finding himself staring at the wrong end of a pistol. "Cousin?" he asked, his eyes widening.

Lord Sherringham lowered the handgun to the bed, but did not release his grip on it. "Roland."

"Please?"

"Why are you here?"

"May I speak to you?" Roland eyed the pistol with a degree of fascination and then raised his eyes to meet Sherringham's, surprised at the hard cold look in them.

"Why?"

"I'm worried." He crept a step or two into the room and then a little more when his lordship didn't object.

Sherringham barked a harsh laugh. "*You* are worried? Has someone tried to kill you, as well?"

Roland blanched. His knees buckled and he sat, hard, on the edge of a chair, catching himself when the chair tipped. "Kill . . . ?"

"My riding accident was no accident," said Sherringham, his eyes narrowing.

If anything, Roland's skin whitened still more. "Then I did not misunderstand," he said quietly. "I did hear him correctly."

"Him?"

"My uncle." Roland leaned forward his head in his hands. "He had a vial. He wanted me to pour the contents into a decanter. You know. One from which you'd drink."

"You said no?" asked his lordship, his voice harsh.

"He would not explain what it was. He said it didn't matter, that I was to do as I was told. Or else."

"Or else." It was a statement, not a question.

"He told me to think it over. That if I did not obey, he'd see my mother suffered for it."

"The bastard."

Roland raised his head, his skin too pale and the skin around his eyes stretched taut. "He called her a whore and that's when I hit him." He bit his lip. "I should not have done it. He's my uncle."

"That fight you had?"

Roland nodded.

Speaking in a more kindly tone, Sherringham said, "A man must earn respect, Roland. I'd say he forfeited it."

"Do you mean that?"

"Yes." Sherringham stared at the boy. "Why are you telling me? Now?"

"Because I must tell him today what I mean to do." Roland looked as if he were about to cry. "I don't know what to do."

"You will tell him you will obey, of course."

Roland's eyes widened. "But . . ."

"And then you will bring that vial to me."

Roland was silent for a long moment. "And . . . ?"

"We will have a bit of a discussion with the local magistrate. He will test it and if, as you, too, suspect, it is a poison, he will arrest your uncle and you will have no need to worry about your mother."

Roland turned it over in his mind and then smiled. "I have never liked him. Mother will not like it if he is arrested, but he is a dangerous man, is he not? He must not be allowed to harm you."

"You would inherit, you know, if he managed it." Sherringham spoke idly, his attention seemingly elsewhere.

"The title?" Roland shook his head firmly. "I don't want it. I have enough to worry me in the estate I already possess . . . and—" He drew in a quick breath, his eyes widening once more. "—with my uncle out of the way perhaps I can bring it back into production. He has been stealing from me! I know he has. Only that makes sense."

"I suspect you have that right."

"It *is* true," said Lady Sarah. She and Julie entered from Julie's room where they had been checking the fit of the habit that Mrs. Lamb had managed to finish once she need not prepare meals for so many.

"How do you know?" asked Sherringham.

He eyed her appreciatively. She had gowned herself in one of her more fashionable day dresses, deciding that now her identity was known it was foolish to continue in disguise. Besides, she was so tired of the few black gowns she'd worn day in and day out she wished only to toss them on the fire, never to see them again—

—*and* the wig. That did go into a fire before Mrs. Lamb could stop her.

"How do I know he stole from Roland?" she asked. "I wrote my solicitor and ordered him to check. His letter arrived this morning, brought to the Cottage along with an order of delicacies you must have ordered from London."

"An order of delicacies? I've ordered nothing. You, Julie?"

Julie shook her head.

"I think," said Sherringham sharply, "that those *delicacies* had better be checked. Very carefully—and *before* anyone eats anything."

"You think perhaps the vial Roland is to receive from

his uncle is a ruse? That the real problem will come from something in this order that everyone will think someone else sent from London?"

"I like that you are an intelligent woman, Sarah," said Sherringham. "You do not need everything explained to you."

Sarah blushed slightly at the compliment. "I'll see that Mrs. Lamb opens nothing until we test it."

"I'll go," said Roland.

"You and I will go," said Julie to him and held out her hand to the boy. He awkwardly offered his arm. She took it gracefully and they exited, talking about what Sarah had told them.

"May I read this letter?" asked Sherringham.

"Yes." Sarah handed it over. "It was not difficult for him to find evidence of misappropriation of funds." She watched his lordship read down through the letter and, at the end, raise his head quickly, looking at her sharply. "I see there is other news as well."

She smiled. "Yes. He thinks he may have found a way to break the will. Then I will have my income."

"I see."

"I will be free," she said, smiling broadly.

"You'll need no one to give you the elegancies you once had," he said. "I had thought perhaps that might be a small compensation for wedding me—that I could give you the life to which you were born."

"I will not wed you. Get that out of your head."

He eyed her. "I will not despair," he said with one of those rare but particularly sweet smiles. "Once I can move about freely, I will woo you as you should be wooed and, in the end, you will agree because you'll have no choice but to agree."

"You are very sure of yourself."

"I must be," he said simply, his gaze holding hers and revealing a sincerity that had her mind reeling.

Sarah backed from his bed toward the door. "I . . ."

He smiled but there was a touch of sadness to it. "You'll not escape so easily once I am on two good legs," he said.

"I . . ."

Sarah could think of nothing to say, no way of freeing him from the delusion that he could win her hand for any reason whatsoever, so, as he'd suggested, she merely escaped. Once in the hall, she stood there, staring at nothing at all.

What will I do when he can chase me down? she asked herself, a wryness twisting into her heart. *Especially when the problem is complicated by the fact I do not want him to give up, do not really wish to escape . . .*

She sighed, then recalled the necessity of consulting with Mrs. Lamb concerning the delivery that had come that morning. She hurried down the stairs and into the kitchen where she found Mrs. Lamb, Julie, Roland, and Lord Cannington staring at an array of items set out on the large worktable.

"This is everything?" asked Cannington, legs slightly spread, arms akimbo, and fists against his hips.

"Everything, my lord," said a slightly frightened and rather flustered Mrs. Lamb.

"You are absolutely certain?" asked Sarah sharply.

"My lady," said the woman, "I assure you, it is everything that was in the three crates that arrived only this morning by carrier. I unpacked only the one, you see, because it contained a ham—as if we did not have perfectly good hams right here in Leicestershire," she added under her breath, "—and those bits and pieces of odd . . . the, er, delicacies? The others contained the wine." She gestured to the bottles lined up at the back of the table.

Cannington picked up and scrutinized each item. When he'd finished he passed it on to Julie who also checked it carefully.

Sarah saw that Mrs. Lamb had arranged a tea tray to be taken up to Sherringham's room and, thirsty, poured herself a cup. She burnt her throat taking too large a sip. Another more cautious sip had her staring at her cup.

"Is this new tea?" she asked. Her eyes widened and her hand went to her tummy. Suddenly she leaned over, dropping the cup. It shattered, very nearly hiding the moan of pain she could not repress.

"Oh dear," said Mrs. Lamb coming to her side. "My dear child, whatever is the matter?"

"Poison," said Cannington. "She's been poisoned."

Julie rushed to Sarah's side and forced her fingers into her suffering friend's mouth, pressed hard on her tongue, and made no move to jump away from the spewing vomit. "Milk," she ordered. "Or cream. Cream is better!"

Mrs. Lamb, her face white stared at her own cup from which she'd not yet taken a drop. "Poison? Is *that* what you seek?"

"The milk!" Julie held Sarah tightly as spasms coursed through her.

Cannington clutched Mrs. Lamb's shoulder. "Cream. Milk. *Now.*" He shook her slightly.

The woman blinked and then scurried off to the pantry where she dipped a cup of milk from the rising pan and ran back with it, neither noticing nor would she have cared that it dripped all along the way.

Julie asked Cannington to hold Sarah as she forced the milk into her. "Swallow," she ordered her voice stern. "*Sarah! Swallow.*"

Barely knowing what she did, Sarah swallowed. Swallowed again when again ordered to do so. And then, weakly, put her hand up to help tip the milk into her mouth. Finished, she groaned.

"Mrs. Lamb, the tea?" asked Cannington, worried about Sarah, but more worried that someone else might suffer likewise.

Mrs. Lamb gulped. She pointed at the cup she'd poured to test the new tea's flavor. "I made it. It was the new tea."

"New? Then what is on the table was *not* the only thing in that unpacked crate?"

"I forgot. I forgot!"

Mrs. Lamb threw her apron over her head and sobbed loudly. "I killed her. I killed my dearest lady."

"No, no," soothed Julie, but did not leave Sarah's side. "Canny, find that blasted tea and make certain it is safely out of the way. And empty that misbegotten teapot before someone else decides to drink."

Sarah chuckled weakly and then moaned. "It hurts," she said.

"Mrs. Lamb, control yourself and bring more milk. Heavy on the cream, please."

"I hate creamy milk," mumbled Sarah, clutching her stomach. She opened her eyes, wrinkling her nose. "Oh dear," she said and gagged at the smell.

Julie laughed. "You'll do. Here." She took the cup from the housekeeper. "Even if you don't like it, drink it. Sometimes it'll save a life," she said darkly.

Cannington, glancing from time to time toward Sarah, sequestered the tea. Mrs. Lamb, penitent to the point of being a nuisance, cleaned up the mess. And finally, weak as a cat, Sarah said she'd like to go to her bed. "I'm sorry," she said apologizing, "but I don't think I can make it by myself . . ." Tears rolled down her cheeks.

"Poor dear," murmured Julie. She gestured and Cannington instantly came to Sarah's side, lifting her easily. Julie led the way to Sarah's rooms and looked around. It was her turn to wrinkle her nose. "This won't do. When you are feeling the thing again, Lady Sarah, we'll move you back upstairs and into a room more worthy of you."

"I don't care if I am above the stables if only there is a *bed*."

Julie smiled. "I'll sit with you. If you can sleep . . . ?"

Sarah whimpered. "It hurts, Julie," she said, pressing her hand to her stomach.

"Yes. I don't suppose we got it all, but I think we got the greater part of it. I am sure you'll be all right, Sarah."

"It was meant for Lord Sherringham, was it not?"

Julie nodded. "Yes. But in such a way! The whole household might have died."

"Not the servants. Maybe Mrs. Lamb, but she would not have brewed tea for the servants from such high quality leaves."

"No and very likely not Roland," said Julie thoughtfully. "He almost never drinks tea."

"Not Roland." Sarah, distracted by the conversation, added, "His uncle. It must have been his *uncle's* doing."

"I think so. I really do think so."

Upstairs where Cannington had just related the whole to Sherringham and then restrained him from rising to go directly to Sarah's side, the two men came to the same conclusion. "That vial Roland was to put into the brandy . . ."

The two men stared at each other and Cannington went off to talk to Roland. A couple of hours later he returned. "I've got it," he said.

"What do you think is in it?"

"I don't know."

Sherringham frowned. "It is time to call in a magistrate. Sarah might have *died*."

"She might have, but she did not. We *all* might have." Cannington snorted. "Can you not see it?" he asked, in excellent dramatic style. "It is late in the evening. Mrs. Lamb brings in the tea tray and we all drink quickly . . . and then—" Cannington mimed vomiting this way and then that. "—and there we are," he finished, gesturing widely. "Sprawled out, dead, lying all around for someone to find in the morning."

"I can do without the vivid description," said Sherringham, his voice dry.

"You always were the squeamish sort," teased Cannington.

"At the moment I'm a worried sort."

Cannington sobered. "Yes. Someone is out to do you in, Devil."

"I'm not worried about *me*."

"You should be."

"Blast it, Canny, she might have *died*."

"She will be fine."

"Thank God."

"Yes, very well," said Cannington, a trifle embarrassed by such fervor. "If we don't want to tip our hand to our villain we must make plans . . ."

All they decided for certain that night was that the magistrate should be contacted in secret. Sherringham was insistent, however, that, one way or another, the magistrate be contacted.

The next morning he reiterated that point. "I will *not* chance anything happening to Lady Sarah," he said, his chin at a stubborn tilt.

Cannington had seen that particular look before and sighed. "We've no proof."

"No, but a magistrate can poke and pry. He can contact

London and ask for information concerning this particular bird in a way we cannot. And he can come up with a means of keeping an eye on him. Perhaps put a man working at the inn where Roland's uncle is putting up. Perhaps he knows of a whore who will put herself into the bastard's way. Amazing what an intelligent woman can learn when in bed with a man."

"The problem with that plan," said a new voice, "is that you need not only an intelligent woman but a brave one. This particular villain is the sort who would not stop at smothering a woman he feared knew too much."

"Julie, I did not see you come in. How is Sarah?"

"My stomach aches abominably," said Sarah, entering behind Julie, "and I'm weak as a sick cat, but I'm alive and *glad*."

"I'd be glad, too," said Cannington.

Sarah made a gesture denoting impatience. "Not for *me*. Glad that we discovered there was a problem before anyone but me suffered." She cast a quick look toward the bed and discovered Lord Sherringham watched her with an intensity that frightened her a trifle.

"*You* suffered," he said. "That is too much suffering." Sherringham, remembering he should not stare, looked down at his tightly clenched fists. "You, Lady Sarah, suffered *in my place* and that is *wrong*. What do you know of the local magistrate?"

Lady Sarah sat in the chair Cannington placed near the bed for her and tipped her head. "Lord Kenwicker?" She frowned slightly, pursing her lips. "Very little. He is not a hunter, so he was not of Father's circle and did not come much in my way. Let me think . . ."

They waited according to their natures. Julie with that intelligent placidity, a peace-inducing manner that had appealed to many men. Cannington was impatient. He was a doer, not a thinker. And Sherringham silently encouraged her.

"He is something of a recluse," said Sarah slowly, "and rarely goes into society, but he is respected and, from what I recall, thought a fair and honest magistrate. No one knows what he does, holed up all day every day there at Stonewall Manor, but he is always polite when he must be disturbed for reasons of his magisterial duties. I think you will find him helpful rather than obstructive."

"An excellent statement."

"And jibes with what I learned of the man some time ago," said Cannington. When Sherringham tipped his head, questioningly, he added, "From Alfred, when your saddle came off."

"You thought of sending for a magistrate then?" asked Sherringham.

Cannington grimaced. "Alfred did, but I thought perhaps I should discuss it with you and you were unconscious and then it went out of my head."

Sherringham, long aware that Cannington's attention to anything could be easily transferred elsewhere, was not surprised. "Lady Sarah, if you'd find paper and pen, I'll write Lord Kenwicker and ask him to call."

"I don't think we *should* ask him to call."

Cannington blinked. "You don't think Sherringham *should* consult with him? But you said . . ."

Once again Lady Sarah expressed irritation and impatience. "Of course they must consult," she interrupted. "But it should not be in such a way that the villain will guess they've done so. Whomever is attempting to kill Lord Sherringham must not escape."

Cannington, who tended, like the bull in the china shop, to ram straight for a goal, nodded. "I remember."

"Yes, that was Cannington's thought when my saddle came off. But all that is changed. We tried, last night, to make a plan whereby we could inform him secretly but now . . ."

"No." Sarah shook her head. "If the man who put poison in that tea thinks he himself is in danger I fear he is the sort of snake who attacks first and thinks after. He should *not* be alerted."

"I wonder," mused Julie, "if I might get lost and find myself somewhere near this manor of which you spoke." She had been so quiet for so long the men looked at her in surprise.

"You mean you might go for a drive and be forced to ask directions?" asked Cannington.

Julie nodded but Sarah shook her head. "That won't fadge. You'd not see Lord Kenwicker. His butler or a footman, whoever answers the door, would give the necessary directions."

Julie grimaced. "I had not thought of that."

Frowning slightly, Sarah added. "But something of the sort should work . . ."

"What if she has an accident, needs succor?" asked Cannington.

"And how would I go about arranging an accident?" asked Julie dryly.

"We might manage it," said Cannington. "Lady Sarah, how far is it to this manor and in what direction?"

Sarah told them.

"Too far," said Sherringham once she had. "I think we better just send the man a message and perhaps meet Kenwicker up on the tops where we are unlikely to be seen talking together."

"Someone will let the cat out of the bag that a message was sent," said Cannington mournfully.

"I've an idea how getting lost *might* work," began Julie. "Surely a magistrate has trusted servants?"

"In other words, you pretend to be lost, deliver a written message and that vial, and tell the butler word is not to get out you've done so?"

Julie nodded. "If I do *not* judge the man trustworthy, then I'll not do it. You always said I am a good judge of people," she added, turning to Sherringham who nodded.

That little interchange depressed Sarah. The implication the two had known each other long and well could not be avoided. She knew the relationship went back years, but had somehow managed to avoid thinking about it. And now wasn't the time to begin. She drooped.

"Sarah, dear, we have kept you up and about far too long. Surely your new room is ready for you. You must go to it at once. Come now," finished Julie and then blushed when Sarah, without thinking, cast her a look of dislike. "I apologize for giving you orders, Lady Sarah, but it is because I am concerned for you," she said more formally.

Sarah sighed. "I too apologize. I do not know why I reacted that way."

"You are tired and sore and don't feel well," said Julie soothingly. "Do come along now. Please?"

"You will tell me if anything new is decided?" asked Sarah. Julie nodded and Sarah turned to look at Sherringham. "We are a pair, are we not," she said, sudden humor lightening her temper. "You tied to your couch by that leg, and me stupidly ill and likewise prone to be prone."

He chuckled. "We are certainly a pair, Lady Sarah," he said softly, holding her gaze.

Sarah took that look to her bed with her, was still basking in the warmth of it when she slid into sleep . . .

Chapter 12

. . . And woke wondering what he had meant by it.

Surely not what I wish he meant, mused Sarah. *It is far from likely that he loves me.* She sighed just as the door opened and Julie peered in. "Julie?"

"I have brought you something. We decided your tummy would not like anything too difficult, so Mrs. Lamb made you a panada—" Julie chuckled when Sarah wrinkled her nose. "—which you are to try to eat even if you are not fond of pap."

"I suspect I could, at this moment, eat most anything that would go down my throat," confessed Sarah. "I am . . . am . . ." Suddenly she grinned wickedly. "I am gut-foundered!"

"Lady Sarah!"

"Well, I am."

"Where did *you* hear such a term as that?" asked Julie as she arranged a tray over Sarah's knees.

"I can't recall . . . oh yes, I can. Long ago. There was a boy who came to my father's stables and asked if he could work for some food. He was ragged and dirty and, as he said, *gut-foundered.* I don't think I ever saw a boy put down so much food at one time in my life." She popped a spoonful of the soft food into her mouth

"Did he *keep* it down?" asked Julie, amused and, just a little, horrified.

Sarah nodded, swallowing. "He did. He didn't gulp his food or swallow it half chewed. He ate methodically but neatly and kept right at it until I was certain he would founder for reasons other than hunger."

"Did your father hire him?"

Sarah lay down her spoon. "We saw that the lad ate with his knife and fork, wiping his fingers on a napkin. His proper table manners made us suspicious. It took Alfred to ferret out the truth, however. A runaway. His mother remarried and he could not like his stepfather. He was trying to reach his uncle so my father contacted the man. I often wondered how it turned out . . ."

Julie watched Sarah without appearing to, ready, if necessary, to supply her with the basin. She was relieved it was unnecessary. They had rid Sarah of very nearly all the poison before it could affect her too badly. Julie shuddered, thinking of what might have happened.

"What is it? Are you chilled?"

Julie explained.

"I know. I woke in the night thinking of—" At the last moment she refrained from mentioning Lord Sherringham in particular. "—us lying dead in the great room and a footman, coming in the next morning to clear the ashes and re-lay the fire, finding us."

Julie nodded. "I too had nightmares."

"I just remembered," said Sarah. "Did your getting lost accomplish our goal?"

Julie smiled. "I was very nearly lost for real," she said ruefully.

"But you arrived at the manor and . . . ?"

"And was admitted by a rather flustered housekeeper. Something sounding very like a Billingsgate row was going on behind a closed door near the entry. I could not distinguish the words, but the voices were not—not exactly polite?"

"What happened?" asked Sarah.

"I was asking the housekeeper for directions, trying to decide if I could trust her, when the door opened and, his hands at collar and the seat of the boy's trousers, Lord Kenwicker himself hustled a lad across the hall, out the front door, and down the steps to the gravel. He returned, brushing off his hands, and in an exceedingly bitter voice, said, '*and good riddance.*' Then he saw me. His scowl faded and . . . he smiled—"

Sarah was surprised to see a rather dreamy expression appear on Julie's face.

"—and . . . and well, he *stalked* toward me, his eyes never leaving mine."

"And?"

"And I very nearly forgot my own name, let alone why I was there."

"A *coup de foudre?*" asked Sarah softly—and was surprised to feel *hope* that it was true that Julie *had* experienced the traditional *flash of lightning* striking love into her heart. She was surprised all over again when Julie blushed hotly.

"I . . . don't know what it was," she admitted.

"Did you manage to deliver our message?"

Julie blinked and then grinned. "I need my head examined. Yes, of course I delivered the message. But I am ahead of myself. Lord Kenwicker invited me to take tea and—" A rosiness spread across her cheeks. "—very properly, he left the door open when we went into his study. A bookroom, Sarah. I have never seen so many books altogether except in a bookshop or a lending library. They were strewn everywhere, across tabletops, on the floor, beside chairs, on the mantel, helter-skelter in the shelving of which there was a great deal. It was wonderful."

"Is he writing a history or something?" asked Sarah, curious.

"Or something." Julie waved a hand dismissively. "He didn't wish to discuss it, whatever it is, but he did allow me to browse the shelves and I have brought home half a dozen volumes. You may wish to see them . . . ?"

"I am sure I will. But then what?"

"Then what?" Julie blinked. "Oh. The tea arrived and I poured and we drank it and discussed books we have both read—Sarah, Miss Austen's work has yet to come his way!"

"Then he has a treat in store, does he not?" asked Sarah impatiently. "Julie, cut line!"

Julie seemed to come back from a long way away and then blinked. "Oh dear, I am making a mull of my tale, am I not? Well, when I saw the footman leave the hall, I told him that my being lost was a ruse, that we wanted to bring him a message that would not look as if we had brought him a message and to ask his assistance without word getting around that we have done so. And then I gave him Larry's letter."

"And?"

"Well, I browsed the shelves while he read it. And then he had questions—very good questions, Sarah—and then we made plans. He saw me to the door, carrying the books I have borrowed, and he said, in his butler's presence—the man, by then, was there as he should have been earlier—that he would come here tomorrow or the next day to discuss my reading and that he hoped I enjoyed the books as much as he has." Julie grinned. "He also ordered me not to get lost again, teasing, you know? That it was dangerous to stop at just any house along the road and ask directions!"

"The butler will tell the upper servants and the upper servants will tell the under servants and word will get to the gardener lads and the stable boys, who will bruit it about the village inn and no one anywhere will have anything in their heads but the thought that you were lost and borrowed some books."

Julie nodded. "After all," she said, "nothing else occurred. Not really," she said wistfully. And then she sighed.

"Nothing at all," agreed Sarah, but, silently, she thought that perhaps a great deal had occurred if Julie was truly as smitten as she appeared to be.

And then reality struck. Julie could not wed.

She was a . . . a *courtesan*. Worse. She was a *well-known* courtesan. What well-bred man would take such a woman as Julie Green in marriage?

Sarah foresaw tragedy.

The next day, after being closeted with Lord Sherringham and Julie for nearly an hour, Lord Kenwicker asked to speak to Roland. The boy, curious, joined the others in Julie and Sarah's favorite room. "Sir? You wished to speak to me?"

Kenwicker held up the vial and Roland swallowed hard as he glanced at Lord Sherringham. "My lord?" he asked.

"I gave it to Lord Kenwicker, Roland. He means to test it to determine what it is. But before he does so, he'd like to know who gave it to you and have you describe the scene during which you received it."

Roland bit his lip. "I've been thinking . . ."

"You are bothered because it is your uncle? Even though you now hold proof he has been draining your inheritance into his own pockets? Has done so for years?"

"It isn't that. He can go to hell in a handbasket for all of me . . . It's my mother . . ."

"She'll be unhappy to discover the truth?"

There was tension showing around the boy's eyes and

in the slightly crooked set of his mouth. "Thing is, you know, I don't think she'll believe it."

"I assure you, lad, that your uncle will be given every chance to prove himself something other than the villain he appears to be. But if I have the story right, there is a chance that he has not only tried to kill your cousin here, but has already murdered at least one and perhaps more to achieve his aim of raising *you* to the earldom."

Roland's eyes snapped to meet Sherringham's. His lordship nodded. "No . . ." breathed the lad, shaking his head in denial. His sun-touched skin paled. "Oh no, surely not."

"You would deny he is a man who could do such a thing?" asked Kenwicker, idly swinging his eyeglass from its ribbon. He appeared totally relaxed and that very stance seemed to reassure the boy.

"I don't know," he admitted after thinking about it for a moment, "but it isn't at all pleasant to suppose I might be related so nearly to a man who can be accused of such things."

"Roland," said Lawrence, "at this point, Lord Kenwicker merely wishes you to tell how it came about you received the vial."

For another moment Roland hesitated and then he sighed. He gave a somewhat garbled account, but Kenwicker patiently probed with sensible questions until he had the whole of it.

"And where," asked Kenwicker when they were finished, "is your uncle putting up?"

Roland's mobile features fell into a vision of consternation. "Is it not odd? I do not know. There are a great number of inns here about, are there not? For the hunters who will come for the hunting season?"

Kenwicker nodded. "Rooms are often booked years in advance, although many are available this early in the fall." He looked thoughtful. "Or perhaps your uncle has an acquaintance in the area with whom he stays so he'd not have to put up at a public inn?"

Roland frowned. "I don't know, do I? I don't really know him. I was at school. Since I've left school, we've either avoided each other or fought about the fact he refuses to teach me how to manage my estate."

"Don't worry your head about that," said Sherringham. His tone was rueful. "*I've* all to learn, you know. You can take lessons along with me from my agent and overseers."

Roland smiled, his eyes glowing warmly. "May I?" he asked a trifle shyly.

"You may," said Sherringham and wondered if he would live to regret the offer.

"Thank you," said Roland. "I have been worrying about it. Now I needn't."

Julie and Kenwicker's eyes met. They smiled at each other. Larry was not so preoccupied he did not notice and glanced sharply at Julie. When Kenwicker suggested to her that they go for a drive—

". . . in order," he said, "to keep up the, hmm, *pretense* that I came merely to see you . . . ?"

—she agreed with alacrity.

Larry bit his lip, hiding concern for her. So far as he was aware, Julie had never allowed her emotions to become involved in any of her previous relationships. Except possibly with himself, of course, and that had been gratitude and the affection of friendship more than romantic love. But if what he imagined these two were feeling for each other actually existed, then . . .

Sherringham predicted disaster.

Once the two were gone and he had answered as many of Roland's questions as his patience allowed, he struggled with his crutches, prowling hither and yon, until he traced Sarah to a seat in the overgrown garden.

"There you are," he said, joining her.

His relief at seating himself was palpable and Sarah scolded him for overdoing.

"If you were not so difficult to find, then I'd not have had to search so diligently," he responded.

"Would it be improper to ask why you sought me out?"

That sobered him. "Julie . . ."

She didn't pretend to misunderstand. She had seen the pair drive off. "And Lord Kenwicker?"

He nodded. "I fear Julie has . . . is . . . will . . ."

"May suffer a *tendre* for the man?"

"She has never, to my knowledge, reacted to a man as she does now."

"When she returned yesterday and told me what had occurred, it appeared obvious to me she was much struck by Lord Kenwicker."

"It can mean nothing but pain for her," he said sadly.

Sarah nodded. "I know."

The two sat there looking at nothing in particular until, simultaneously, they sighed. Then they looked at each other and smiled—although there was something a trifle sad about those smiles.

"Is there nothing we can do?" asked Sarah.

"I can think of nothing. I know there was nothing I could do for myself when it happened to me . . ."

Sarah cast him a sharp glance and instantly looked away. "What do you mean?"

"Hmm?" He blinked, reddened, and swallowed. "Umm, when I fell in love. Of course, I didn't really want to do anything about it, not then, so maybe that doesn't count . . . ?"

"I don't know that I have ever loved." She thought of her infatuation with her made-up ideal man and it was her turn to blush slightly. "Not really." She blushed more deeply when she recalled admitting to herself that she had exchanged this man, the real man for the dream man, that that love had deepened into another sort of love, one which was not mere self-indulgence. "Or . . . No—not really," she repeated.

"If not really," he asked, curious, "then does that mean you have pretended to love?"

The blush deepened. "I suppose one might put it that way . . ."

"Playing at love as the young do?"

She bit her lip.

"You do not wish to tell me?" he asked gently.

"Do you wish to tell me when and with whom *you* fell in love?" she countered.

He hesitated. "Perhaps not just now . . ."

"I doubt I'll ever wish to talk of *my* folly."

"Love is not folly. Although first love rarely lasts, even it is truly love while one suffers with it," he said and wished he knew how to make her fall in love with him.

"Yes, but it is also so very personal, so *private,* that it is difficult to speak of it."

He glanced at her. "That is a perceptive comment, I think."

She glanced at him and their eyes met, held. "Yes," she said. "I think it was."

They lapsed into silence, each morosely thinking thoughts that were surprisingly similar. Each wondered if they would ever share the sort of love they wished to share with another. Each worried they would not. Each longed to do so . . . *and each longed for the* other *to be that person.*

And as *they* mused, Julie and Lord Kenwicker enjoyed an entirely different interlude. The rapport they first felt over the teacups was strengthened as their conversation ranged beyond books and into the philosophies they had adopted, their ethics and ideals. From that they progressed to a discussion of social ills and possible solutions—and disagreed.

Julie understood the problems as Kenwicker never could. She did not tell him why, of course, but revealed, now and again, knowledge she should not have had. Not if she were the proper lady she appeared . . .

Kenwicker knew she was not. He had seen Julie Green in London. He knew exactly who she was and it made no difference to his rapidly deepening feelings. He couldn't put his finger on why this particular woman was not merely tolerable—he was something of a misogynist—but was, instead, intriguing and exciting—both physically and intellectually. He debated telling her he knew the truth, but could not get beyond a ridiculous wish that *she* tell him.

What he knew for a certainty was that Mrs. Green was as unlike as possible to the well brought up young women who were, whenever he dared go into public, thrown at his head. He hadn't the patience to tolerate those young women for more than ten minutes at a time. On the other hand, Mrs. Green, *Julie,* was someone he wished to know far more deeply than mere acquaintance would allow. As they returned to Blackberry Hill, he swore he would find a way of making her trust him so she'd confide in him—

Julie interrupted his personal thoughts. "Have you a plan?"

"A plan?"

"For catching whoever it is that threatens Larry."

"Larry."

Julie thought she'd forgotten—if she ever knew—how to blush, but felt heat in her throat and ears at the soft unaccented repetition of the nickname. "I have known his lordship forever, my lord. Since long before he became Lord Sherringham. I do not stand on points with him."

"He is important to you."

"Very. If anything happened to him—" Cold steel entered her tone. "—I would hunt down his killer and kill the bastard myself."

Kenwicker felt a chill up his spine. That Mrs. Green was that deeply involved with Lord Sherringham was not to be tolerated. He clenched his jaw and vowed he would find a means of replacing his lordship in her affections. He had waited far too many years for the woman with whom he could share his life. He had, in fact, given up the search for her. Now that chance had put her in his way, he was not about to step back and allow her to remain with another man.

Kenwicker was not an illogical man and, since he'd seen nothing stronger than a brotherly concern for Mrs. Green in Lord Sherringham's manner or tone or words, he decided to watch and wait and see what he would see . . . but Lord Sherringham would not keep her.

Julie had no way of knowing what went through Lord Kenwicker's mind but, ruefully, she admitted to herself that, after so many years and so many men, she had discovered one with whom she would like to spend the rest of her life. She was a realist, so her dream was that she could rent a cottage somewhere near Kenwicker's estate, where they could carry on a properly discreet relationship—so discreet that they would do no damage to his reputation in the neighborhood . . .

Julie determined to ask Larry for advice. For the first time in her long career of pleasing the male of the species, she felt out of her element, unsure of herself.

"I've some notions," said Kenwicker belatedly, "concerning my duty to protect Lord Sherringham." But he added nothing to that and his clipped tone did not encourage Julie to probe.

* * *

Kenwicker returned two days later. Sherringham and he were closeted, for well over an hour, in what Sarah called her father's office and, upon exiting, they looked more than a trifle grim.

Sarah looked first at Lord Sherringham and then turned to Lord Kenwicker. "You cannot find Roland's uncle," she said.

Kenwicker admitted it, a muscle jumping in his jaw. "There is a man I use for inquiries. He has searched the whole of the region and Mr. Neverling is staying at none of the inns or the houses that take in hunters at this time of year."

"Could the man have used another name?" asked Julie.

"I gave him the description Roland gave us. He went around pretending to be angry, pretending the man owed him money. Locals would be angry for him, would help to the best of their ability."

"Perhaps Neverling returned to his sister's," suggested Cannington. "To Roland's estate."

Kenwicker nodded. "I've a man on his way to check that very thing."

"Would Neverling suspect his nephew had given him away?" asked Sarah a trifle diffidently.

"He threatened Roland's mother," Sherringham reminded them.

A cold chill ran up several spines and silence reigned for some minutes. Kenwicker's eyes narrowed. "I will send a message to a fellow magistrate, a man who will check that all is well." He thought about it and then shook his head. "But surely such a threat was nothing but the blustering of a bully. His *sister*, after all."

Sherringham pursed his lips. "Four men are dead. He

wants a fifth dead. Assuming our logic is correct, of course."

"He didn't kill *all* of them, surely," said Julie.

"No. The father and his eldest son died in the way of things, the one in battle and the other from over-indulgence and apoplexy aggravated by grief. The younger brother . . . Well that death might not have been what it appeared. He was found bludgeoned to death in an alley not far from a gambling hell, stripped of all he had. Questions *were* asked concerning the death of the heir preceding me but came to nothing . . ."

"I sent a detailed letter to London to Bow Street concerning this situation," Kenwicker said after everyone absorbed that information. "Perhaps they will come up with something that catches the man out." He drew in a deep breath and blew it out. "I must immediately send someone posthaste to tell my friend to check on Mrs. Caldwood. Roland's mother is unlikely to be in danger, but it is not impossible."

"Danger? My mother? But you said . . . !"

They turned to where Roland stood in the doorway to the card room.

"What are you saying?" the lad asked, moving nearer in the half awkward, half impulsive manner that was the way of youth not yet comfortable with a growing body and burgeoning maturity.

They read alarm in his eyes and Sarah moved nearer, laying a hand on his arm. "Roland, tell us again what your uncle said to you that day he gave you the vial." Still holding the lad, she turned back and, before Roland could reply asked, "Have you determined what was in it?"

Lord Kenwicker nodded. "An opiate. Anyone imbibing a dose would have slept soundly. *Very* soundly."

"This becomes ridiculous," said Julie, her hands spread against her hips and arms akimbo. "He asks *Roland* to add an opiate to something we'd all drink. *He* sends poisoned tea. What is the man doing, that he does both?"

"We are certain the tea came from him?" asked Sarah diffidently.

Kenwicker nodded approval. "An excellent question. In my letter to London I asked that the order be checked. We know, after all, where it originated. There should be records concerning the person who placed the order."

"Might the order have come by letter? One purporting to be from me?" asked Lord Sherringham. "Or the housekeeper?" He winked at Sarah who blushed.

Kenwicker pursed his lips. "That is possible, but my hope is that someone put in the order personally, a man who can be identified by whomever served him. Still, handwriting is distinctive and I doubt he can have had a sample of Lord Sherringham's writing which could be copied."

"This is not to the point," said Roland, glaring. He had stared with painfully open eyes from one to the other as each spoke. "What did you say concerning my mother?"

"You have yet to tell us what, exactly, your uncle said to you that day," reminded Sarah. "Come. It will help us determine what we must do."

"Do." Panic was obviously rising in the young and untried lad. "Do! Yes, *do* something. *Now.*"

Julie strolled nearer and quite calmly slapped Roland across the face. He blinked. "Now tell us," she ordered.

He swallowed. "He said I'd be sorry if I didn't do it. He said Mother would suffer and it would be my fault." Once again he fought down panic. Sarah patted his arm when he won control. "Please," asked the lad. "What is wrong?"

"We cannot discover your uncle's whereabouts. We wondered if he might have returned home. And then Lady Sarah recalled your words about your mother. I will send a man with a letter asking a friend of mine to check the situation. My agent will bring me back word."

"But . . ."

"Roland—" Lord Sherringham spoke calmly, soothingly. "—we will do what we can to protect your mother, but if your uncle feels he is being hunted, he is likely to become still more dangerous. We cannot simply ride *ventre à terre* to her side. It is not the way." Roland did not appear to relax at all. "Trust me, Roland. We will not allow her to be harmed." The words were spoken firmly and with grim determination.

At just that moment, a loud knocking was heard at the front door and all swung to look that way. The knocking was repeated, a hollow thundering through the room. Sarah looked toward the back for her footman. When the knocking came for a third time, she started across the great room.

She was forestalled by the dignified but swift passage of the first footman. He opened the door and all, silently, waited.

"I must speak with Roland Caldwell," said a groom who looked as if he'd ridden hard. Beyond him one could see a roan gelding standing with legs very slightly splayed, his head hanging. "At once."

"I am here," said Roland, hurrying to the door. "What is it, Jimmy?"

The young groom looked relieved. "I'm come to the right place then. Praise be," he muttered and handed over a twist of paper. "Said to give it to you. At once."

"Who said?" asked Lord Sherringham who had maneuvered on his crutches to stand behind Roland.

"Mr. Neverling, sir."

"My uncle," said Roland and all color faded from his face.

Sarah came forward then. "Joseph, take . . . Jimmy, is it?"

When the groom nodded, Sarah continued. "Take Jimmy to the kitchen and see he has what he needs in the way of food and drink. Thank you for coming quickly," she added.

Her mild praise put color in the groom's cheeks but he looked uncomfortable coming inside where he was unused to being. He slouched through the great room in Joseph's train, but turned before disappearing under the stairs. "Big Beauty. My horse . . . ?"

"Joseph will send a groom to care for him," said Cannington, going forward to move the lad along.

Roland, his hands shaking, tried twice to untwist the bit of paper. Finally he gave up and handed it to Sherringham, his face white, a pleading look in eyes made huge, so wide open were they. Sherringham spread the paper and smoothed it before handing it back. Roland tried to read but his hands were too unsteady.

"I cannot. I am so afraid," he said, one hand rising to cover his eyes, which were, he feared, revealingly damp. "Tell me what he says."

Sherringham read the brief note and looked up from the dirty crumpled piece of paper. "He tells you, Roland, that your mother is safe for the nonce, but that you will not see her again until you have accomplished what you were ordered to do." He looked around, especially at the women, his mouth set in a grim line.

"That is not all, is it?" asked Julie.

A tiny movement of the corner of Sherringham's mouth might have been the least hint of a smile or, alternately, a twitch of irritation. "You have guessed there is more."

"Please," said the lad. He bit his lip, stress putting lines into his youthful features. "I must know how things are."

"Yes of course you must." Again he handed it to his young cousin. "Here. Read it for yourself."

"You might as well tell us," said Julie sharply, realizing

Sherringham hoped to keep it from Sarah and herself. "If you do not, we will dream up worse horrors than can possibly be the true case. The woman is Neverlings's sister. Surely, it cannot be so very bad."

Sherringham grimaced. "I doubt your imagination is quite this inventive." He drew in a deep breath and let it out slowly. "Neverling informs Roland that he will sell his mother to a certain man who owns . . . hmm . . . houses of ill repute here and abroad."

"You are right. My imagination was inadequate," said Julie nodding. She moved to put her arm around Roland who turned into her embrace, his head bowed to her shoulder, his shoulders shaking with emotion. "Lady Sarah is still less capable of conjuring up such horror. Come now, Roland. Your cousin, Cannington, and Lord Kenwicker will not allow this to happen even if it were possible. I suspect your uncle dreamed up the worst threat he could in order to frighten you into doing as he ordered."

"But I cannot. Even if I wished to, which I do not, I could not obey. I gave over that vial." His head came up and he thrust Julie away from him a trifle roughly, his eyes wild as he looked from one to another of the men. "He is greedy. I fear his greed is such he will do exactly as he says. *He will sell my mother!*"

"A week ago you merely thought him incompetent at handling your affairs. Why do you suddenly feel he is utterly evil?" asked Cannington, his eyes narrowing.

"You did not see him that day I—" He glanced at Sarah. "—accosted him."

"You mean the day you engaged in fisticuffs with the man?"

Roland nodded and a fleeting expression of satisfaction crossed his face at the memory—only to disappear in more horror. "My fault! *It is my fault.* He is angry with me so he will punish me through my mother."

Cannington nodded. "Not an impossible notion. Unfortunately." He turned to the magistrate. "Kenwicker, what resources have you for tracing Neverling's movements? He cannot have gone from here to there and departed with Roland's mother and have left no trace."

Kenwicker nodded. "I must organize an investigation at once."

"One question before you go," said Sarah quietly. "Mr. Neverling has lived most of his life not too terribly far from here, has he not?" She turned to Roland who tipped his head. "Roland?"

"Since my father died, he has. I'd never met him and don't know where he lived before."

"What is your question, Lady Sarah?" asked Kenwicker impatient to be gone.

"I am probably wrong," she said and bit her lip. "It is just . . . this man to whom he would sell Roland's mother. Would he be someone who lives near here? It occurred to me Mr. Neverling would be more likely to know such a person *here* than *elsewhere*."

Kenwicker's eyes narrowed. "There is a man . . . not that there has ever been proof of any sort of wrongdoing . . . but suspicions . . . rumors . . ." He nodded his head sharply, once. Then he grinned, a rather demonic look. "It is just possible that this investigation will result in netting more than one bird."

"You will avoid putting Roland's mother in danger, will you not?" asked Sherringham, his tone sharp.

"At this point I have no clue what I'll do," said Kenwicker blandly, "but I do not use women for pawns if that is your fear."

Sherringham nodded.

Julie felt something inside her still. When Kenwicker, seeing no one had more to say, moved to leave, she followed him.

Chapter 13

After seeing that Roland's groom was fed and settled for a well-deserved rest in empty quarters above the stables, Sarah went to her room. She felt drained. As if emotions and fears and temptations and a variety of other emotions had spilled from her, leaving behind an empty region in heart and mind.

She dawdled about the room, straightening this, moving that, using her handkerchief to wipe the dust from the top of a small table, and ended by staring out her window over the raggedy garden at that side of the house.

What is the matter with me? she asked herself.

The uncared for flower beds and uncut lawn bothered her as they had not done previously and she turned away.

"Something . . ." she muttered. "But what . . . ?"

Not Roland, although she worried for the lad who was out riding with Cannington and Sherringham, who if he were careful and went slowly, could now cross a horse. And not Julie, although what could possibly come of the growing attachment between the courtesan and the magistrate bothered her a great deal. And not Sherringham's broken leg. That was healing nicely, the splints removed. He was adept at using a single crutch when walking and he rode again.

"So what is it?" she asked her reflection. Her reflection

in the standing mirror made no response and Sarah moved on.

Thoughts concerning Sherringham circled in her head, repeating but adding nothing new. Finally Sarah stamped her foot. "This is absolutely and utterly foolish. Why can I not get the man out of my head?"

Because you love him.

Luckily Sarah was standing beside the low chair she used when putting on her stockings of a morning. She grasped the back and, with something of the care of an old and arthritic woman, seated herself. And then she scowled. Although she had more than half admitted the truth once or twice, she was shocked to discover the full measure of her feelings.

"Of course I love him. Or, not *him,*" she blustered, "but my version of who he is."

You love him.

Sarah stared at the images racing through her mind. Sherringham, as she'd seen him turning from the fire in the great room. Sherringham, teasing Julie. Sherringham, his head thrown back and laughing. Sherringham, brought into the kitchen on a hurdle, unconscious. Sherringham, as he conceded a chess game, neither angry nor chagrined at being beaten by a woman. Sherringham, being kind to and patient with Roland, even when tired or suffering the ill-effects of a morning after.

Love? Real, deep, a forever kind of love?

"No. And no." She gripped her hands so tightly the nails bit into her palms. "No-no-no."

Yes.

Sarah forced her mind to go blank. She stared at nothing at all for a very long time. Finally, focusing, she sighed. "Yes," she told herself. "I love him with all my heart. The *real* man and not a made-up man. When did it happen? How has it happened?"

Again the answer required little thought. The same images flitted through her mind and, added to them, many more of the same ilk.

Over the past weeks, she had discovered that much of what she wanted in her ideal *could* be found in the real but, beyond that, had discovered the real man had other traits she liked, traits she had not considered when dreaming up a *perfect* man.

"But he isn't perfect," she said. "He swears. He brought a courtesan with him, and allowed the others to bring their doxies."

He hadn't a notion you would be here. He did nothing that was out of the way when a hunting party comes to a hunting box. Besides, you like Julie.

"Yes, I do." Sarah felt herself pouting until she realized what she did and cleared her countenance of all expression. But then, softly, she also admitted, "I do not like *Sherringham* liking her."

He knew her before he ever saw you.

"She is a . . . a . . . *whore*."

Lacking in generosity, are you not?

The biting tone of her conscience was a slap. "I am not supposed to like a . . . oh, all right. A courtesan! It isn't at all proper. I should not even know her."

So?

Sarah was tired of arguing with her inner self. "I don't know," she said and sighed still again. "I just know I want the man I love to love *me*. *Only* me. I want him to understand me, to be there for me, to . . . to . . ."

Forsake all others?

"Yes."

Old friends? Friendship? Friends to whom he owes a debt?

"Surely he has paid that debt?" She thought of how petite Julie had come to his rescue, wielding a broom against young ruffians. She sighed again. "It is not a debt one can ever repay, is it?"

Her conscience only smiled.

"I *do* like her. She is interesting as many of the women I *should* like are not. She is never boring. She is intelligent. She likes many of the same things I do." Sarah smiled slightly. "I suppose I should not be surprised Sherringham likes her? Since I do?"

There was no inner answer and Sarah rose to her feet. "But do I really love him? The *real* him? *Really?*"

She searched her mind and heart and concluded she did. For a time she felt happy, lighthearted, content . . . and then she remembered that Sherringham did not *wish* to marry her. He *would*. He *insisted* on it. But only because he felt she had been compromised, and for that reason alone. All her happiness in her newly admitted love evaporated as if it had never been.

For a time she wallowed in self-pity.

For a time she wondered if she dared wed him and teach him to love her.

For a time, knowing she did not, she despaired.

And then, for a time, she berated herself for a fool. She stiffened her spine and scowled. Once he had stared across rooms at her, had watched her from afar. Surely that meant that he'd had strong feelings for her? Once upon a time?

Sarah nodded. She would *not* wed him and teach him to love her. She would teach him to love her—love her *again*—and *then, if she was sure he did, then* she would marry him!

But only if she were certain.

That settled, if not quite to her satisfaction, Sarah left her room and, after searching the house, went into the kitchens. "Where is everyone?" she asked Mrs. Lamb.

"Out."

Sarah closed her eyes, her lids fluttering ever so slightly. *Patience,* she thought. "Any notion of where they are out *to?*" she asked.

"The men went riding. I don't know where they went, do I? Mrs. Green went off with the magistrate in a gig."

Reminded that Julie had an interest other than Sherringham, Sarah relaxed slightly. "I'd forgotten that. Lambsy, I'm bored. What can I do?"

Mrs. Lamb looked up from the birds she was preparing for the spit. "Don't call me that."

Sarah felt instant contrition. "I'm sorry. I should not have done so when I know you dislike it. But what can I do?"

"Put on your habit and go riding," suggested the cook-housekeeper. "I should warn you I am having the maids back before everything goes to rack and ruin. *And* letting go the extra footmen. Now most of the guests have left we don't need them."

"Bring the maids back by all means, but, while the house is leased to Sherringham and he pays their wages, let the footmen stay. Work is hard to come by these days."

"They knew it was temporary."

"Yes, but it can be a longer temporary! Sherringham can afford it."

Sarah turned and went back upstairs to don her habit before going to the stables. She would ride. She was used to riding daily and she had been out only irregularly ever since the house party began.

For the next three days Sarah rode at her usual early morning hour, taking the same route each day. The fourth day, Cannington rode with her. The day after, old Alfie saddled up a horse and followed along behind her. He did so the following day as well, and the day after that, Roland, yawning and only half awake, joined her.

"What is this?" she asked. "I have always ridden alone."

"Don't want you endangered. Have someone with you and you are less likely to run into trouble, you know?" The lad yawned again.

"You haven't been sleeping well," said Sarah accusingly.

He flushed. "No. Worried about m'mother?"

Sarah softened. "I know, and I am sorry for you. And for her."

He shrugged. "Everyone is doing what they can. I know that. I just wish there was something *I* could do. But they will only say I am too young."

Sarah nodded. "*You* are too young and *I* cannot be allowed to do anything because I am merely a woman. It is very irritating, is it not?"

Roland managed to smile at that but it faded quickly. He sighed. "Let us go, shall we?"

"You've no desire to go with me."

A muscle jumped in his jaw. "There is nothing else to do. And Lord Sherringham's horses—well, he owns the best blood I've ever crossed, so it is no penance to ride with you, you know."

"Very true. Very well, let us go."

Roland threw her into the saddle a trifle too enthusiastically, but she caught herself and managed to settle herself without falling over the other side. He was unaware he had done anything out of the way and Sarah debated asking him if he would like lessons in how to properly mount a woman.

Just before she opened her mouth to speak, it occurred to her that that comment could be interpreted in an exceedingly suggestive manner and she decided that she had better *not* mention it. Mounting a woman in her world meant a gentleman helping a lady onto her horse—in a man's less tonnish world, the phrase involved behavior in which *horses* were not involved. Roland was quite old enough to misinterpret what she'd have meant innocently—and either be shocked out of his wits or, worse, take her seriously.

They were more than halfway around the course Sarah had set for her daily ride when suddenly, out of nowhere as it were, four mounted men surrounded them. Roland was pulled from his horse and the horse struck across the flank by a crop. Sarah's bridle was grasped and she was pulled along beside a second rider.

It was over so quickly that, for a moment, Sarah could not believe what had happened. Then, fully aware, she yanked hard at her reins, which jerked her mare's head up and out of the unsuspecting man's grasp. Free, she put her heel in Swallow's flank, leaned low over her neck, and rode across country, flying over hedges, and outdistancing the man who had the lesser horse—to say nothing of his not handling the creature very well.

Sarah tore into the stable yard and almost fell from Swallow's back before rushing into the house. "Sherringham! Cannington! *Someone*, for heavens sake! Where are you?"

She was nearly to the door to the great room when it was thrust open. "What is it?" asked Julie.

"Where are the men?"

"They went to Lord Kenwicker's. Why?"

Sarah swore. Mrs. Lamb, coming up behind her, scolded her. "But it is enough to make a saint swear," insisted Sarah. Then she explained. Mrs. Lamb was so shocked she fell against the wall, looking aghast.

Julie's mouth pursed and her eyes narrowed. "So . . . they want another hostage, do they?"

"Perhaps that is why they wanted me, but Roland! What has happened to the lad? The men must rescue him."

"Perhaps he will show up here when he either catches his horse or manages to walk home—but then again, perhaps not." Julie nodded. "Mrs. Lamb, is there a groom other than Alfie in the stables or have they gone off to the pub while the men are away?"

"I don't know." Mrs. Lamb pressed a hand to her heart, her skin overly pale.

"Oh dear, I have shocked you," said Sarah contritely. She put an arm around Mrs. Lamb's shoulders and led her back to the kitchen where she seated her on the settle in the inglenook. She sent a footman running to the stables with a message while Julie set about making a pot of tea and finding something sweet to go with it. Once they were certain Mrs. Lamb would be all right, they conferred as to what more they should do.

"A note," said Julie. "And someone to take it to the men at Lord Kenwicker's."

Sarah nodded. Alfie stomped in the back door at that point demanding to know why Sarah had gone off that way and not even tied up her mare. Treating an overridden animal that way was no way to behave.

". . . I taught yer better nor that!" he ranted.

His muttering would have gone on if Sarah had not managed to ask if Roland's horse had come in.

Alfie stilled. "What's to do, m'lady?" asked the old man, his eyes narrowing.

She told him and then asked if a young groom was available to take a message to Kenwicker's.

He nodded. "Yes, but they're all strangers and don't know the way. I can go cross-country, which those town bred grooms never could. I'd be there in a trice."

Sarah bit her lip.

Alfred's eyes narrowed. "You think I'm too old to ride hard that little distance?"

Sarah smiled at his tone of outrage. "You could outride us all any day of the week. No, I have no fear you'd not manage the distance. What I'm concerned about is Roland. It is because you know the area I need you here.

To lead help to where I left the lad—abandoning him is something for which I'll never forgive myself."

"And what could you have done if you'd stayed?" asked Julie.

Sarah grimaced. "Why do you think I did not? That makes it no easier to deal with the knowledge I ran off and left him."

Paper and ink were fetched while Sarah explained where it happened.

"Not so very far," said Alfred, nodding. "Those lazy town lads can find their way and see to Master Roland. *I'll* take the message."

After giving the other grooms careful directions to where Sarah and Roland ran into trouble, he left, cutting across country as he said he would do.

Sarah, talking to Sherringham's head groom, was ready to go with them to find Roland and was arguing her point, when Roland's horse trotted onto the cobbles before the stables. The gelding held its head off to one side to keep the reins from under his feet and was skittish when they tried to catch him.

"Leave him and *hurry*," ordered Sarah and explained her curt order by adding, "I'm more than ever worried."

Jeremy dithered for half a moment, tried once more to grab the gelding's reins with his one arm, was evaded, and shrugging, mounted his own nag to lead the other grooms out of the yard.

Sarah looked after them angrily. They had not saddled another horse for her and her own mare was too tired. She looked at the remaining saddled animal. *Not*, of course, a sidesaddle . . .

Julie came out just as Sarah, who had taken what she felt an inordinate amount of time gentling the beast so she could catch and lead the gelding to the mounting block.

"You mustn't," said Julie, running up.

"Why not? Roland is in difficulties, perhaps hurt, and I am to do nothing?"

"The others have gone. Despite his only having one arm, Larry's groom will be far better at rescuing Roland, if that becomes necessary, than we. Sarah, you cannot ride astride!"

Sarah had done just that when much younger, wearing britches under her skirts so that her legs were covered where bared by the hiked up skirt. She sighed. "I feel so inadequate, Julie. If it were not for me, Roland would not be in difficulties."

"Do you think so? To my mind, it is because of *Roland* that *you* were in trouble."

Sarah thought about it. She sighed still again. "I still want to do something."

"You've done a great deal. You've sent for Larry and Cannington. You've sent off the grooms to find Roland. Now you need to come in and change out of that habit so that you'll be ready when the men return—or if the grooms return either without Roland or if the boy has been harmed in some way."

"Do not suggest such a thing!"

"The world is a cruel place, Sarah." A muscle jumped in Julie's jaw. "I prefer to be prepared for the worst. Then I can rejoice when the worst does not occur."

Sarah nodded. "I know that now. It was not a philosophy that concerned me until after my father died. Only since then have I understood that life can be truly miserable."

Julie did not say that it could be *worse* than miserable, that it could be dangerous in ways Sarah could not even imagine. And she thanked God that Sarah escaped the trap set for her. If she had not, she might have been compelled to live in the sort of hell only a woman can be forced to endure.

"Don't be a damn fool, Larry," snarled Cannington, grasping Sherringham's bridle with an iron-fisted grip. "She is all right. She is home and safe. You will return to Blackberry Hill Cottage at a reasonable speed or I will order out Kenwicker's carriage and stuff you into it trussed up in such a way you cannot get out."

Sherringham trembled, closed his eyes, regained control, and relaxed. "You are correct. It will do no one the least good if I break this blasted leg all over again."

"I can let go?"

Sherringham grinned. "I am sane again." The grin faded. "Someday, perhaps, you'll know what it means to worry about someone you love. Someone so dear to you her loss would mean that half of you was missing."

"I hope not," said Cannington bitingly. "Not if it turns one into the blithering idiot you've become."

As he spoke he too mounted up and the three men, followed by Alfie, who was proud of himself for managing a ride he would not have attempted for any lesser reason. It had been many years since he'd ridden like that and—although he would admit it to no one—he feared he'd suffer for it. Tomorrow, if not yet tonight.

I'll warm some blankets to wrap my old bones in, he decided. *That'll help as much as anything will. And a goodly tot of grog before I sleep. And maybe that groom of Sherringham's will rub me down with some liniment . . .*

The old groom's musing continued all the way to the Cottage stables where, since no one was there, he set about grooming the horses—which was not altogether a bad thing. He didn't realize it, but that relatively mild exercise kept his old muscles from stiffening and aching nearly so badly as they would have otherwise done.

A groom arrived some little time after they returned, sent by Jeremy to explain. "Tracked 'em," he said, his eyes looking everywhere but at Lord Sherringham.

"They are watching the place?" Sherringham questioned.

The taciturn groom nodded, his lip between his teeth. He was unused to speaking to the nobs, tending to efface himself whenever any of them arrived in the stable and had mumbled Jeremy's message so quickly he had been forced to repeat it.

"You can guide us there?"

The groom nodded. That he *could* do. If only they wouldn't demand he speak to them.

"How many men are in the house? Guards and others?"

The groom frowned.

"You don't know?" Sherringham's experience as an officer to green troops came in useful. He intuitively understood the man's problem and didn't press for more than was needed. "Guess?" he asked gently.

The groom held up four fingers, changed it to eight, back to six, shrugged and dropped his hands.

"Knowing that much helps," said Sherringham, still speaking gently. "Now try to tell me how far away they are."

This time the groom was quicker, holding up five fingers and pointing.

"Miles?"

The groom nodded.

"Near a road?"

The groom hesitated.

"Not too far from it?"

The groom shrugged and held up one finger, bending it at the knuckle.

Larry nodded. "Half a mile from the road."

"I know the place. A ramshackle cottage, long abandoned," said Kenwicker.

Sherringham's eyes narrowed. "We must have a carriage in case Roland is hurt or if it is where his mother is being held. Kenwicker, have you constables available to increase our numbers?"

The men laid careful plans. Sarah and Julie listened, silent, wishing they would finish and get on with it. Sarah smiled a rueful smile that Sherringham caught, looking across the table at that moment.

"Something strikes you as humorous?" he asked. "Perhaps you would share it. Our mood could do with lightening."

Sarah grimaced. "You will not find it at all comical, I think, but I suddenly understand those London politicians you so dislike. The ones who want Lord Wellington to get on with it, and not indulge in so much backing and filing. It is the same with me. All this planning. I know it is important. But I want you to leave, to go, *now*, and rescue Roland *immediately*—and his mother, of course, if she is there."

He smiled. "I see. You empathize with those who want the war ended *now*."

She nodded, then grimaced again. "And that when I am one who *knows* that if Lord Wellington followed the orders they'd send him, that, although the war might end *sooner*, it would *not* end in our favor!"

Kenwicker cast Lady Sarah a surprised look. "I had not thought of that. I fear I am one who would have his lordship chase down the French troops and massacre them."

"The thing is, it wouldn't happen that way," said Sherringham, "but we've no time now for a discussion of tactics. Are we decided?" he asked looking around the table.

They were and went off to take care of the things each must do. Sarah and Julie, not agreeing, but knowing the men would feel better if they were known to be protected, packed small portmanteaus and went out to the stable where the gig was harnessed for them. Kenwicker and Cannington escorted them to Kenwicker's home while Sherringham and the groom drove a carriage slowly toward the ancient cottage that was their goal. With luck, they would time things so as to arrive not long before Kenwicker brought reinforcements.

"You will be safe here," Kenwicker assured the women after giving orders to his staff, which was large and varied.

Kenwicker was a landowner who tried to ease the poverty found all over the countryside by hiring more workers than he really needed. Some of his men rode off with him. Some were stationed around the garden and in the house near doors and windows that offered easy access.

"You ladies make yourselves at home. We will bring word to you the instant we've managed the trick."

Julie nodded. "Both Lady Sarah and I will enjoy the freedom of browsing your library with no one to see what we do. As for you, do be careful, please. We would dislike it of all things if you were hurt during this little adventure. Any of you," she added quickly so it would not be obvious her order to be careful had been meant for Kenwicker. "We know there must be danger, but do nothing rash."

She spoke lightly, but Sarah recognized that Julie was deadly serious. "Amen," breathed Sarah softly.

"We value our skins. I doubt we'll allow anything to happen to them," said Kenwicker a trifle sardonically—and then he joined Cannington who was already mounted and impatient to be gone.

Sarah and Julie stared after the cavalcade until it disappeared and then they turned to look at each other.

"Do you think things will ever be different?" asked Sarah as they went into the house.

"Different? You mean that *we* ride off and the men remain at home to do the fretting?" asked Julie wryly.

Sarah, surprised, laughed a short sharp bark of a laugh. "I think I meant that we *all* ride off and *no one* must stay behind."

Julie thought about it as they moved into the library. She put a hand on Sarah's arm. "Have you read Wollstonecraft's *Vindication of the Rights of Women?*"

Sarah nodded. "I agree with much of what she says."

"That sort of thinking could lead to a relationship between the genders which resulted in the sort of behavior you suggest," said Julie thoughtfully. "Yes, I think it might happen. I think a time might come when men and women work together in ways the likes of which we have never dreamed."

The comment sparked another from Sarah—and the two were quite surprised when, some hours later, the butler informed them the table had been laid in the dining room and, if they were agreeable, dinner would be served now.

They were, it was, and half an hour after they took their last bite a footman appeared telling them a carriage awaited them and that they could return home.

It was not a carriage they recognized.

Chapter 14

Neither did Sarah recognize the groom who, rather obsequiously, held the carriage door for her. She hesitated—but decided he must be from Kenwicker's stables. She was about to take his hand when, seeing a sudden change in his expression, she backed away, stumbling into Julie.

"Run," she said, turning and pushing Julie along.

Sarah was too late. While Julie, shouting for help, picked up her skirts and raced toward the house, Sarah was caught, returned to the carriage, and swung up into it. The door slammed. She reached for it—and discovered there was no handle on the inside. She pushed aside the leather flaps covering the window and leaned out, but the carriage was already bowling down the drive.

It would, she knew, be necessary for the horses to slow for the awkward turn out of Kenwicker's drive. She heard shouts and running feet coming along behind but they were too far away. Taking all her courage in hand—as well as her skirts—she inserted her legs into the opening. As the rig slowed, she dropped down the side, clutching the rather flimsy wood from which the door was made. The rear wheel turned much too near for comfort and she feared the material of her skirts would catch, would pull her against it, roll her under the iron bound wheel . . .

The carriage slowed still more. It was her only chance. She looked to the side of the drive, saw thick grass and, sending up a prayer for help, pushed herself away from the carriage—and, at the same time, dropped. One leg buckled, but even as it did so, the other pushed and she rolled onto the grass.

There was a shout from the back of the carriage where the groom clung, but, looking behind, he judged Kenwicker's men too near. He urged the driver on.

Sarah was carried into Kenwicker's house where she was treated by Mrs. Malone, who had, over the many years she had kept house for Lord Kenwicker, been forced to learn a great deal about aiding the wounded. The felons brought to his lordship's attention often required rough and ready care and, more often than not, she supplied it.

Julie hovered over Sarah. "That was too close for comfort, Sarah," she said, watching what littler color remained fade from Sarah's face as the housekeeper manipulated her ankle, testing whether it was broken or merely sprained.

"Well?" asked Sarah faintly, when the woman looked up.

"Don't think it's broken," said the housekeeper, "but it is bad. Sprains often hurt more than a break, I think. I'll order ice brought in from his lordship's icehouse. Ice helps."

"You and Larry will be a pair, will you not?" asked Julie, smiling.

Sarah chuckled weakly and then, having injudiciously moved her foot, moaned. "I hate this," she said.

"You would hate it more if you hadn't had the courage to escape," said Julie. "That must have been Neverling's doing and, believe me, you would *not* care for what he had in mind."

Sarah shuddered. "You are correct. A sprain is a small price to pay to avoid his revenge."

"You think that is what it was?"

"I suspect it means our men will soon return to tell us all is well—except that Neverling escaped."

Julie relaxed as Sarah's color returned and then chuckled. "They will be surprised to hear it was nearly to do all over again!"

Sarah smiled. "I wish they would come," she said wistfully. "I hate not knowing what is happening. If I have not said thank you for distracting me all afternoon, I do so now."

"We distracted each other," said Julie.

The day moved into dusk and this time they could find distraction in nothing. Sarah envied Julie's continued ability to pace, wishing she too could move and thereby burn up some of the nervous energy fear induced.

And so they waited, Julie pacing and Sarah fretting.

"It is over, Mama. Please do not refine on it still again," said Roland, holding his mother's hand.

"How could he? How dared he?" She turned her head into her son's shoulders and sobbed.

Cannington cast Roland a sympathetic glance. "Your son is correct, Mrs. Caldwood. Your adventure is over and you are none the worse for it. Please, cry no more. Your tears will do no one any good and they are distressing your son."

Roland gave Cannington a grateful look as his mother turned from his shoulder. But she glared at Cannington, sharing the glance with Sherringham. "What do *you* know of what I have suffered? You were not there. You do not know what was threatened." Reminded of what her fate might have been, she wailed, "How *dared* he?"

"But he has already dared a great deal, has he not?" asked Kenwicker softly. "He dared to strip your son of his inheritance. He dared to kill at least one, perhaps two, of four men standing in his way and planned the death of still another in order that your son might inherit. *Another* inheritance he wished to steal for himself. Surely you do not think he would balk at using you to see that your son was kept in line, that he would do what he was ordered to do?"

Mrs. Caldwood frowned. "Ordered to do?"

"Roland was expected to give my houseguests and myself a soporific which would have allowed your brother to enter our house, ransack it safely, and, very likely, as a mere bagatelle, murder me—leaving Roland free to take up the honors of the earldom."

"He wanted *Roland* . . ."

"You may thank your son's training and his character that he would not do so."

"Would not . . . !"

"That he came to us and told us what had happened, gave us the drug which we tested."

"He would not . . . !" She turned horrified eyes on her son, backing away from him. "You would have let that monster sell me? Your own mother? Into you cannot know what horror?" Mrs. Caldwood pushed herself into the corner of the carriage. "How could you? You unnatural boy! You snake in the bosom! You . . . you . . ."

Cannington leaned forward and grasped her chin firmly. "Enough nonsense," he said sternly. "You know very well it was your son who saved you. What is the matter with you that you talk such utter balderdash?"

Mrs. Caldwood burst into tears still again. "You do not understand. Men never understand a woman's nerves."

"Maybe we do not, but to my mind, you owe your son an apology. You have not thought of what hell *he* has

gone through since that note arrived telling us of his
uncle's plans."

"*Not* his uncle."

The words were almost undecipherable as Mrs. Caldwood continued her sobbing even as she spoke.

"Not?" asked Sherringham softly.

She shook her head, sobbing still harder. Then she
peeked through her fingers to see how her sobs were
being taken. Observing the hard cold expressions on the
older men's faces, she sighed. She sat up straight, and
wiped the tears from her face with her gloved fingers.

"I see how it is," she said. "You think I should have
known he was evil, but I am merely a woman and when he
offered to help—when everything was *such* a mess—I was
so relieved you cannot know. He knew *just* what to do. And
he explained it all very carefully, not at all like my husband's solicitor who would have made life *ever* so difficult."

"But it was difficult anyway," said Roland, frowning.
"And if he is not my uncle, as you said he was, then who
is he? You allowed a *stranger* to control our lives?"

The woman rounded on Roland, her fists clenched and
her eyes wild. "I tell you you don't know how it was. That
solicitor would not have paid those debts, all those men
dunning me. We would have lived forever under the burden of them, had strangers at the door forever and ever,
demanding money I could not give them. Wally, Mr. Neverling I should say, took care of that problem right away."

"By selling Roland's land, correct?" asked Sherringham
a trifle harshly.

"Yes. There was no other way."

"And then?" asked Kenwicker politely.

"Why, he began making it possible for Roland to have
a future with what was left, of course."

"There must have been income from renting your
manor. Where did it go?"

She looked bewildered. "I haven't a notion. What business of mine was it? Wally took care of all that. He took that burden from me. All those years he cared for us, saw the bills were paid, did what he could with what was left to improve things . . . ?"

Suddenly she recalled that she had been kidnapped, threatened with the horrors of being sold. "Or did he?" she asked, her wide eyes going from one man to the next. "You would say he did not?" she asked in a small voice.

"I do not doubt he paid Roland's school fees. And bills for coal and food, but Roland says you were in straitened circumstances, that you had to make your own clothing and had few servants?"

"So?"

"So, if every cent was put into improving things, why did they not improve?"

She relaxed. "Oh, there was one bad year after another. You do not know all the trouble we have had. He explained . . ." Once again she tensed up when she saw derision in the men's faces. "You do not believe me."

"Every landowner I know," said Kenwicker, his voice silky, "has done exceedingly well the last half dozen years. It amazes me that you have not."

Mrs. Caldwood was not a particularly intelligent woman, but by the time they reached Stonewall Manor, she finally understood her savior had been anything but. She was a subdued and unhappy woman and, not having had to deal with her during the long ride home, Sarah and Julie felt nothing but pity for her and soothed and coddled her and did everything they could to help her forget her incarceration and the mistake she made in trusting Neverling.

"But why did you tell Roland he was your brother?" asked Julie when, after words with Kenwicker, she understood the situation.

"Oh, you know," said Mrs. Caldwood, waving a hand airily. "Old friends are aunts and uncles to one's children. It is just a way of referring to them."

"But it is my understanding that he was *not* an old friend. That you met him only after your husband died."

Mrs. Caldwood looked from one woman to the other and burst into tears. Roland, about to enter the room, backed out, his expression one of disgust. As he left, Sarah heard "not *again*" from the boy, but was too occupied attempting to soothe the woman to ask what he meant.

Before the evening ended, both Sarah and Julie had decided Mrs. Caldwood was a very silly woman. They both, silently, wondered how long they would be forced to put up with the creature before it was safe to return her to her own home.

Sherringham and Kenwicker consulted, wrote letters to Sherringham's solicitor who, before posting north, consulted with Sarah's who told him what he had discovered of fraud and the misappropriation of funds by the man known as Neverling.

Before too many days the solicitor, with Kenwicker who wished to lay the whole before the appropriate authority in Roland's home region, and the Caldwoods, drove off, leaving Sherringham, Cannington, Julie, and Sarah to put their lives back together at Blackberry Hill Cottage.

And, of course, Kenwicker's men continued the search for Neverling and his cohort, the man who had thrust Sarah into the carriage the day she'd escaped that particular plot, spraining her ankle in the process.

"Julie is correct," she said to Sherringham who, on one crutch, swung along beside her as she limped along a newly graveled garden path.

"How so?" he asked.

"She said we were a pair." Sarah lifted her cane and tapped his crutch.

"I too think we are a pair, Sarah," he said quietly and stopped her by the simple means of thrusting the crutch before her, holding her back.

"Don't," she said, turning her head away.

"Don't tell you I've loved you for years and looked for you in London after my inheritance of the peerage was confirmed? Once I knew I was, finally, an eligible suitor for your hand?"

She glanced at him and quickly away, biting her lip.

"You were never out of my mind the whole of my years in the Peninsula, Sarah. Thinking of you, remembering you, dreaming about you . . . that kept me sane. War is not . . . nice," he finished, unable to find another way of ending that particular sentence.

The hope that filled Sarah when he said he loved her faded. "You dreamed of me." She stared straight ahead. "But did you dream of *me* or of a woman you made up, using my form and style to embody her? You didn't know *me*, my lord. The person I am. You never once spoke to me before you left England. You could not have known the real me," she finished, remembering how *she* made up a character, *her* ideal, and used *him* to embody it.

"You are wrong," he said. When she wouldn't look at him he continued softly, "I knew you very well indeed, my dear. I watched you. I saw how you interacted with all sorts of people. How you were kind to elderly women who were lonely and wanted someone to talk to about their youth. How you were friendly to shy young girls, those who did not *take*. You would introduce them to men who, for your sake, asked them to dance or go down to dinner, or walk in the garden. You would laugh at old men's jokes and laugh again when you heard the same story repeated on another occasion. And you managed your father's houses with ease and fairness to all who were forced to look to you for their livelihood. I think I knew you very well, Sarah. I fell in love with you when I'd no hope of ever winning you. Now it *is* possible. Now I have wealth and status and cannot be called a fortune hunter for pursuing you."

"Is that what kept you from me?' she asked, interrupting, once again hoping.

"Of course. It was laughable, the me I was then, to even think of wedding you."

"Why?" She turned, glaring at him. "Were you evil? Were you dishonorable? Were you under a cloud or deeply in debt? *Why* would it have been so wrong?"

He cast her a stern look. "You are not stupid. You know our world. You know how our peers would have made a union between us one of misery. The whispers. The snide remarks. The sly looks. Such would have been the death of any relationship we might have tried to build."

She sighed. Reluctantly she nodded agreement. Then she turned aside, forgetting her decision to wed him if he could only be brought to love her—wishing she believed he did but unable to accept it. "I thank you for the honor you do me—" She spoke primly, automatically using the response she'd always given. "—but I cannot wed you."

"Why?"

She turned back, her eyes wide. "Why? That is not something you are supposed to ask. You should accept that it is so and . . . and go away."

He smiled ever so slightly but the expression in his eyes was cool. "I should not press you for reasons?" He eyed her stubborn expression. "Perhaps it is merely that I am too soon with my request for your hand. I have loved you forever, but you did not return the feeling then and you do not now love me as I do you . . . Not yet."

She bit back a chuckle at that last bit of arrogance—to say nothing of wrong-headedness—but at the same time shook her head. "It is not that. My feelings for you do not come into it." What could she say, she wondered. "I decided long ago I'd not wed and I will not change my mind."

"Decided?" He tipped his head, a querying expression giving him that devilish look that was so intriguing to almost every woman who saw it. "Long ago? Sarah, are you merely stubbornly holding to that decision or is there a rational reason that keeps you from wedding?"

"Reason? One exists." Sarah bit her lip. "*Rational?* I don't suppose it is. But it is real and deep within me and I cannot see that anything in the world will ever change the way I feel."

"Can you not explain?" he coaxed.

How could one explain one wished to be loved? Truly loved? She shook her head. "Just accept it."

But there was sadness in her that caught at Sherringham's heart. "I don't think I can, Sarah." They walked on in silence for a bit before he asked, "Can we put this conversation to one side and—" He paused searching for words. "—not forget it, exactly, but not allow it to interfere?"

Sarah prodded the path with the cane. Her good leg was tiring and the bad ankle ached. "I . . . don't know," she said and looked up, meeting his eyes. "I would not like to . . . to lose your company. I enjoy playing chess with you and talking with you and . . . and all sorts of things. I would miss your company if you did as I suggested and went away, forgot me." *Miss that and so much more!*

He smiled but his eyes held a somber look. "I did not forget you while in the army. I doubt very much I can forget you now I'm home. Let us go in. The sun is low in the west and the warmth it generated is leaving the garden." He held his arm out for her, glad of having only one crutch to manage so that he could play a gentlemanly role again. "Shall we go?" he said and they moved off together and into the house.

The next day Kenwicker returned from Roland's home. He came immediately to Blackberry Hill and was admitted to the great room where the others sat or stood, undecided as to what they should do with their day. Sherringham was in one chair, his healing leg stretched across a padded stool. Cannington leaned against the fireplace, his arm laid along the ledge above it.

Sarah had a chair across from Sherringham—and another footstool. Julie, sitting on the raised hob before the fire, rose at Kenwicker's entrance and went to greet him.

"What can you tell us?" she asked.

He took her extended hand and raised it to his lips rather than shaking it as she expected. Julie felt herself blushing and wondered at it. She hadn't blushed for ever and a day. Perhaps never. But she could feel the heat in her face and felt it more strongly when Kenwicker chuckled softly. He put her hand on his arm and strolled over to where the others awaited him, Lord Sherringham struggling to rise. Kenwicker waved him back into the chair.

"You all look relaxed and in good humor," said Kenwicker, smiling at the small group.

"Good humor, perhaps. Relaxed . . . not at all," said Sherringham. "I, at least, am worried about the whereabouts of our villain. Have you any word?"

Kenwicker nodded. "He and his servant were traced to a small fishing village on the coast. It is possible that he left the country on a smuggler's boat or that he hired a fishing boat to take them across the channel, but no one will admit to doing so—even when granted immunity."

"Granted immunity?"

Kenwicker grimaced. "Smuggling goes on. We cannot stop it. We hoped that someone would admit taking Neverling where he wanted to go, but we are beginning to doubt it happened. It seems—" He spoke with a dry note that caught their attention. "—that he *tried*, but refused to pay what was asked, so no one would take on the job."

"Refused to pay . . . ?"

"The man is parsimonious to the point he will cut his own throat before allowing an extra groat slip through his fingers. He will be unable to leave our shores surreptitiously for what he is willing to pay."

"Cut his own throat," repeated Julie. "You mean that, even if it means capture, he will not spend the necessary?"

"I feel it is so. You cannot imagine how much he stole from young Caldwood. They are only beginning to find out the whole and already it is a fortune."

"Poor lad. Do you think any of it will be recovered?"

"Some. What they can locate. He had a trunk in the set of rooms Mrs. Caldwood gave over to him that contained several deeds to what had been Roland's property. That will be returned to him. The trunk was nearly full of bags of coin. Several bags appear missing from one corner. It is thought he took them with him." Kenwicker looked grim. "Or perhaps that groom of his stole them. What remains is only a minor portion of what is missing, of course." Kenwicker shook his head. "I don't know what the end will be. Poor Caldwood is not only having to deal with it all, but with that impossible mother of his as well. She wants him to take the coin and herself and go at once to London. Every time he comes within range of her voice, she is after him again."

"I feel guilty," said Sarah softly.

"Why should you?" asked Sherringham, casting a glance her way indicating surprise and disbelief.

"I disliked her. I wanted her gone from here. I was selfish."

"How so?" asked Cannington, blinking in confusion. "We *all* wanted her gone."

"Roland is young. He is dealing with something that would make a far older man tear his hair with frustration, not knowing where to turn. And, on top of that, he must deal with his mother. The woman is a nag and a shrew and—" Sarah looked a trifle thoughtful. "—rather stupid, I fear."

"*Very* stupid," said Kenwicker in that dry tone that made one smile. He turned to Julie. "Mrs. Green, I came to ask if you'd care to go for a drive? The day is crisp, but not too cold and I, at least, would enjoy it. May I hope for your company?"

"I'll get my pelisse . . ."

"Julie," said Sarah, "you'll find a fur lined cloak in my armoire. Take that. It will be warmer."

Julie, already part way up the stairs, paused, her hand on the banister. "I'll do that. Thank you." She continued on her way.

The men had questions for Kenwicker who answered as well as he could when suddenly, every head swung toward the upper story.

Julie's scream rang out a second time.

Chapter 15

Kenwicker and Cannington leapt for the stairs. Sherringham, swearing, struggled to rise and Sarah went to help him, knowing he would hurt himself if she did not, but wishing, somehow, she could keep him from going into what she feared must be danger.

He was on his feet and setting the crutch in place, his face a grim mask, when Julie appeared and ran down to them. "I should not have screamed. There is no danger," she said and got Sherringham back into his chair.

"You would not scream for no reason," said Sarah, looking at her white face.

"I had reason, I guess." Julie looked flustered. "Up there. In your room, Sarah . . ."

"What is it, Julie?" asked Sherringham.

"Miss Murphy—"

Cannington appeared at the top of the stairs. "She's dead." His voice was harsh, his usual, somewhat inane, expression hardened.

"Yes of course she's dead," said Julie, her tone angry.

"Miss Murphy? In *my* room? Dead?" asked Sarah. She seemed unable to comprehend the news.

"Very dead," said Julie and shuddered. She met Sherringham's eyes. "Knifed . . ."

"Poor girl," murmured Sherringham and shook his head. "I wonder how, when . . ."

"Not long ago," said Cannington, coming down the stairs to join them. He looked older. "She's still warm, Devil."

Sarah wanted to tell Cannington not to call Sherringham by that stupid nickname but she was too horrified to say anything at all.

"That's not all," said Cannington, catching and holding Sherringham's gaze. "She is clutching your tie pin. That regimental pin you lost?"

"Clutching it . . ."

"As if she'd torn it away from your cravat . . ."

"Nonsense." He lifted his hand toward his throat where the emerald gleamed. "It has been lost since before I broke my leg."

"Yes. Kenwicker knows that and is not about to arrest you for murder, Devil, but he is not happy that someone has attempted to make it look as if you were guilty."

"Another attempt—"

Sherringham's brows formed those devilish check marks and, because of them, Sarah realized he would never rid himself of the nickname.

"—to rid the world of my presence? The hangman is to take care of that little problem, is he? But surely Neverling does not think he can still profit by my death!"

"He *may* think it," said Julie slowly. "The man is not sane. You cannot predict what such a one will say or do or believe."

"Very true," said Kenwicker, coming down the stairs. "The man is clearly mad, completely irrational, and exceedingly sly. No one saw him approach the house, enter it, or leave it."

"Not *leave* . . ." Sarah rose too quickly and yelped at the twinge to her ankle. "Perhaps he has not," she said as the pain faded. "Has a search been ordered?"

"From the attics down." Kenwicker nodded. "If he is

still in the house he'll not escape, but I think he is gone. Your window is unlatched, Lady Sarah. A ladder leans against the side of the house just there. It cannot have been easy for Miss Murphy to scrambled up and into your room, but I think he made her do it."

"That poor woman," said Sarah again. "I did not like her, but she did not deserve this."

Julie was still white. "No one deserves such a death," she said quietly.

They sat in silence for a bit, listening to the search as it progressed on the floor above them. The footmen and grooms were soon on the ground floor—and then were done. Merit, neat as usual, came quietly into the great room. Sherringham, looking up, motioned him forward.

"You've finished?"

Merit nodded, his hands folded before him. "No one was found, but your room, my lord, was searched. So too, I think, was Lady Sarah's." He bowed slightly in Sarah's direction. "Mrs. Lamb is putting things to rights," he added when she looked alarmed.

"Later," said Kenwicker, speaking to both, "I'll want you to see if anything is missing." He looked from Sarah to Sherringham. They nodded. "I doubt anything is, but we should know."

"You do not think it was merely an attempt at theft with a falling out among thieves?" asked Cannington.

"When Miss Murphy clutched one of his lordship's possessions as if she'd ripped it away from him in a struggle?" Kenwicker shook his head. "No. This was a deliberate plan to implicate his lordship in murder."

"How can you be absolutely certain I did not do it?" asked Sherringham quietly.

Kenwicker grinned. "You, my lord, have been sitting in that chair for two or perhaps three hours and, according to any number of servants who have been in and out and around for a variety of reasons, you have not been above stairs since early morning. Stairs are still difficult for you to manage and you have nothing to do with them once you've come down until you must go back up to bed. You were not above stairs, so you did not do the deed. Q.E.D.," he finished, using the formula all schoolboys learned to put at the bottom of their geometry problem proofs.

"Ah. I finally have reason to be glad for a broken leg, do I?"

Cannington, recovering his equanimity, chuckled. "Neverling was foiled in this attempt because of the results of another of his ruses!"

The men grinned at each other at the irony of that.

"But, it means he remains nearby," said Sarah unhappily.

Julie moved a bit nearer to Kenwicker. Sarah thought it an unconscious move, one she would be surprised to know she had made. *But it is,* thought Sarah, *another hint to Julie's feelings for and about Lord Kenwicker.* Again Sarah wondered what could come of it. And again she concluded that nothing good would result. She sighed. Softly.

But not so softly that Lord Sherringham did not hear. He wondered what exactly had upset Sarah—not that there was not a great deal about which one might be upset. Two disasters were immediately obvious. A murdered woman in her bedroom and a determined villain, cause enough to frighten the strongest woman.

Sherringham, however, thought that neither of those were the reason for Lady Sarah's sigh. Unfortunately, he could not guess what *had* caused it.

Chapter 16

Kenwicker looked around the great room. His gaze settled on Julie and a series of fine lines creased his forehead. "This will not do," he said.

Cannington, who had been plotting how he might catch Neverling, jumped, startled. "What will not do?"

"The women are not safe here. The house is old and too easily breached. Proof of that lies upstairs."

"We had no notion we would be attacked. We thought our enemy long gone," said Sherringham. "Now we know, we'll set guards . . . you shake your head."

"My house is more modern and far better protected. I want you all there. Order your traps packed while I arrange for carriages and carts to transfer you and your possessions to my home." He held up a hand. "I know you think you can protect yourselves, but I would rather you were where I *know* you will be safe." Once again his gaze moved to Julie. When she met the look squarely, it flicked away, red spots glowing along his cheekbones.

Sarah, noticing, shook her head ever so slightly, her concern for Julie growing. *Would it,* she wondered, *be better if they were parted now—or should they be allowed as much time together as possible, before he discovers who she is, before his affection for her turns to disgust . . . ? For Julie,* she decided, *gathering memories is best, even if the hurt is greater in the end.*

"I will," she said, "ask Mrs. Lamb to help me pack. That

is—if that . . . if the . . . if she . . ." Flustered, unable to phrase her question tactfully, she looked around for help.

Sherringham perceived her problem. "Is the room free?" he asked. Kenwicker, understanding, nodded. Sherringham turned to her. "Go, Sarah. If you prefer we move to Kenwicker's, then we will."

"I admit it is selfish of me. I do not want my retainers attacked, hurt by mistake—or on purpose, for that matter. I think we should leave here with as much noise as we can so that word reaches the villains' ears that we are no longer here, that it would be useless to try any more tricks at Blackberry Hill."

"My invitation can be extended to your servants, Lady Sarah," said Kenwicker. "Or you could send those with nearby homes away and we take only those who make this their home."

Sarah nodded. "Thank you. That means Mrs. Lamb and Alfred. The rest are local. I will continue paying them, so that they will not lose by our closing up the house until that man is caught and the danger ended."

Kenwicker bowed. "An excellent suggestion."

Everyone moved in different directions to accomplish what must be done before leaving. Sherringham conferred with Kenwicker and arranged for guards to be left behind, men who could guard against fire or any other revenge Neverling might devise. He was not sane. Everything he had done spelled that out clearly. He would try something.

"And insane, he is unpredictable," said Sherringham.

Kenwicker agreed. "Unpredictable and therefore impossible to outguess. I will be very glad, for a variety of reasons, to have this finished. I wish I could think where the man might be hiding." He frowned. "I have lived in this region all of my life. You would think I'd know all the ins and out, but I have checked every possible house."

"Could he have bivouacked up on the wold? It will be nearly impossible to find him if that is the case."

"Living rough? He did not seem the sort to find that tolerable."

"A caravan, perhaps?"

Kenwicker's eyes narrowed. "He would need a track to pull it up, away from everyone . . ." He rubbed his chin thoughtfully.

Sherringham, seeing that Kenwicker had the matter in hand and would organize a new search, went to his room, disgusted that he must either sit ignominiously on the stairs and scoot himself up them or hop ingloriously one step at a time.

Of all times to have a broken leg that must be allowed to mend, he thought, *it would be when I am needed to protect my Sarah.*

Sarah, her ankle no longer so very bad, could manage the stairs by grasping the banister and climbing slowly from step to step, had similar thoughts. She knew that, if it were necessary, if Sherringham were in difficulties, she'd be unable to run for help. Nor could she again evade capture as she had done before.

It is she thought—her thoughts echoing Sherringham's—*really too bad that this happened now when I would wish to be in perfect health.*

The move was accomplished smoothly, Mrs. Lamb changing hats to act as Lady Sarah's abigail. Alfie grumbled about moving into stables managed by another man, but accepted Sarah's order after only a little argument. Understanding her concerns did not, however, mean he would be content. He would be happy only when he could return to his own place and ways and not champ at the bit, wanting to interfere at every turn with Kenwicker's head groom.

The rooms to which Kenwicker's guests were shown caused a certain amount of humor in two breasts. Julie was amused that she and Sarah were domiciled in one wing while the men were put into the wing where Kenwicker had his apartment.

Cannington, realizing the proprieties were to be maintained, glanced at Sherringham, who had brought Julie north with him, and wondered how his friend would manage the relationship when not only separated by several halls, but with Devil on crutches—a fact which would make sneaking around at night something of a problem. But then Cannington recalled his odd suspicion that there was no relationship. He shook his head at the notion.

Sherringham, on the other hand, didn't so much as notice that problem. *His* reason for arguing that the men and women were too far apart was that he and the other men could not protect them properly.

"I'll have guards walking the halls and I release dogs on the grounds each night. I doubt we need worry about intruders," said Kenwicker when Sherringham approached him. "The hunting box was smaller, of course, so you were all on top of each other, but here we may do things properly. There will be no need for reputations to suffer as they would if I were to put the women in rooms in our wing."

Sherringham nodded. Again it occurred to him that Kenwicker was treating Julie as he did Lady Sarah, treating her as if she were a lady. Sherringham and Julie had been friends, *merely* friends, for a long time now and Julie had retired a year or so earlier. Still, her reputation was what it had always been. It crossed his mind there was a certain irony to the situation.

* * *

Kenwicker did one thing that he did not bother to discuss with anyone. The guards at Blackberry Hill went there secretly, in hopes Neverling *would* try something and, thinking there was no danger, be caught at it. When nothing happened for several days, the man he'd left in charge sent a message, asking if they should remain or if they could leave. Kenwicker returned orders that they were to leave—but should sneak back under cover of night for another try.

If he had needed proof that the hunting lodge was watched, he had it when, around three that morning, a fire was set in Lady Sarah's stables. He was exceedingly unhappy, to say nothing of a trifle embarrassed, to have to report that the damage was greater than he liked and the arsonists uncaught.

"I don't know what to say, how to apologize," he said. "I was certain nothing could happen to either persons or property with my guards there."

"Apologies are not in order. Thanks to your advice, no life was lost. We and the horses removed here and the other servants to their homes," said Lady Sarah. "Property damage?" She shrugged. "What is that in comparison to the loss of a life?"

"You are generous," he said. "It helps that you forgive me, but I do not know if I can forgive myself for such an error."

"You have done your duty from the first," said Julie. "What more can one do than one's best?" she asked.

"Something . . ."

"Those stables should have been replaced years ago," said Cannington, smiling lazily. "Now their owner—" He glanced pointedly at Sarah "—*must* do something, which is all to the good."

Sarah laughed. "Lord Kenwicker or Lord Sherringham must write my solicitor, describing what has happened."

"He will blame me and demand I make good on the damage," said Sherringham, but didn't appear particularly perturbed by the notion.

"I will see he knows the truth of the situation," said Kenwicker who was still blaming himself. "You will not bear the cost. If anyone does, it is I."

"Nonsense," said Sarah. "Lord Cannington has the right of it. Instead of doing harm by burning the stables, Neverling has done me a favor. New stables *were* needed and now they must be provided."

Kenwicker shook his head at Sarah, but forbore belaboring the point. Instead he turned to the men. "We need to find where Neverling is staying. The men I sent up into the wold found nothing . . ."

He was interrupted by the entry of his butler.

"Yes," he asked abruptly.

"Old Jimson Mercer is here. He wishes a word with you," said the butler, a hint of disgust in his voice

"Ha! Finally!" He turned to Sherringham and Cannington. "Come with me. Here's someone who can tell us something if anyone can!"

Lady Sarah and Julie, although not invited, trailed along, too curious to remain behind. Sarah was surprised when she saw Mercer. He looked very like a man from her home district, a poacher who made his living by illegally taking birds, fish, and occasionally a deer, to sell in the London markets. This man had the same long, scraggly graying hair and unshaven pockmarked features. The same sort of long filthy coat that everyone suspected contained large pockets for concealing birds but no one had ever managed to check because *her* poacher never, ever, summer or winter, removed the thing. At least, not where anyone could see him. And this man wore the same sort of boots, run down at the heel and unpolished for so long their original color was lost forever.

The man glowered under his brows. He spat.

"Enough of that. You've come to me with news. What do you know?"

"You looking for a man," snarled the poacher.

"I am. I'll willingly pay for word of him—if you know anything and if we take him. Alive."

"Oh, you can take him. *And* that rank rider he calls a groom." The old man's voice was harsh with dislike and, almost, he spat again, but, when Kenwicker scowled, he refrained. "They've a camp."

"Where?"

"Want paid. Now."

"You'll be paid and paid generously once we've our man in irons."

"Now."

Cannington dug into his pocket and pulled out a handful of change. "Here's for going on with," he said and, moving in a lazy manner, approached near enough he could drop the coins into the fellow's outstretched hand.

The poacher scowled, poking at the coins. "'Tain't enough."

"It's all you'll get until we catch our man," said Kenwicker sternly. He shook his head at Sherringham who would have given the man more.

"Pikers." The poacher glowered from under grizzled brows.

"You'll get what is due you," said Kenwicker. "It will be sufficient."

"Yes, and who decides what's enough?" growled Mercer.

"You know me, Mercer. Have I ever been unfair about these things?" asked Kenwicker.

Mercer's lower lip pushed up against his upper, forming an upside-down bow. He glowered, staring at everyone beligerently. Finally he pursed his lips, his head slightly tilted. Grudgingly, he opened his mouth just a trifle and said, "Farmer Parnotter's glade."

"Parnotter's glade!" Kenwicker's eyes widened. "But that is almost within sight of the road. He can't have a fire there."

"Caravan. Stove. Don't use it much."

Kenwicker nodded. "And Parnotter needs the cash he undoubtedly receives for the use of the land. Moreover the man is unlikely to know anything of what has been going on." He noticed skeptical looks sent his way at that. "He is more the hermit than I've ever been. I don't think he speaks to anyone from one month to the next."

"If that is where they are," said Sherringham, "then let us organize a force to surround and take them."

"I will see to it. *You* will remain here."

"What?" asked Cannington laconically. "You mean to deprive us of the best entertainment to come our way since we arrived?" Cannington had gone out once or twice with the pack since things had gotten bad, but, given how much an aficionado of the hunt he was, he had given up a great deal for his friendship with Sherringham.

"I mean just that. We may be certain they'll resist and I'll not endanger you or Sherringham. You will remain here and see to the women."

"You think he might escape your trap?" asked Sherringham quietly.

"It is not impossible. I will feel better if you four remain here."

Cannington was not happy, but Sherringham asked him to cooperate and he did. "We will expect to hear every detail when you return," ordered Cannington, pushing his finger into Kenwicker's chest and glowering.

Sherringham was impressed as Kenwicker outlined his plans to the force he gathered to surround and take the two felons into custody. "You should have gone into the army. You are an excellent tactician," he complimented the magistrate.

Kenwicker grinned. "I have read a great deal of military history. Such books detail the plans of famous battles and then analyze them. I learned something of the tricks one uses."

He said goodbye, lingering a moment over Julie's hand, and then was gone.

"And now we wait," said Cannington, not even attempting to hide his disgust.

"Perhaps we could play a round or two of whist," suggested Lady Sarah—and then looked quickly toward Julie to see if she knew the game. She did. "Shall I ask the footman to put up a table and find the cards?"

So it was arranged and if no one concentrated on their hand to the usual extent, neither did anyone play so badly they felt they should stop. The hours passed slowly, however, and they were pleased when, finally, Lord Kenwicker strode into the drawing room.

Both Sherringham and Cannington threw down their cards and stood. Julie folded her cards and laid them neatly before her and Sarah merely sat staring at him. "Is all well?" she asked.

"Very well. I have both men in custody. Both are ranting and raving that I had no business arresting them, that they were merely enjoying the good weather, minding their own business, et cetera, et cetera." He grinned. "What is more, as we turned in our drive, a traveling carriage followed us up to the house. It contained a solicitor *and* a red breast!"

"A Bow Street Runner?" asked Cannington.

Kenwicker nodded. "Bow Street found information that ties Neverling to London at the time and near where your immediate predecessor died so they are interested in discussing that with Neverling. The man who put in the order for those supplies sounds like Neverling's groom. He'll be faced with the clerk."

"And the solicitor?" asked Sarah.

"Yours, my lady."

Sarah grimaced.

"From the little he said, I think you'll be pleased to see him."

Sarah straightened. "Oh?" she asked and then thought it an utterly idiotic response—but she could think of nothing more so closed her lips tightly, staring at Kenwicker.

"He is settling into a room and washing away the dust of the road, but he wishes to speak with you privately as soon as he has done so."

Sarah nodded. "If you've no objections, I will see Mr. McAfferty in your book room."

"That will do very well." Kenwicker offered his arm and led her to the door, speaking as they went. "I will, in the meantime, see to the runner's needs so that we may begin our interrogation of Neverling and his accomplice." They disappeared into the hall and those remaining in the drawing room looked at each other.

"Did I or did I not demand to know what happened the instant he returned?" asked Cannington.

"Perhaps you didn't say *instantly*," said Julie, smiling. "I can't recall. But I know just how frustrated you are. I too wish I knew what happened."

Julie felt shivers as she recalled her feelings when Kenwicker walked through the door a few minutes earlier. She could not believe the relief that flooded her at the knowledge he was safe and not lying somewhere with a bullet in him, his life's blood seeping away.

"I think," she added after a moment, "that I will go up to my room for a bit . . ."

"What is wrong with Julie?" asked Sherringham looking at the door she closed behind her.

"Hmm? Who knows what goes on in a woman's head?" asked Cannington who was still fuming that he hadn't a notion how the villains had been taken. "It is outside of enough that we were refused a part in what appeared to be a fine entertainment and then we are refused even so much as the entertainment of *hearing the tale!* It is not to be borne." He stalked from one end of the long room to the other. "I tell you I'll not have it." He made another round. "I believe I will just go see . . ."

"You are not wanted, Canny."

"Nonsense. We'll see what is what."

When Sherringham didn't move, Cannington went to him, pulled him to his feet and handed him his crutch.

"You know you want to," he said, accusingly.

Sherringham grinned very slightly. "Yes, of course I do. But I don't want to do anything that might result in Neverling getting away."

"Hmm." Cannington, hesitating, scowled.

"How about this?" asked Sherringham. "We'll ask the butler if there is a way of observing without being a bother to what passes between the law and the lawless?"

"Ah *ha*." Cannington's lowering expression lightened. "Let us go."

Soon they were seated in chairs beyond a door connecting to the room in which the interrogation was proceeding. The butler set it ajar just before he left them.

It required no more than a little eavesdropping for the hidden listeners to decide all was not going well.

Sarah awaited Mr. McAfferty with a combination of hope and fear that amazed her. Had his letter been a lie? Had he not managed to break the trust? Why else would he come this far if it were not bad news? But perhaps he merely felt responsible for her well-being and, having discovered where she was, had come to see that she was all right?

Well, she was. As right as could be, considering she had been compromised in the eyes of the world by Sherringham's presence under her roof and no chaperone in sight. Or perhaps *not* so well—when one added to that that she had given her friendship to a woman whom she should never have met. Or that she had escaped the machinations of a villain who had killed and wished to kill again . . .

Sarah found she was gripping her hands tightly together and forced herself to relax. "Mr. McAfferty," she said a few minutes later when the solicitor entered the room a trifle hesitantly. "I hope you've good news for me?"

He nodded, coming forward to bow over her hand. "It was not easy to arrange, but you have full control of your fortune with only a nominal oversight by your trustees."

She barely restrained a blink of surprise. He'd gone beyond what she'd only half expected of him, which was to set aside the restrictions on the use of her *income*. "Since it took so long, I assume it was not easy. You will give me, I hope, chapter and verse, concerning what I may and may not do."

"Yes my lady, I will be happy to do so." He gave her an overview right then and there. "We may continue this in more detail as you will. There is a great deal you must know concerning not only your inheritance from your grandmother, but all that was left you of the un-entailed property from your father's estate."

That did make Sarah blink. "I was unaware there was any."

"Oh yes. The townhouse was not entailed and it is yours. Blackberry Hill Cottage, is another instance. And Seaview House still another. There are two farms attached to the latter. Then there are several smallish houses around and about London, which your father either purchased or won at cards. Those are leased, of course, except for the one you were to occupy."

"You did not explain that a house would be made available." Sarah forced the accusing note from her voice. "I had only my pin money once that first year ended, you will recall, and was to support myself with that."

He nodded. "It was part of the will that you be told only that. I was not allowed to tell you more until the year ended . . . and you disappeared before I could," he said. There was the faintest of accusing notes in his tone. Unable to control himself longer, he gave vent to some of his long restrained emotion. "Have you any notion how frightened I was to learn you ran off in such a harum-scarum fashion?"

"I had no desire that anyone know where I went. I could not—I *believed* I could not maintain the life to which I was accustomed. I was not about to sink into some sort of shabby-genteel style of life that I would abhor. Nor would I live as the poor relation in someone's house. My pride would not allow it."

He sighed. "If only you had waited one more day."

"But I did not." She smiled a slightly sly smile. "Actually, I have enjoyed my enforced leave from a tonnish life. It is amazing how much I have learned. It was not an altogether bad thing."

He was unconvinced. "You will, of course, return to London under my escort," he said.

Her brows arched. "Why?"

"Well . . ." He closed his eyes and shook his head, once, as if he could not comprehend how she could think she would do anything else. "If nothing else," he said sternly, "you must not continue living with no companion to act as chaperone. I cannot comprehend how you have managed all this time. Especially after Lord Sherringham and his party arrived. Where did you go?"

"I managed," she said shortly. "That is all you need to know. I will not go to London until I know all is well here. You may stay, if you will, and continue my lessons in my inheritance, or they may wait until I return to London— which I would prefer."

"*All is well?* Ah!" he said, his eyes widening and his body stiffening. "That Bow Street Runner. I don't know how he discovered I was driving north, but he did and demanded room in my carriage. Why? Surely it has nothing to do with *you*, my lady? How could it?" demanded McAfferty.

"Nothing directly and nothing you need worry about," said Sarah and stood. "I will go to my room now. If there is something else we need discuss before you leave, we will do it later. I must change for dinner."

She nodded regally and swept from the room, wondering if there were any way of keeping it from the man that she had been at Blackberry Hill all the time Sherringham and his party were there. There was also the problem of Julie. Would he recognize her? Would he know her for who and what she was? Would he embarrass everyone when he saw her . . . and what of Kenwicker!

"Julie," said Sarah, entering her friend's room after permission was granted. "I'm worried about the arrival of my solicitor. What if he recognizes you? What if he says . . . something?"

"Hmm. I see." She turned from Sarah. "I would not wish him to embarrass you. I will remain in this room while he remains in this house."

"It isn't me I'm worried about. It is you. And your relationship with Lord Kenwicker."

Julie swung around, her face white. "I have no relationship with him."

"But you want one."

Julie smiled a rueful little smile. "I will admit I have wondered if some . . . arrangement might not be made between us."

Sarah's eyes widened. "You mean . . . you would become his mistress?"

"But what else?" asked Julie, bewildered.

"I don't know." Sarah controlled her agitation. "I guess . . . well—marriage . . . ?" she blurted

"I? Marry?" Julie laughed but there was little humor in it. When Sarah cast her a mulish look, she spoke gently. "He could not, Sarah. Not me."

"Oh, the devil . . ."

Julie laughed and this time with only the merest touch of bitterness. "You had hoped for a happy ending, is that it? You do not understand, my dear. If Kenwicker and I come to an agreement, I will be happy. I'll sell my property in London and buy a cottage near here where he may come when he can. I don't suppose I should tell you this, but obviously you were thinking of something far different and I would not have you suffering from such a misapprehension."

"Julie . . . does Lord Kenwicker know who you are? Is *he* thinking of the sort of arrangement you have in mind?"

Julie blinked. Her hand went to her cheek. "You cannot mean . . ."

"Why not? He has lived the life of a recluse. I am of the *ton*. He cannot have thought I'd live amiably with a . . . a courtesan. That, you being you and me being me, we'd be friends."

Julie dithered for a moment and then spoke quickly. "But there is still the problem of your solicitor who very likely would recognize me and would be unhappy that you have become acquainted with me. He must not see me. I will remain in my room until he goes."

"Then I will see he is on his way in the morning so you are trapped for only a little while," said Sarah. She wasn't happy, but saw the wisdom of Julie's decision. "Now I'd better do as I told him I meant to do. I'll change for dinner."

"And I will change as well—into something more comfortable," said Julie, laughing.

But she sobered the instant Sarah left the room. "Marriage . . . ?" she said softly. And then, impatient with herself, added, "*Impossible.*"

Chapter 17

Before Kenwicker could voice the thought that was on his mind, Lady Sarah shook her head at him. Since he was not a stupid man, he shut his mouth, but soon after made an opportunity to question her. "Is Mrs. Green unwell?" he asked.

Sarah opened her mouth to reply and then realized there was a difficulty. She could not plainly tell him that Julie feared to be recognized by Mr. McAfferty, for the simple reason that Lord Kenwicker was, so far as she knew, unaware of Julie's identity. She closed her mouth and cast Lord Sherringham a faintly anguished glance.

Lord Sherringham, also not a fool, realized the problem instantly. "Julie having one of her spells?" he asked quietly.

Pleased he was so quick, Sarah smiled at him. "Yes. That is it."

"Nothing serious, I hope," said Lord Kenwicker, his brows arched.

"No. Not at all serious," said Sarah quickly—just as Lord Sherringham replied, "Rarely."

They looked at each other.

Lord Sherringham added, "I don't mean that it is anything *serious*, of course," as Sarah, backtracking, said, "One never knows how these things will go."

Mr. McAfferty neared and Kenwicker, who suddenly

realized the real problem, grinned. "One never knows, of course," he echoed Lady Sarah and turned toward the solicitor. "You are a conscientious man to have come so far yourself," he said admiringly and, as he led the gentleman away, added, "Tell me about that trial in which you played a part last winter . . ."

"A very minor role, my lord." McAfferty could not help but be flattered that Lord Kenwicker knew he had helped Counsel prepare a defense for his client. "A minor role . . ."

"What," asked Sarah when they were beyond hearing, "did Lord Kenwicker mean by that last comment?"

Sherringham frowned. "When he echoed your comment, which nicely foiled my attempt to right things?"

"Which I too was attempting," said Sarah, her hackles rising at his accusatory tone.

He grinned. "We both tried, which never works." The frown returned. "But as to his meaning . . . surely he has not recognized her?"

"And if he has not?"

The frown deepened. "Would it be such a bad thing? His marrying her?"

"And then, sometime, in the not too distant future, when someone *does* recognize her and tells him her history? *Yes*. A very bad thing." Impetuously she reached out to lay her hand on his. "I am so unhappy for them. I have never seen two people so obviously meant for each other."

"Ah, Sarah." He covered her hand, enclosing it between his. "There is another ideal couple here."

She looked up. Should she, she wondered, object to his use of her name? But it felt so right . . .

"*We* are such another, my love," he said, his voice softening.

Very carefully, she removed her hand from his. She put it behind her where she clenched it. "Don't," she said.

"Don't love you? Don't wish to wed you?"

"Don't embarrass me!" She turned and moved to Cannington's side.

"Feeling lost, a lone woman among the men?" asked Cannington.

Sarah looked around. She shrugged. "I was hostess for my father and at times the only female. He would come home from his club or a sporting event, for instance, and half a dozen of his cronies would have joined him. They'd expect a dinner put before them and my father insisted I preside with him on those occasions when his friends took pot luck, as he called it."

"You didn't answer my question, did you? Nicely evaded, too," he said admiringly.

Sarah cast him a rueful look. "You are correct in thinking this is not the same situation. It is too bad Julie cannot join us. The numbers would still be uneven, but not entirely skewed."

"Why hasn't she . . . ?" His wandering eye fell on McAfferty. "Oh. Of course," he interrupted himself.

The meal was endured with only a trifling discomfort for Sarah, but Mr. McAfferty was obviously unhappy with the situation and made it clear to her the instant the men came into the sitting room once they had drunk off a glass of port.

"You should not be here," he said bluntly. "It will get out and your reputation will be in shreds."

"If my father had not made my life such a misery," said Sarah just as bluntly, "then I would *not* be here. I would still be in London or in the country if I had left town when the season ended. I would not have felt forced to run away."

"But you have no more excuse for running away, Lady Sarah," he said rather plaintively. "None at all."

"None except that I have experienced an adventure

and made new friends and have no wish to change the situation at just this moment. Mr. McAfferty," she continued quickly when he opened his mouth in order to offer another argument, "unless you yourself spread the tale abroad, I cannot see how anyone is to know."

He bowed. After a moment he asked, "There is another woman here? I think I heard mention of a lady named Julie or some such thing?"

"She is indisposed this evening," said Sarah shortly.

"I would like to meet her," he said.

"You leave early in the morning," said Sarah as if it were a settled thing, "so I doubt you'll have the opportunity. I understand the runner wishes his prisoners on the way at an early hour."

Mr. McAfferty stiffened. "Not in my carriage! I will not have it! It was quite bad enough that the runner requisitioned himself a seat in it for the trip north."

Sarah grinned. "As to that, I believe Lord Kenwicker means to supply not only a carriage but extra guards. He has no desire for these particular prisoners to disappear, which they managed to do for far too long."

McAfferty nodded. "Excellent." But he pouted ever so slightly. "I will order my carriage brought around at eight. It is an awful hour to ask one's host to rise in order to see one off, so, before we retire, I will say my goodbyes and give my thanks to Lord Kenwicker for his hospitality."

"And I must give you *my* thanks for all you've done on my behalf and wish you a good journey." The courtesies out of the way, she added, "And now, Mr. McAfferty, you may rest easy. I mean to leave you men to yourselves and go up to bed." She offered her hand, decided once again that her solicitor's hands were far too moist to be quite pleasant, and then made her way from the room.

"Are you awake?" she asked, putting her head into Julie's room.

"How could it be otherwise at such an early hour?" asked Julie. "Come in."

Sarah shut the door behind her and strolled across the room. "McAfferty leaves in the morning. You'll not be shut up for long." She eyed Julie's peignoir, which made her think of a particularly diaphanous cloud of pale blue surrounding the other woman. "How lovely."

Julie looked down. She shrugged. "I've a dozen from which to choose. Perhaps more—not that I brought them all north, of course." She got the pixie look Sarah loved, her mouth forming a funny little "V" and her eyes twinkling merrily. "In *my* business . . ." she began and then laughed when Sarah blushed.

Sarah did not allow faint embarrassment to interfere with what she wanted to know. "May I ask the name of your mantuamaker? I have nothing half so lovely."

Julie tipped her head. "You'd not look right in the sort of thing I wear." She pointed. "On the dressing table there. That pad of paper . . . ?"

Sarah retrieved it and then watched, amazed, as, with a few quick lines, Julie designed a robe. It was high at the neck with gathers at the back, the material flowing down the length of the figure's body like water moving over rounded stones in a streambed.

"A medium to heavy weight silk, I think," mused Julie. "Deep colors." Julie looked at Sarah and nodded her satisfaction with that thought. "Blue," she continued. "A deep dark blue the color of your eyes. I wonder if we could find a good heavy silk of the right color anywhere near . . ." She put the tip of the pencil between her teeth. "It would require a smooth silk . . ."

Sarah gave an embarrassed laugh at the blatant sensuality of the design. "It is outrageously beautiful. I don't know that I'd have the courage to wear it if I *did* own it."

Julie cast her another quick glance, this one full of

humor. "I will order it for you as a wedding gift. Now you *must* get married or you will never know the delight of a man's hands smoothing silk over one's naked body."

Sarah put her hands over her cheeks, shaking her head. She closed her eyes against the instant mental picture of Sherringham touching her, sliding silk over her skin—but closing her eyes made the sensations worse and her eyelids snapped up. "You are evil, Julie Green! Oh dear. I will never forget . . ."

"Sarah," interrupted Julie abruptly, "explain to me once again why you refuse to wed."

Sarah's shoulders dropped and her head drooped. She moved heavily toward the chair near the window and sat. Staring into the dark, she drew in a deep breath. "Julie, I don't think I can. Unless you had known my father, his dictatorial manner, you would never understand how anyone could set up another's back to the point they could not even think of certain subjects with any sort of rationality."

"That's it, is it not?" asked Julie softly.

Sarah lifted her head slowly. Slowly she turned to stare quizzically at her friend. "That's what?" she asked, not exactly clearly.

"On the subject of marriage you are irrational. I can understand why you rejected your first suitor." Julie shuddered. "I knew a woman he had in keeping. You were well out of *that* marriage! And perhaps I can understand why you rejected the next. A naval officer, after all! He would have been gone year in and year out. But the next? He was a good man, Sarah."

Sarah frowned. "I suppose in your, hmm, way of life, you see the real side of men. The side never shown a tonnish woman."

"Oh, their wives and daughters know. Or most do." Julie spoke with a certain dryness. "A man cannot hide such things from those closest to him. If he is a tyrant and cruel, his family suffers."

"My father was a tyrant but I could not say he was cruel."

"He was neither, Sarah," said Julie quietly. "You think he was a tyrant because he had one bee in his bonnet, a belief that a woman must be married in order to be fulfilled and happy—and protected, of course. He didn't want you worrying your head about such things as finances, estates, that sort of thing—" She held up her hand when Sarah frowned and opened her mouth to interrupt. "—and he'd no understanding that a woman could *enjoy*—could actually find *great satisfaction*—from dealing with her own finances."

"He *ordered* me—"

Julie grinned and nodded.

"—in *such* a way . . . you know?" she asked when Julie's grin broadened.

"I told you I knew him. His belief that women were a lesser breed—lovable, necessary, a burden and a joy—was obvious in the way he treated 'Cousin' Aurelia. She, of course, supported his beliefs by acting the part he expected her to play. No," she said, "now it is you who does not understand. Aurelia was *paid* for that acting. Since she wished to continue to enjoy his patronage, she willingly played the role he asked of her."

"And," said Sarah somewhat bitterly, "by doing so, reinforced his beliefs that a woman must be coddled and has no mind of her own?"

Julie merely smiled.

"You would say it was the way he was and I should not resent it."

"Oh, I'd not go quite so far as *that*. Resent it as much as you will, but *understand* it. And accept that now he is gone, you must no longer allow his beliefs to push you into a rebellion you cannot win. My dear Sarah, you will regret it for the rest of your life if you do not reassess your future." Julie looked down at her hands as the pencil broke between her fingers, revealing the intensity of her desire to convince Sarah, for Larry's sake.

Sarah, at the snap, rose to her feet. "Did you hurt yourself?"

"Hmm?" Julie shuddered ever so slightly. "Hurt myself? No, of course not."

But inside, where it did not show, she felt like crying. She had done her best. She could do no more. It was up to Larry to convince his love she must not continue in her idiocy. *He* must convince her to wed him. Deliberately faking a yawn, Julie tossed the pieces of the pencil to the floor.

"It must be later than I thought," she said, hoping Sarah would take the hint and go.

Sarah did, muttering her good nights and closing the door silently, quietly going to her room. Julie had given her a great deal about which she must think.

Had her father's insistence she wed been more than a mere determination to have his own way? Had he truly believed marriage was the only way to protect her, allow her a happy life? *Could* he have been so blind to her real nature?

Sarah moved to her window. Stars sparkled in clear skies and, to the west, a gibbous moon cast down its light. Lord Kenwicker's gardens were quite lovely. Sarah felt an urge to go down and walk in them, fill herself with the peace of them . . . and then she saw the glow of a cigar, saw one man approach another, watched the first say something to the second and then move on to where, dimly, she made out another such meeting.

"Lord Kenwicker," she muttered. "Checking his guards?"

Very likely, but she was reminded that the gardens were not populated by flora alone and that a stroll there would be under the eyes of who knew how many men? She sighed and, fending off a yawn of her own, prepared herself for bed.

Tomorrow she would make an attempt at straightening out her mind. A moment's irritation passed through her: It was too bad of Julie to upset her preconceived notions in this fashion! Discovering one might have misunderstood one's parent—and been so badly misunderstood by him—was not comfortable. Far better to never have known the sort of man Lord Staunton had been than to deal with rearranging her whole philosophy of life.

And then she laughed silently. Better to live life under a misapprehension? What nonsense! She should bless Julie for opening her eyes.

Except . . . her eyes would not remain open and sleep flowed into her mind and body. Refreshing sleep.

Cannington sipped his brandy as he studied his friend. "Glad that's over," he offered.

"Hmm?"

"The villains under lock and key. The danger done. The women safe."

"Hmm."

"We can get back to important things."

That caught Sherringham's attention. His head snapped up. "Important . . . ?"

Cannington waved his glass about. "The cubbing. The way the youngsters are shaping. Do you know how long since I've been out?" Cannington pretended outrage. "I'll have forgotten the youngster's names."

Sherringham chuckled. "You have never forgotten a hound's name in all the years you've been hunting."

Cannington grinned. "You must agree it will be good

to return to the reason we came to Melton country so early in the year."

"The reason *you* came," retorted Sherringham, gently swirling his brandy before raising the bulbous glass to his nose.

Cannington tipped his head. "You had another reason?"

Sherringham shrugged, uncomfortable with having revealed so much. "Yes."

Cannington waited. When that was all, he asked, "Well?"

Sherringham's lips compressed and then he heaved the slightest of sighs. "I was tired of it."

"Tired of it," repeated Cannington without expression.

"The whole social thing, the feting of my coming into the title, the absurd feeling I was hunted . . ."

"Absurd? Nonsense—because you *were*."

"Hunted?"

"Of course. An eligible, in terms of title, wealth and age. How could it be otherwise?"

A bleak look chilled Sherringham's expression. "Maybe I'll buy back my commission. At least there are no matrons with that gleam in their eyes, dragging poor bewildered misses into my orbit and insisting we be introduced."

"I doubt many of the chits were at all bemused. Most young ladies are quite up to snuff," said Cannington with the cynicism of experience.

"Worse."

"So?"

"So . . . blast and bedamned."

"Don't think that's the answer," retorted Cannington, amused.

"*Why won't she marry me?*"

"Lady Sarah?"

"Who else?"

Cannington thought of the years since Sherringham

met Julie, his loyalty to the courtesan, but didn't say anything.

"I love her," continued Sherringham. "I think she loves me. I don't understand why she insists she'll not wed."

"Ask her."

"I have."

"Ask her again."

Sherringham thought about that. He stood, set his half finished glass on the sideboard, and stretched. "I will," he said and headed for the door.

"Hey!"

"Hmm?"

"You *can't* ask her now. She's gone up to bed."

"I didn't mean now." Sherringham, his hand on the knob, turned. "In the morning."

Cannington frowned. "Morning . . . but I thought it was decided. We'll catch up with the master. Follow the hounds . . ."

Sherringham grinned. "Maybe *you* mean to ride out. I do not." He nodded and slipped out of the room before Cannington could come up with an objection.

Chapter 18

Lord Sherringham was not the only one to come to a decision concerning a woman. Lord Kenwicker was also out of patience. He rose early that morning, saw Lady Sarah's solicitor off, and then, less than a half hour later, the carriage with the runner, his prisoners, and the extra guards. Thankful that that bit of business was settled—

If for nothing worse, Neverling could and would be tried and convicted of embezzlement.

—he returned to the house where he told his butler to inform him the moment the two women came down to breakfast.

He had nearly finished bringing his accounts up to date, a job he detested and did often so that it was never so *very* irritating, when a tap at the door heralded the information he had requested. Hastily setting aside his work, he went to the breakfast parlor.

The meal was nearly ended when he cleared his throat. "Mrs. Green, I noticed a particularly lovely rose has come into bloom. I'd like to show it to you if you are agreeable to a short stroll in the gardens?"

"A late rose?" asked Sarah, looking up from the last cup of tea she was pouring for herself.

"Yes," said Kenwicker shortly and turned back to Julie. "Will you come?"

He spoke in such a way that Sarah realized the invitation

was for Julie alone. She cast a worried look toward her friend but, seeing the tiniest of head shakes in response to her silent question, went back to stirring her tea, into which she had dropped a lump of sugar.

"I would very much like to see your rose," said Julie calmly. The time had come. Once it was over, once Lord Kenwicker had turned from her in disgust, she would ask Larry to arrange for her to return to her house in London . . . assuming the conversation she was about to have with Lord Kenwicker went as she expected rather than as she hoped.

Lord Kenwicker smiled. "Whenever you are ready?"

"I need a shawl," said Julie. "I'll join you in the hall."

When the door closed behind her friend, Sarah rose to her feet. "My lord," she said, a trifle of urgency in her tone.

Kenwicker caught her eyes and held her gaze. "I know," he said softly. "I know *exactly*. Do not concern yourself."

He smiled such a sweet smile Sarah was reassured—until he excused himself and left the room and it occurred to her to wonder what it *was* about which she was not to concern herself! She was still mulling it over, frowning deeply, when Lord Sherringham entered the breakfast room.

"What is it?" he asked, speaking more sharply than he'd meant to do. "Oh! Sorry, but your expression . . . ?"

Sarah looked up and then down at her tea. "Lord Kenwicker has taken Julie for a walk in the garden . . ."

Sherringham tried to make sense of that. "And that concerns you?" he asked when there was no sense to be found.

"I fear . . ." Sarah bit her lip. Then she sighed. "Never mind."

"How can I not mind? Something has upset the woman I love and I am not to care?"

That brought Sarah's eyes up to meet his gaze. "Love?"

He nodded, holding her look with his own steady look. "I have told you I love you. I have loved you for a very long time. Has that no value in your eyes?"

Now her concern was for herself. "I . . . yes, of course it does. How could it not? It is just that . . ." She stopped, her conversation with Julie the evening before coming to mind. "Oh, I am so confused!"

"I wonder if we might discuss it, whatever it may be, and try, together, to unravel the problem?"

"It is so embarrassing."

"Love?"

She nodded.

"Marriage?"

More slowly she acquiesced to that, too.

"The two of us?"

A muscle twitched in her jaw as she clenched her teeth.

"Ah. There is no two-of-us?"

"I . . . don't know."

"Well."

After a moment she asked, "Just 'well?'"

He grinned. "I'm not sure. I *think* I meant that that is an improvement over your former adamant denials that there could *ever* be a two-of-us-together. Will you come driving with me if I ask that an open carriage be harnessed for us? The sun shines and there is no wind," he added. "It should be warm enough if you wear something warm?"

Again Sarah hesitated, but, with somewhat the same feeling of resignation that Julie had experienced, she agreed. "I'll send for my cloak," she said.

Lord Kenwicker did take Julie to where a sheltered bush had produced a lovely show of peach colored roses. "Like your complexion," he said, smiling down at her—

and then frowned when she frowned. "*Not* like your complexion?" he asked softly.

"Oh, very likely," she said a trifle crossly. "But it is not like *you* to hand out trite compliments, and I do not like it."

"Then, since it is my earnest desire to please you, I must think up a compliment that is not trite, must I not?"

"Compliments are unnecessary, my lord."

"Torrence."

She didn't respond, reaching out to touch the petals on one particularly beautiful rose.

"Or better yet," he said quietly, "Torrie. That is what my mother called me. I would like to hear the name on another woman's lips." He took out his penknife and cut the rose's stem, snapped off the thorns, and handed it to her. His eyes met hers.

"My lord . . ."

"Torrie." He waited. "*Say* it," he ordered.

Reluctantly, Julie obeyed. "Torrie . . ."

He smiled brilliantly. "There. That was not so hard, was it? And now, Julie—" He grinned. "—ah, Julie, my dear."

"You should not . . ."

He interrupted her. "Now you've used my name I may use yours. I have wanted to do so ever since I first saw you."

"You can use my name anytime you wish. It is the endearment . . ." She held up a hand when he would have spoken and turned away, hoping it would be easier to speak if she did not look at him. "My lord, there is something I must tell you. And then if you wish to continue speaking to me, I think we might—" Julie swallowed. "—come to an arrangement."

He was silent until she turned back, her eyes raised

to meet his. "My dear," he said softly, holding her gaze, "there is nothing you need tell me."

"Oh but there is. You are under a misapprehension. I should have informed you weeks ago . . ."

Realizing she was about to confess, he changed his mind, realizing he didn't *wish* her to suffer the embarrassment she was obviously feeling. "Julie," he said softly, "I first saw you a number of years ago. You were in Hyde Park driving a sweet little cabriolet. I asked about you."

Her eyes widened. Again, she swallowed. "You . . . know?"

He smiled. "I have known from first seeing you here at my door when I wondered what loving Providence had brought you to me."

She relaxed. Her plan might actually become a settled thing. "Then may we not avoid all the usual dilly-dallying maneuvers and simply discuss how we might bring about a situation that would be to our mutual advantage?" she asked. Instantly she went on, not allowing him time to suggest anything at all. "I must inform you I have my savings, an income on which I live simply, but comfortably. I am retired and have no desire to, ever again, find myself a kept woman. Instead, I have thought, if you desired me to do so, I might buy a cottage nearby or lease one if there is nothing for sale. A place where you might visit me whenever . . ." She stopped, his fingers over her lips.

"I've a better suggestion."

She stared over his fingers.

"Marry me," he said softly.

Julie's eyes widened.

"I have never before met a woman who entered into my interests as you do. When I first saw you, I fell into lust for you. I admit it. Knowing you for the woman you are, I have grown to love you. It would be less than satisfying, indulging in the hole-in-corner relationship you suggest. Not with the woman I love."

"You cannot wish to wed me," she wailed. "Not *me*."

He chuckled. "Of course I can."

"But . . ." Julie drew in a deep breath. Controlling her emotions if not the rapid beat of her heart, she tried again. "You cannot have thought. Someone would recognize me. Someone would inform your neighbors you have married a whore . . ."

Once again his fingers covered her mouth. "Hush. Do not call yourself by such a name. You are so far above a common whore . . ."

She nipped his fingertips with her teeth and he pulled them away, his brows arching. "Although I prefer to be termed a courtesan," she said with dignity, "that is only a whore by a prettier name. I cannot wed you, my lord. I will not sully your reputation by joining mine to it."

"You will, I think," he said, studying her. "Marry me," he added quickly, fearing she might misunderstand. "You will do it because it is what we both want. I will not be the first man to wed merely because I have found a truly exceptional woman whom I wish to take to wife. Nor will I be the last. Anyone who will not accept you as my wife is someone I do not wish to know."

"I would be snubbed by every decent woman of your acquaintance."

"That will bother me only to the extent it bothers you. *Will* it bother you, my dear?"

Julie frowned. "You cannot mean that."

"My dear Julie—" His mobile brows arched once again and a smile twitched at the corners of his mouth. "—you forget that I am a scholar, living a reclusive life. Do you really think I will worry about a falling off of invitations to social affairs I have, in any case, no desire to attend?"

The brows dropped and the smile faded entirely. "I *will* be upset, however, if *you* are bothered by it."

Julie shrugged. "I have known very few tonnish women. Those I have observed are not women I would find interesting. Lady Sarah is an exception and would be exceptional whatever life she lived. I doubt there are many like her." When he continued looking at her expectantly, she added, "I doubt I'd find it difficult to forego local society."

"I enjoy Lord Sherringham's company. We can have them to dinner whenever they are at Blackberry Hill so you would not be entirely devoid of agreeable acquaintances."

"Them? They?"

The brows climbed high up his forehead. "Do you think there will not be a *they?*"

"I know Larry hopes to wed her," said Julie, turning away. "Lady Sarah has . . . difficulty coming to the point." She took a few steps from his side, a subtle but unconscious indication that the subject was not one she would discuss.

For once Lord Kenwicker either didn't understand or—more likely—decided to ignore her hint. "Can you tell me—or is it truly a private matter?" He led her to a nearby bench.

"Private—" She frowned, *wanting* to speak to someone about the problem. "—but not, I think, secret." She described Sarah's rebellion against her father, listing the men she'd turned down over the years. ". . . and she cannot accept that all is different now Lord Staunton is dead. She has not accepted that it is *herself* she must please."

"And not his lordship whom she must *displease?*" Lord Kenwicker chuckled. "Poor dear," he added, sobering. "It must be very difficult to be an intelligent woman in the world as it is today. I suspect, my love, that you have had far more freedom in your life than Lady Sarah has had in hers."

Julie nodded. "I know what you would say. You do not mean I have had an *easier* life, for freedom is *not* easy, is it? Freedom cannot be separated from responsibility, can it?"

He nodded in turn. "I knew you would understand. Can you also understand that I truly want you to wife? That I am not so stupid that I do not foresee difficulties, but that I am willing to face them in order to have you at my side?"

Julie fiddled with the ribbons hanging from the bow between her breasts. He put his hand over hers, stilling it, and, using his other hand, tipped her head around until they faced each other. Slowly, giving her time to object, he lowered his mouth to hers.

Warmth, tenderness, a soft request for more, roused something in Julie she had rarely felt. She released her fingers from his and put her hands to his face, framing his cheeks and drawing him nearer. His arms went around her and the embrace deepened.

When he drew his mouth from hers and backed enough to stare into her eyes, she stared back, those eyes widened with amazed delight. "Can love make such a difference?" she asked softly.

"Love makes *all* the difference," he said and kissed her again still more enthusiastically.

Chapter 19

Lord Sherringham turned into the lane to Blackberry Hill and glanced at Lady Sarah. "I thought perhaps you might wish to inspect the damage done the stables. You'll find they were not harmed to the extent we first thought, but you must make a decision concerning their repair—or replacement—assuming it is to be done now and not next spring."

"In all that has happened, I forgot about the fire," she said and stared ahead. The drive had not gone quite as Sarah had expected. She had thought Lord Sherringham would, again, urge her to wed him and was, she discovered, more than a trifle disconcerted that he had not.

Has he changed his mind? she wondered. She peered around her cloak's hood, but the blandness of his features revealed nothing

"Which means," he said, continuing his interest in her stables, "you have given the problem no thought. Do you wish to delay making a decision?"

She avoided an exact answer. "I should see what happened, should I not?"

"I thought perhaps you should," he said and cast her a fond but knowing look.

Pulling up near the partially burned structure, he dropped to the ground and tied the reins to a post.

Then he came to her side and lifted her to the ground, leaving his hands at her waist just that fraction of a minute too long for propriety. Sarah, knowing he had *not* given up on her, relaxed.

Then she wondered *why* she worried. *Did* she wish to wed him? *Would* she say him yea if he asked again?

"You'll see there was damage to both sides—" Lord Sherringham pointed. "—but that the central structure is pretty much unscathed."

Sarah put questions of their future from her mind. "The middle is the oldest, however. When I first arrived and made an inspection, I thought it would soon need re-thatching."

"Fire got into a portion of it." He pointed to a corner of the roof. "They pulled it down and got it out before it did too much damage."

"Still," she said, thinking, "if it needs thatching, then should not the whole come down and be replaced with a more modern design?"

The discussion continued with each raising points and then, together, finding answers. Finally, Sarah said, "I think that settles it. You think more stalls are needed, which means more horses, which implies more grooms, which demands more rooms for the grooms . . . so—" She cast him a mischievous smile. "—I assume you also have a favored design for proper stabling! Tell me."

He grinned. "Minx. You have your own favorite, do you not?"

She nodded. Her smile faded, "But, even so, I would hear yours. I have not been allowed to hunt as often as I'd have liked and haven't heard arguments concerning proper stabling, so I am unlikely to know all I should for making such decisions."

"I like it that you can admit you need help. I had wondered if you were so independent you'd not want it."

She grimaced. "Independence is all very well, but no one can know everything."

He smiled and led her away from the acrid smell of damp burned wood. She tugged him toward the house.

When Neverling was caught, Sarah asked Mrs. Lamb, who was still with her at Lord Kenwicker's house, to order the servants back to Blackberry Hill. Someone would be available to provide refreshments. She entered by the kitchen door. A maid and a footman sat at the table drinking tea.

"Do not worry," she said as they jumped to their feet, embarrassed. "Lord Sherringham and I mean to sit in the sun in the summer house at the end of the garden. We'd like a tray. Perhaps a few ham sandwiches and, if some of Mrs. Lamb's fruit cake remains, a slice or two of it? Fruit if there is any, but nothing fancy," she added and returned to the garden where Sherringham awaited her. "We'll have tea soon," she said and moved toward the vine-covered structure that was cleaned when she had ordered the garden cared for.

Entering the arched front for the first time in years, she looked around curiously. "I do not recall that mural along the back," she said, studying it.

Sherringham glanced at it and then moved nearer, peering at it. "Surely not," he said in a bemused tone.

"Surely not *what*?"

"It looks very much like a Ferneley. I wonder. Did your father order this from him?"

"Ferneley . . . ?"

"John Ferneley of Melton Mowbray. He specializes in hunting scenes." As he spoke, Sherringham searched the mural for the artist's signature. "Thomas Assheton Smith is one of his patrons . . ." he added absently.

Sarah watched Sherringham search the oddest places

for the signature and was amazed when he finally found it, painted very small, on the rail of a gate at one side.

"What an odd place for him to sign the thing," she said.

"He has been known to do no more than scratch his name into the wet paint of a canvas with something like the head of a pin," said Sherringham. "I was lucky to acquire one of his paintings not long ago. Unlike most sporting artists, he has had few reproduced as prints, so I don't suppose he'll ever be so well known as, say, Henry Alken, another sporting artist. Nearly all *his* work is prepared for sale as prints."

"You are interested in art and artists?" asked Sarah, staring at the lively scene. Without waiting for him to continue, she added, "I think something must be done to protect it—" She gestured. "—or the winter and the damp will ruin it. Perhaps," she said, thinking aloud, "glass in the windows and some sort of door to shut off the opening when no one is in residence, one which could be removed in good weather."

"I think you would also need a fireplace," suggested Sherringham, "or perhaps a small stove, to keep out the damp." He ignored her question concerning his interest in art, an interest almost as new as his title. Previously he could not have afforded patronizing any of the modern artists and had had nowhere to hang their work if he had, but he'd recently discovered a desire to learn more.

Sarah merely nodded. The mural in which hounds streamed up a hill alongside blackberry bushes entranced her, a fox racing on up the hill beyond them. "I think I could find the exact place that scene occurred," she mused, but turned away when the scrape of foot against raked gravel indicated the footman approached with the tray. A maid followed with a cloth for the table and a vase into which she had tucked a few late blooms.

The food was laid out and Sarah nodded. "You may go. We will serve ourselves."

She poured and indicated Sherringham should choose from the plates whatever he wished to eat. For herself, she sat back holding her cup and saucer before her and stared out the opening into her newly improved garden. "I wonder why I did not have this done sooner," she said, indicating the view.

"Because you were in hiding and wanted as few as possible to know it."

She nodded. "It seems so long ago," she mused.

"And unnecessary."

She glanced at him and then away. "You refer, of course, to Mr. McAfferty's saying there was a London house for my use about which he was unable to inform me. But unnecessary? Perhaps, but not time wasted. I learned a lot. Not only about myself but about others."

"Julie?" he asked softly.

"In my old life I would never have met her." She frowned. "I hope there is some way we may remain friends . . ."

"Marry me and we will snub our noses at society by inviting her into our home whenever she will agree to a visit," he said promptly.

Sarah grinned. "And have the *ton* assume we are a ménage à trois?"

He laughed. "They would, would they not?" He sobered. "That would not do. I'll not have them gossiping about you in that way."

"You *will* not?" she asked, her heartbeat racing.

"I assume you are a rational creature, Sarah, and will, eventually, do the rational thing."

"Rational . . ."

"You insist you will not wed, but admit, the decision is not rational," he reminded her.

"I have admitted it, have I not?"

"Then . . . ?"

She sighed.

He remained still. Very still. Not, in fact, moving a muscle, his teacup held partway to his mouth. When she continued silent, he lowered it slowly, setting it into his saucer with only the faintest of clicks, and the saucer onto the table.

Soft as the sound was, it brought Sarah back from the reverie into which she had fallen. She looked at him and set down her own cup and saucer. "You have the right of it."

"The right . . . ?"

"I cannot continue as I have. Julie pointed out how idiotic it is to feud with a man dead and buried. My father *is* dead. He is no longer a factor in my life. Even his *will* no longer controls me. Mr. McAfferty saw to that. Moreover, Julie convinced me I misunderstood my father's motives just as he lacked knowledge of the woman I am. I have acknowledged all that. Now it is time to change how I react to . . . things."

When she said no more he could not bear it. "Does that mean," he asked carefully, "that you will wed me?"

"Do you," she asked daringly, "truly love me?"

"Oh Sarah—you can never know how much."

The intensity of his response could not be misunderstood. Sarah believed him. Love. The one requirement she'd not surrendered . . . she drew in a deep breath. Finally, exhaling, and with that gust of air relinquishing the past, she nodded.

He whooped and rose to his feet. He came to her. Picking her up, he swung her around and around, whirling down the path and then back again. Carefully, he set her on her feet.

Breathless, she grinned. "I suppose that means you are pleased?"

"Very," he said and hugged her.

"I assume something else," she said. His brow arched questioningly. "Your leg has healed?"

He grinned, loosening his hold on her. "I heal quickly, thank God." He released her. "And now we must return to Kenwicker's."

"We must?" Sarah was rather amused to find she was disappointed he'd not kissed her.

"We must. At once," he insisted. Then a flicker of self-deriding amusement crossed his features. "I don't trust myself to remember I am a gentleman or that we are not yet wed." He took her hand, drew it into his arm and stalked off with her.

She tugged herself loose and ran back into the summerhouse where she picked up one of the maid's sandwiches before she rejoined him.

When he looked at her, amused, she grinned. "I find coming to such an important decision has made me hungry."

"I too am hungry," he said softly, "but not for food."

The four did not meet again until dinner—Cannington having sent word he was dining in Melton Mowbray with a member of the Old Club. Since Brummell, one of the four members, was not in residence he needn't worry about evening dress.

Lord Kenwicker, when Julie insisted she must change, had also gone to his room and, in honor of the occasion, donned far more formal clothes than usual. Lord Sherringham and Lady Sarah also changed when they returned to Kenwicker's manor.

Sherringham went from his room to the garden for a

cigar. Kenwicker retired to his office to finish the accounts he had put off that morning. Julie sat in the library where, instead of reading her current book, she stared at nothing at all, worrying she'd done the wrong thing. And Sarah did her fretting in her room, staring down into the garden, hungrily eying Lord Sherringham who had no idea he was watched.

All four heard the dinner gong and appeared immediately from four different directions. They seated themselves in their usual places, allowed the footman to place bowls of broth before them and, simultaneously, they picked up their spoons.

At the continued silence, Kenwicker grinned. "I haven't a notion why everyone *else* is mute, but I find I cannot wait for the end of the meal for the announcement I planned to make then along with the champagne cooling in the icer." He indicated the bottle sitting in the corner. "We'll have it later in the library, Biggs," he said. The butler nodded and carried it away.

"An announcement?" asked Lady Sarah, casting a questioning look toward a blushing Julie and then a doubtful one toward Lord Sherringham.

"Julie has done me the honor of agreeing to wed me. I mean to purchase a license as soon as possible and . . ." His brows arched. "Yes?" he asked shortly, a hardness in his eyes as he stared at Sherringham.

"I too have an announcement. And a suggestion," said his lordship, smiling at Julie who looked worried. "Sarah and I are also to wed. I assume, knowing Julie as I do, that you are not ignorant of her background. My suggestion is that you put off your wedding until Sarah and I have said our vows and that, *then,* Julie be married from our house. Sarah's support will not smooth Julie's way in the *ton* entirely, but it will help."

Kenwicker, who had looked very much like an angry

terrier ready to leap into a fray, relaxed. He nodded, his eyes on Julie. "My dear?"

"Nothing will smooth my way," she said with no bitterness. "And the *ton*'s reaction if your new wife comes to my support? They will not be fooled into thinking I am acceptable, Larry, but will believe Sarah is urging the wedding so that I will be out of your way." *There* was the bitterness not to be heard when speaking of herself.

The other three frowned. They looked at each other. "But that is nonsense," exclaimed Sarah. "I *like* you. You are my friend."

Julie's mood shifted and she smiled, reaching a hand toward Sarah. "I know. And I value that friendship. But, Sarah, I know our world. It is unforgiving and much prefers to think the worst when given the alternative. Also," she added musingly, "the truth *is* somewhat difficult to swallow."

The last was said with such wry humor the men chuckled. Sarah's smile flickered but she sobered quickly. "It isn't fair."

"My dear Sarah," exclaimed Julie, grinning, "surely you do not think life is *fair?*"

Sherringham frowned, ignoring the banter. "I will think of someone who *can* sponsor Julie, someone who has the standing to rub the *ton*'s collective noses in it, so that she ends up smelling like a rose."

"Such a person does not exist," said Julie, shaking her head.

"There is the prince . . ."

"Prinny?" asked Julie, startled, just as Sarah, equally astounded, said, "The Prince Regent?"

"Flying high," suggested Kenwicker, his eyes narrowed. He, after all, had the highest stakes on the table. If Sherringham could find a means of making Julie acceptable in the eyes of at least some of the *ton*, then he, for her sake, was all for it. "From what I have heard, he is unpredictable at the best of time."

"But a romantic to the core," retorted Sherringham. "One would need to put the story to him in just the right way, of course."

"I cannot believe you are serious," said Julie, uncertain whether to laugh or cry.

"I'm *serious*," said Sherringham. "Just uncertain I can pull it off . . ."

"The Beau could," said Sarah softly.

"Brummell?" Sherringham's lips pursed. "I wonder . . ."

"This must be nonsense," said Julie, shaking her head, afraid to hope

"Nonsense? Perhaps. But worth a try. You, I know, are worried about marrying Lord Kenwicker because you know your past cannot be kept a secret. Sarah likes you and would like to retain your friendship but knows it will be difficult once she and I are married." He stood and struck a pose, raising his glass in mock toast. "What we need is a *deus ex machina*."

Kenwicker's brows crouched low over his eyes and his mouth was set in humorous lines. He shook with laughter. "But Sherringham, you cannot have thought!"

Sherringham lowered his glass. "Thought?"

"In ancient Greece, in their plays, the god in the machine was lowered in a basket from above. I cannot think where you are to find a basket large enough to contain our Prinny!"

They all laughed, the jest, tainted as it was with just a touch of *lèse majesté*, lightened the mood and somehow, in the ensuing banter, the notion was set aside. Rather than think of a means to their future, the four settled down to enjoy the knowledge the future was, in the more general sense, decided. The celebration was lively and carried on well into the evening—until the champagne ran out.

Kenwicker poured the last drop from the last bottle into Julie's glass. "I should have saved some for the wedding," he said a touch regretfully. "It isn't as if we can replace it. Not with the war dragging on and on." He held up the empty bottle and then tossed it over his shoulder. It landed in the fireplace with a satisfying crash and tinkle of glass.

"That is not something with which we need concern ourselves," said Sherringham. "I possess, according to the wine list I inherited, several dozen cases of the real thing, put away for special occasions. We'll have enough for all." He made one last toast with his eyes, a silent one, and drank off the last of his sparkling wine while holding Sarah's gaze with his own.

Chapter 20

Lady Sarah settled into one of her favorite chairs. Seated on the edge of another, Julie looked around the small room in the back of Lady Sarah's townhouse. "Very cozy," she said, approvingly.

Sarah laughed. "If it is so cozy, why will you not relax? We have just accomplished the speediest journey of my life and I, at least, need time in which to convince myself the world will no longer jounce me or throw me half across the carriage at unexpected moments."

"The men were in something of a rush, were they not? Larry is an excellent whip, but that journey was outside of enough!"

Sarah grinned. "It appeared as if they thought the world would end if they did not implement their plot instantly."

"Their plot." Julie sobered and slouched back into her seat. "Such foolishness."

"Do you think so?" Sarah leaned her head back. "For myself, I pray they succeed." She turned and trapped Julie's gaze with her own. "Julie," she said, her tone assuring the other she was absolutely serious, "even if they do not, I want you to know we will find a way to keep our friendship alive."

"There are always letters," said Julie.

"Not half so satisfying as having you there across from me talking to me."

"Have you any notion at all how—" Julie searched for a way of expressing what she felt. "—deeply grateful I am that you accepted me for the person I am—even though you knew my history?"

"Grateful! Gratitude has no place between us. After our adventures, the danger we both endured, we would be fools if we had not grown close." Sarah cast Julie another quick look. "Besides, I always wanted a sister. You are just the sort of whom I dreamed when I dreamed such dreams."

"Sister?" Julie flushed hotly. "I think not."

"Not?" Sarah sat up and turned to stare at Julie. "You sound as if I'd insulted you," she said, a trifle hurt.

Julie shook her head. "No, no. You don't understand. I had sisters. I would not wish such a relationship on anyone!" She relaxed and smiled. "Far better that we be friends, Sarah. For that I bless you."

Sarah relaxed. "I see. But not *all* sisters are a millstone about one's neck. I have known many who appear quite pleased to depend on each other."

"You have also," suggested Julie, "known the other sort. The trouble with relatives is that you must take the good with the bad. Friends can be chosen." She fell silent and then, after a moment added, "Perhaps the very best would be if one had a relative who was also a friend?"

Sarah nodded. She closed her eyes until a tap at the door heralded the entry of a footman with a tray. She bestirred herself long enough to pour their tea. The footman passed Julie a plate of tiny sandwiches and, at a gesture from Sarah, left the room. "Dinner," said Sarah, picking up her own dainty sandwich, "will be in a very few hours, but I could not eat at that last stop."

Julie nodded. "I know exactly what you mean."

Between the two of them, they cleared the plate, discussed the possibility of ordering more, but then

decided it required too much energy. Neither had
moved when, some time later, Sarah's butler announced
the arrival of Lady Sarah's favorite aunt.

"Aunt Mandy! Where did you put her?" she asked,
rising to her feet.

"The blue salon, my lady," said the butler. He cast a
brief glance toward Julie and then turned to look at
nothing at all. "She said you were *both* to come."

Julie blinked, turned a wary look toward Sarah. "She
knows I am here?"

"I don't know how she knows *I* am here," said Sarah.
"Lord Sherringham, perhaps?" she asked after a moment.

"Would he tell Lady Mountmart of my presence in
your house?"

"He might . . ."

Julie sighed. "Let us get it over. I told you I could not
remain here, that I would go on to my house in Chelsea."

"Don't be a faint-heart," said Sarah. She linked her
arm with Julie's and, with only a tug or two, led her to
the blue salon. "Aunt Mandy! How did you discover so
quickly that I had returned?"

The tall bony woman lifted a lorgnette and stared at
the two younger women. "Harumph. He said it, but I
didn't believe it. I have come to chaperon you. The *both*
of you," she added in her abrupt fashion. "I'll have the
yellow room, Sarah. If Mrs. Green is in it, you will move
her to the mauve room. I told Rutherford."

"Chaperon?" said Sarah, the point far more important
than which room was occupied by whom. Besides, if her
butler knew, then it was unimportant.

"Lord Sherringham arrived on my doorstep not an
hour ago in all his dirt and insisted I come immediately
to see to the proprieties. Although if half the tale he told
is true, then—" A touch of acid colored Lady Mountmart's voice. "—it is far too late to be worrying about

such niceties." Her eyes narrowed and she stared from Sarah to Julie and back again. "How dared you, Sarah? What idiocy did you take into your head to run away like that? Have you any notion how worried I have been?"

"Father's will. My year's grace ended." Sarah scowled. "I could not face the *ton.* I could not bear the thought of a life as a dependent, the poor relation, hanging on someone's sleeve. The fact I was rich and could not afford to maintain any sort of establishment was . . ." She attempted to think of the words to explain her feelings, but everything sounded trite. She settled for, "I could not bear it."

A muscle jumped in Lady Mountmart's jawline. Jumped again. "But Sarah, to remain at the Cottage once you knew it was rented to a hunting party!"

"Aunt . . ." Sarah shook her head, knowing there was nothing she could say in defense of her decision.

Lady Mountmart drew in a breath and huffed it out. "Lord Sherringham says the two of you are to wed. I suppose the gossip will die down eventually. And you, Mrs. Green..." She pursed her lips and studied the courtesan about whom she had heard rather unbelievable tales. She sighed. "I don't know. I do not see how his lordship can possibly manage..."

Julie's head rose. "Manage," she continued for her, "to make me acceptable in the eyes of the ton? He cannot. It is impossible. I know that. I do not mean to become a burden to Lady Sarah. I have told her I cannot stay here."

"Oh, as to that, of course you must. There is nothing in *that.*" Lady Mountmart waved her hand at Julie's astonishment. "Do not be missish. I cannot bear the least hint of missishness and, besides, it does not become you. I have no objection to the wife of Lord Kenwicker as friend to my niece. It is not that. It is . . ."

Again her voice died away.

"Aunt Mandy, this is not like you. Come now. What is it you wish to say?"

Amanda, Lady Mountmart glared. "Mind your manners, Missy. I will open my budget in my own good time." She drew in a breath. "What I would say is I do not see how his lordship can arrange two weddings in less than a month. It cannot be done! You know it cannot. There are announcements, celebratory functions, trousseaus to be ordered, invitations must be sent—" She threw up her hands. "—and far too much else."

Julie blinked. "I suppose," she said, her voice utterly bland, "I could announce my engagement at the next Cyprian's Ball. It would be *most* appropriate and I would know there would be *someone* in attendance."

"Do not act the fool," snapped Lady Mountmart. "If Sherringham brings the Regent up to scratch, then you will not lack for guests. I would put my money on him, if I were you. A most competent young man. I always thought him better than most of your suitors, Sarah. Far more sense in his cockloft and not a greedy bone in his body."

"He was never a suitor. He knew Father would have nothing to do with him," said Sarah. "That is why he didn't put himself forward."

"More's the pity. On the other hand, a man who wishes to avoid a snub is not stupid. Nor is he a coward. He is merely realistic in his knowledge of our world. Since he has inherited, he is *more* than eligible and you are not to turn up your nose at that. Despite the current rage for losing the world for love, such things *are* important." She hesitated again and then added, "Besides all else, I believe he feels . . . affection for you."

"He loves her," said Julie softly.

Lady Mountmart sniffed. "Oh. Love. The poets *love*

the sentiment, but I do not. Love is proved only by behavior. We will see what his amounts to." She sniffed again. "As to your gentleman, Mrs. Green, I found him still more sensible. He thinks just as he ought on any number of subjects. I like him."

"You had time to discover his thoughts on your pet concerns?" asked Sarah, astounded.

"Of course." Her brows arched. "You may be certain I asked. I would not put my reputation on the line for a man I could not stomach. Not even for you, Sarah." She stood. "Now, you both look worn to the bone and no wonder if you made that journey in the time his lordship claims, so you are to go to your rooms and rest until dinner when the gentlemen will join us."

The word that Sherringham and Kenwicker meant to come to dinner brightened both young women's outlook. But their thoughts were in turmoil—although for different reasons—and each welcomed the notion of having an hour or so alone.

"What have you done?" asked Lady Sarah once the servants left them in peace to enjoy the last course of what had seemed an overly long meal.

Sherringham glanced toward Kenwicker who motioned for Larry to speak for them. "We went straight from where I stable my horses to your aunt's, Sarah. That—" He cast an indignant look toward Lady Mountmart. "—took far longer than expected."

"I have already explained to the girls—"

She ignored Julie's raised eyebrows. She hadn't been a girl for a very long time. Perhaps, never.

"—that I could not oblige you in this ridiculous plan if I did not approve of Lord Kenwicker. As you know—" She cast a benign smile toward Torrence. "—I found him quite superior to the general run of men parading themselves as gentlemen."

"Yes," objected Sherringham plaintively, "but that meant we were too late to catch Brummell before coming here, as you demanded we do, to dinner."

"We mean to find him later at his club," said Kenwicker who was quite as impatient as Sherringham to set their plans in motion.

"Much later," said Lady Mountmart. "You will first escort the three of us to the theater. I had thought to allow my cousin and his wife the use of my box this evening. How fortunate that, for one reason or another, I had not gotten around to offering it."

"But . . ." Julie half rose from her chair.

"Do not pretend to be lacking in poise at this point in your career," scolded Lady Mountmart. "We will show our faces, allow a few gentlemen to visit during intermissions, and say not one word concerning imminent weddings."

"But . . ." Sarah caught Julie's appalled gaze and returned it with one of irritation. She drew in a deep breath. "Why?" she asked, turning, slightly belatedly, to face her aunt.

"To rouse the *ton* to curiosity, of course. That I, with my interest in poor women, would take up with a courtesan would not be thought particularly out of the way. Particularly a cyprian of Mrs. Green's reputation. Especially since it is known she has retired. That I allow her to be seen with *you*, Sarah, will cause a sensation. That *and* that you've returned to town from no one knows where."

"You do not think I should first see Brummell and have him drop a hint in Prinny's ears?" asked Sherringham.

"The news of our foray into the theater should reach the royal ears first. He will be full of curiosity. He will wish to be informed of what is afoot. He will listen and, assuming Brummell manages with his usual flair, he will be delighted to play a role in your plot."

"I wonder if he will not feel insulted that his role is secondary. That we have upstaged him, so to speak, by appearing before he is apprised of the situation?" said Kenwicker with a touch of diffidence.

"You will mention to Brummell that we hope he will hint our Regent into coming here for a visit to discover all. Perhaps hint at the adventure. He will find it most romantic that, in the process of saving you, Kenwicker fell in love with Mrs. Green. He will be amazed by the girls' roles in it all. He will be entranced by the fact they beg for his aid in bringing about Mrs. Green's reformation."

Sherringham and Kenwicker stared at each other. Kenwicker shrugged and said, "You are far more familiar with the personalities involved than I. If Lady Mountmart believes this is the road to take, than certainly I am not the one to object."

Sherringham fondled his wineglass, a faint frown putting a vertical crease above the blade of his nose. "I . . . cannot predict how he'll react. He will have heard that our villain was taken into custody. That is old news but he *will* want details. It is very likely he will demand we tell him the whole . . . but do we dare?" His eyes, which had turned from one to the other, settled on Sarah. "I will not have Sarah's reputation damaged by the weeks we were under the same roof and unchaperoned."

"As to that—" Lady Mountmart waved a hand as if batting a fly away. "—I will manage it somehow."

"You will also explain all away when it becomes known, as it will, that four whores were in residence?" asked Julie with something of a bite.

"No, no," objected Sarah, her features perfectly bland. "Three whores and a courtesan!"

Sherringham chuckled but sobered instantly. "Lady Mountmart, I assume you've something to suggest?"

"No one knows where you were, Sarah. Not exactly. Perhaps I will say you were at Rosehill, of course—and that you and I traveled together to Leicestershire, unware Blackberry Hill had been rented to Lord Sherringham. Lord Sherringham, as was proper, rid himself of his friends and their companions the instant he realized who had arrived."

"Except for me?"

"You, Mrs. Green," said Lady Mountmart, "are retired. I asked that you remain, of course."

Lord Kenwicker once again met Lord Sherringham's gaze. "Will it fadge?" he asked.

Sherringham's teeth moved sideways, his jaw very slightly off-kilter. For a long moment he seemed to stare at nothing at all. "Yes . . ." he said slowly. Very slowly, he smiled, his lips spreading and his eyes gradually beginning to twinkle in a faintly devilish fashion. Then speaking far more firmly, he said, "Yes, I do believe it will. Sarah, were you aware of what an excellent conspirator your aunt could be?"

"Aware?" she asked, a trifle bemused, "Not at all. In fact, I would have said she was—" It was her turn to look impish, "—more than a trifle stuffy—even though she has always been my favorite relative."

"You will discover, Sarah, that appearing to the world to be—what was that abominable word? Stuffy?" Her ladyship shuddered. "Very well. That appearing stuffy *to the world* is excellent cover for doing exactly as one wishes when the world looks elsewhere." Her ladyship rose to her feet. "Come along and leave the gentlemen to their port—We'll have sherry in the blue salon. You will—" She glared at the gentlemen. "—join us so we may leave for the theater in reasonable time. I willingly miss the farce, which is usually so full of low humor as to be intolerable, but I will not miss the opening scenes of the drama." She nodded firmly and swept from the room.

Behind her Sarah met her fiancé's gaze. "Sherry?" she mouthed.

He grinned. "She said one could do as one pleased—when the world looked elsewhere. One must assume she is more pleased by sherry than tea."

Julie shook her head in mock horror. "Come along, Sarah. She will send for us if we do not join her at once. And, frankly, I would avoid the peal she'd ring over us if she were forced to that extreme."

Arm in arm, Julie and Sarah removed themselves from the dining room and strolled on to the salon where Lady Mountmart was already enjoying her sherry—which the younger women were shocked to discover looked and tasted very much like port.

"*Sherry*," insisted Lady Mountmart grandly. "A lady *never* drinks port."

Seated by her in the theater box, Lady Mountmart's words drew Sarah's attention away from the conversation between Lord Sherringham and a man who seemed to know him—and Julie—far better than Sarah could like. She leaned a trifle nearer.

". . . retired, of course," continued Lady Mountmart to the crony who had come to her box out of curiosity. "Couldn't show my gratitude if that were not so."

All the world appeared curious about the quintette in Lady Mountmart's box but only the rudest or the most oblivious to other's sensitivities had knocked at the door.

"Mrs. Green," her ladyship explained, "saved Sherringham's life. He was attacked in the alley where she lived and she came to his rescue when he was about to be bludgeoned by a young thug. I have long wished to thank her. Sherringham's mother was a dear friend and he has always been a favorite of mine."

Sarah fumed when she could not make out the grumbling response from the deep voiced peer.

"*Of course* I know how she has survived," retorted Lady Mountmart with more acid that Sarah had ever heard in her aunt's voice. "A woman with no family. A woman alone in the world. How is she *supposed* to support herself? You and men like you are not philanthropists, willing to set up young and pretty women in their own establishments and ask nothing in return. Well? Are you?"

Sarah stifled a giggle when she saw how red the gentleman's ears grew. She wished she could understand his response, but again his words were unintelligible.

"Why should I not? Not only is she an intelligent and interesting woman, she is also on the verge of marrying the man she loves, a man who loves her. Of course I mean to stand her friend!"

The man mumbled some more.

"Whom will she wed?" Lady Mountmart grinned evilly. "You, along with all the world, can await the announcement. It will be in the papers sometime soon."

After only a few more words and, with a glance the man shared between Julie and Lord Sherringham, he left the box abruptly. He was soon to be seen in another box and then another, and, soon, many eyes were turned toward them. Sarah gritted her teeth and smiled.

And smiled.

And, by the time the play ended and they could go home, had smiled herself into a headache.

Once the three women were settled in the blue salon with a last glass of Lady Mountmart's *sherry,* Sarah could wait no longer. "How dared you, Aunt!"

"Dared I what?" asked Lady Mountmart and tried, unsuccessfully, to hide a yawn.

"How dared you imply to that . . . that . . . old gossip that Julie and Lord Sherringham are to wed!"

Julie, who had been stifling yawns far more successfully, straightened in her chair. "Sarah! Whatever do you mean?"

"My dearly beloved aunt set off rumors that you are about to wed advantageously —and did not bother to explain that Larry—" Sarah was so upset she forgot to be formal. "—was *not* the prospective groom."

"Why?" asked Julie, turning her dark lashed eyes toward Lady Mountmart.

"Because," said Lady Mountmart with more than a trifle of smugness, "I wish Prinny to be in a fret of anticipation when Brummell finds him. He will be shocked that Lord Sherringham would wed you—and so relieved a hermit like Lord Kenwicker is the actual culprit, he will willingly aid and abet the two of you."

Sarah shook her head, reluctantly amused but, simultaneously, appalled. "I cannot approve."

"No of course not. You wish the world to know that Lord Sherringham is yours. They will soon, dear. Do not let my little plot upset you unduly."

"Fine words, Aunt, but what if they upset Larry?"

"Upset Lord Sherringham? Why should they?"

"Why should they not?" asked Julie. "He is known to be my friend—but it is *Sarah* he loves. He'll not like the world thinking otherwise." Julie was surprised to find that, even after falling in love with Lord Kenwicker and discovering her love returned, the knowledge Larry loved Sarah caused a mild pang. She berated herself, silently, for acting dog-in-the-mangerish and, silently, apologized to both Sarah and Larry for her foolishness. She rose to her feet. "I'm for bed. It has been an exceed-

ingly long day and I cannot think how I managed to remain awake this long." She left the room after curtseying
to Lady Mountmart and blowing a kiss toward Sarah.

"Julie has that right, Aunt." She too rose to her feet
but then she frowned. "Aunt, if your meddling causes
me problems with Larry I will . . ."

"Will?"

Sarah laughed, but there was little humor in it. "Perhaps I will disappear again. I wonder. Do convents take in
desperate women who are not of the Roman persuasion?"

"Sarah!"

But Sarah departed, leaving Lady Mountmart to wonder if, in her zeal to help Julie, she had truly alienated
her niece.

Chapter 21

"You understood me," said Lord Sherringham.

Brummell, who had, at Sherringham's request, allowed only the two men into his boudoir during his morning toilet, turned from his mirror where he watched with a critical air as his barber clipped his hair. "You want me to go to Prinny and beg his assistance in bringing Mrs. Green into respectability? *That* is all you ask of me? Why not send me to Napoleon to beg that he come forward and make peace!"

"Come down off your high horse," said Sherringham. "You are the only man in London who could possibly succeed in such an impossible quest so of course we come to you."

"Bah." But the beau was, it appeared, amused by Sherringham's all too obviously complimentary attempt to manipulate him. "You'd best be careful. I am not one of your mannikins who is turned by easy flattery."

"You mean—" Sherringham made instant retort, "—it didn't work?"

Brummell shouted with laughter. "I guess it did," he admitted. "Have you, along with your outrageous demand, advice as to how I'm to accomplish the deed?"

"Lady Sarah's aunt, Lady Mountmart, has set in motion her own little plot which, if she is correct, will aid and abet the end we wish to achieve."

Brummell waved them to silence, took up a hand mirror, studied his coiffeur carefully, and then laid the mirror aside. "A trifle more off the back," he ordered and then asked, "And her plot?"

"I don't know how she dared," said Lord Sherringham.

"You sound a trifle put out," said Brummell when Lord Sherringham didn't continue. "Come now. Open your budget. I cannot help if I don't know it all. In fact, begin with how all this came about? Where, by the way, did you stumble across our lost heiress?"

Sherringham and Kenwicker took chairs and waited for the barber to finish and—obviously regretting he was not to hear the tale—take his leave. They then launched into the carefully expurgated tale of villains and captures and everything but the facts of Lady Sarah's pretending to be the housekeeper and remaining at the Cottage among a handful of hunting-mad bloods and their doxies . . .

". . . *and* Mrs. Green," finished Sherringham. "Julie has been retired for some time now. She was not there under my protection but as my hostess. And while there, thanks to our adventures, she met Lord Kenwicker."

"I understood that bit. I still wish to know how Lady Sarah came into this saga—" He looked from one man to the other. "—but I perceive that particular story is to remain untold. Very well. I've an excellent imagination and have watched Lady Sarah from afar as her ladyship progressed through her seasons. An admirable woman. We need not concern ourselves with the exact moment you two met. My lord," he continued, turning to Kenwicker, "am I to understand that you and Mrs. Green do not mean to take the *ton* by storm and set everyone's ears on end with your antics?"

A muscle jumped in Kenwicker's jaw, but he replied calmly enough. "We mean to retire to my estate in Leicestershire and live a quiet life. We will invite those few friends who are willing to treat my wife with the respect she deserves into our home. It is possible that—assuming the war ever ends—we will travel on the continent, but neither of us has any desire to cut a dash in London society."

Brummell nodded. "I had to ask," he said gently, understanding Kenwicker's irritation exactly. "If I am to take on this task of convincing Prinny—" His brows arched and he snapped his fingers. "—which reminds me that you did not explain to me Lady Mountmart's interference in your plans."

Kenwicker did so, succinctly and exactly. ". . . We did not approve her hinting that it is Sherringham Julie would wed," he finished, "but it is done and the rumors must be all over London by now."

"Oh certainly. And half of England when the first mail is delivered!" Brummell chuckled. "Yes, I see exactly what her ladyship had in mind." He put two fingers into his waistband and ducked his head into his cravat. After a moment's thought, he nodded. "And," he said, looking up, "I believe I see how to do the trick . . ."

The note from George, Prince Regent, arrived at Sherringham's rooms as the two men enjoyed a small brandy before picking up Sarah and Julie who had expressed a desire to view the pictures at Somerset House. Sherringham's brows rose at the seal and he showed it to Kenwicker before opening the missive.

"We are ordered to appear at Carleton House within the hour. His royal highness, it seems, is curious to meet the man who could turn Mrs. Green's head. He also, it appears, wishes to quiz me on my managing to bring the Golden Spinster to the point."

"You cannot mean that he referred to Lady Sarah in such terms!"

"But he did. See for yourself." Sherringham handed over the thick paper with the royal crest at the top. He moved to his escritoire where he scrawled a note to Sarah excusing them from their outing.

The note, delivered by Sherringham's groom, sent Sarah and Julie straight to Lady Mountmart's side. "I have a sudden feeling of doom," said Julie. "What do I do if his highness refuses to lend his support? How could I wed my love if that marriage is forbidden by royalty!"

"Bah. Kenwicker is not so lacking in courage that he would turn you off merely because Prinny turns up his nose."

"But a royal command . . ." insisted Julie, biting her lips.

"You are looking for boggles under the bed," insisted Lady Mountmart a trifle wrathfully. "Sarah, ring for service. We will have tea. And then you will, each of you, settle with your sewing or a book or practicing at the pianoforte. What you will *not* do is pace a path into the rug."

Julie stopped pacing. Sarah did not.

"Well, missy? What has you in a lather?"

"The prince may be angry. He may take it out on Lord Sherringham. He may . . ."

"He may also go on a diet and lose fifty pounds, but I doubt it."

Julie bit back a laugh. "Lady Mountmart, that comment makes you very nearly a traitor to the crown, does it not?"

"Given how sensitive Prince George has become about his weight, it was, as you say, rather unwise. Come now. Sit down before you make me lose my temper."

Sarah swung around. "It is not you who may be the cause of a rift between the man you love and our prince!"

"Oh yes it is. It would be my playing games with that old gossip, Hayworth. Do you think I cannot turn Prince George up sweet? I'd rather not, mind, but I will if I must." Lady Mountmart, having come as close to an apology as she ever did, straightened, pointed imperiously toward the sofa opposite, and ordered, "*Sit.*"

Sarah and Julie sat. They were still sitting when Sherringham and Kenwicker were announced. Both jumped up and moved with more speed than grace toward their visitors.

"How . . . ?" began Sarah just as Julie asked, "What did he say?"

Sherringham grinned. "I am to inform Lady Sarah that, since her father is dead and cannot have that honor, he means to give the bride away. As to you, Mrs. Green, he will invite you and Lord Kenwicker, once you are wed, to his next soiree." When Julie paled and shook her head, he added, "You will, without a doubt, attend. As the new bride of a peer it is, of course, required of you. You'll not go as Mrs. Green."

Julie sighed. "Is there no avoiding it?"

"No." The word was abrupt but understanding softened the look that went with it. "You will not be alone, Julie. Lady Mountmart will present you, of course, and Sarah and I will support you. Nor do you need stay much beyond your presentation. You will manage very well."

"I cannot."

"Julie," said Sherringham sternly, "you are a courageous woman. For Kenwicker's sake, you will do this and you will carry it off with aplomb."

Julie blinked. She turned to look at Kenwicker who scowled at Sherringham. "No, Torrie, do not say it," she ordered, laying a hand on his arm. "Larry is right. Once we have done this thing, then we need never do so again. We can do just as we planned and go home."

"Home?"

"It felt like home, Torrie," said Julie softly, looking up into his face. "The only true home I think I've ever known. And all thanks to you."

"Here now," said Lady Mountmart.

Sarah was surprised that her aunt looked a trifle embarrassed.

"Enough treacle," continued her aunt tartly. "You don't need to turn the man up sweet now you've caught him."

"It is not *treacle* but the *truth*," said Julie, her chin rising.

"I like treacle," said Lord Kenwicker, his eyes twinkling, "but if Lady Mountmart finds it offensive, why do you not bundle up and we will walk a bit in the garden before Lord Sherringham and I must leave."

"Are you not to stay for dinner?" asked Sarah.

"We are bidden to a neat little supper at Brummell's. I suspect he still hopes to get the story of your disappearance out of us," said Sherringham, grinning. "Do not worry. He'll not learn of it from us."

"No, that isn't right," said Lady Mountmart slowly. After a moment's thought while they stared, she explained. "I think you *should* trust him. Oh, not with the *true* version, but a form of it. Assuming he is alone, of course. And that he promises it will go no further—not that you can believe that. But if he promises, then it would be diplomatic to reward him with a story, the one we want, which may ooze out into our world."

Sherringham nodded. "Very well." Then he grinned. "And now, dear lady, will you tell me what our version might be?"

"Does anyone know if he has ever visited Blackberry Hill?" No one spoke and Lady Mountmart sighed. "I would be helpful if he has not. Since we do not *know*, you must be a trifle vague. A cottage. Somewhere not too near the house, but near enough the two of you ran into each other. Perhaps when out riding. You became better acquainted . . ."

"No," interrupted Sherringham, "it is well known I had a tendre for Sarah before buying my commission. Now, as an eligible, I *dared* become better acquainted with her. I will admit to spending more time alone with her than the *ton* would approve, but, since we are to wed, no one need concern themselves . . . ?"

Lady Mountmart nodded. "Yes. Very good. And if he asks about a chaperon . . . hmm. Sarah, did you not have a starched up governess? One who retired once you told your father you'd had enough of her?"

Sarah chuckled. "The Iron Maiden? That is what I called her when angry with her. Once she was gone I managed to remember all the things I *did* like about her, her wry sense of humor, her intelligence, the guidance she gave my reading—anyway, I wrote her, apologizing for being such a charge on her patience. You would like her, Julie, although I suspect she'd be horrified if she were to discover your background. She has a very strict sense of propriety."

"There you are," said her ladyship, nodding. "If you must reveal a chaperon, then you will say it was an old governess with whom Lady Sarah has stayed in touch."

"And," said Sarah, "we will hope that no one takes it upon themselves to ask her about it, because she would not lie and then we *would* be in the suds."

"You needn't use vulgarities, Sarah," said Lady Mountmart. "It would be quite suitable, however, to suggest we would be up to our necks in—" With a hesitation very nearly too subtle to notice, her ladyship's tongue poked into her cheek before she ended her sentence politely. "—trouble."

The men grinned and Julie hid a giggle. Sarah shook her head. "You are a complete hand, Aunt."

"I am, am I not?" said her ladyship, pretending to preen.

Sherringham rose to his feet. "As much as I enjoy the banter, we must be off. It will not do to be late to this particular entertainment. Sarah, you will, I hope write a graceful note to our prince, thanking him for his generous offer and telling him we mean to be wed at the end of the week—assuming he can manage to fit it into his schedule, of course."

Lady Mountmart was still expostulating about the date when the door closed behind the men's well-tailored backs.

Lady Mountmart had her way and it was very nearly a month, banns requiring three readings in church, before the wedding occurred. A much smaller wedding followed immediately after the first, Sarah and Lawrence leaving St. George's and driving to a nearby church where, before a small group of well-wishers, Lord Kenwicker and Mrs. Green said their vows.

The newly married couples then returned to Lady Mountmart's townhouse where she held a wedding breakfast in their honor.

Lord Cannington, who had torn himself away from Melton Mowbray long enough to support Sherringham, gave the final toasts. ". . . so, to this pair—" He gestured to his left. "—I wish a long and happy existence, one graced with prosperity and fascinating friends. And to these two important people in my life—" He gestured to his right. "—I wish great happiness and constant prosperity. I also wish to congratulate my friend—" He grinned at Sherringham. "—for bringing to such a happy conclusion what must be the longest courtship ever. And," he added, "I hope they continue as generous as they've begun. Thanks, Larry. I and young Caldwell, when he can join me, will enjoy my months at the hunting lodge which, you insist, you'll not be needing this year!"

As soon as the two couples were waved on their way, Canny disappeared around the corner to where his own travel carriage awaited him. He tossed his hat inside, looked up at his driver, and with a grin, ordered, "Blackberry Hill, Ambert. And spring 'em!" With a muted tallyho he disappeared inside and, all the long trip north into Leicestershire, dreamt of the long runs he would enjoy with the Quorn—and, on two of the three days when the Quorn did *not* meet, he fully expected to be occupied with either the Cottesmore or the Belvoir hunt. Unfortunately, no one hunted on the Sabbath. On the other hand, once church was out, one could, of course, meet with friends and *talk* foxhunting.

Cannington settled into his seat, set one foot on the seat opposite, and felt a great deal of satisfaction. No more mystery to solve. No more danger to his dearest friend. No more lovebirds mooning about to interfere with his major interest in life.

Yes, everything had been agreeably settled—and when he wished a good meal and a quiet evening, he had that standing invitation to Kenwicker's . . . Julie had always set a good table with no nonsense about feminine sensibilities. And, much to his surprise, Cannington discovered he actually looked forward to meeting Lord Kenwicker again.

Yes. Life was good.

Epilogue

Our villains? At the Crown's expense, Neverling had shipped out with a following wind, arriving in Australia more quickly than might have been expected. For the rest of his life, he plotted . . . not that that life was all that long. There were too many *other* villains there, all of whom disliked being cheated, villains unrestrained by notions of civilized behavior. Neverling, egoist to the end, was quite surprised one day to look down and discover a knife protruding from his chest.

As supposed next of kin, Roland Caldwood was so informed and felt nothing but relief—and then disgust to discover his mother shedding tears for the man. He had, however, once his finances were in order, discovered a means of dealing with her. When she would not stop crying, he ordered her maid to pack her up and sent her off to Bath.

Sherringham did not forget his promise that Caldwood could share his lessons in estate management, so Roland became a regular visitor when they were in the country.

Life took on a regularity that might have become boredom after all their adventures, but none of those involved were the sort to sink into ennui and their existence never became mere routine.

* * *

Julie agreed with Canny's sentiment. Life *was* good. A small item appeared in one of the journals describing the soiree at which she officially met Prince George. Her future, except with the highest sticklers, was eased. Actually, from her beloved lord's point of view, it resulted in far too many of his feminine neighbors arriving at Stonewall Manor to pay their respects to the bride. Mostly, of course, from curiosity about what a former courtesan might be like than any other reason—but they went away impressed and, reluctantly, finding they liked her.

And Lady Sarah? She could not have been happier. She and her beloved, whenever they wished to be alone, would visit Sherringham's most obscure estate. It was a delightful little manor in Devon, quite isolated, and staffed with well-trained retainers who quickly learned they must not enter any room before they first were granted permission.

It was not possible for life to be better than this, she thought on one such occasion while smiling fondly at her husband. Another thought crossed her mind, surprising her into raised eyebrows.

"What is it?" asked Larry, pushing a lock of hair behind her ear.

She chuckled. "It just occurred to me, dear one, that my father may have been correct."

"Hmm?" he asked, nuzzling that particularly sensitive spot just below her ear. He raised up. "Your father?"

She smiled. "When he insisted I should be married. I am," she said as her hands ran up his bare back to his shoulders, "finding it a quite delightful state."

She tugged gently and, obligingly, Lord Sherringham kissed her. Again. And again . . .

Dear Reader,

I hope you enjoyed reading about my very odd housekeeper—and her new friend, Julie. It was almost impossible for someone of Julie's background to marry into the upper classes in this period of history, but such marriages were not completely unknown. There was a Lady Lade who had, according to rumor, been the mistress of a highwayman. It is also true that more than one peer has defied family, friends, and peers, in order to wed an actress. Still, that Julie found love with her Torrie and that the two of them might be supported by not only Brummel, but the Prince Regent as well, is a bit of a stretch, I fear!

Published for the first time in paper, my next book, *A Handful of Promises*, comes out in July. It first appeared in the early nineties, a small print run, hardback edition that few of my readers will have seen. This was the first time that I had real problems producing a book to contract deadline. My then-editor and I had agreed on a synopsis. I wrote the book—and did not like it. I said as much to my editor and she agreed. We had discussed possible solutions to the problem for nearly an hour, by long-distance, before it occurred to me that the reason we didn't like the book was that my conventional hero and heroine were, well, more than slightly boring. On the other hand, there was *another* couple in the story who were not boring in the least. I hesitated to suggest I change the book to *their* story for the simple reason that Regency heroines in those long-ago days were very young women—and this particular female character was a spinster in her mid-thirties. We took a chance and (I hope you agree) the result is a very satisfying romance indeed, a case of lovers parted and then, years later, finding each other again.

Wishing you happy reading,

Cheerfully,
Jeanne Savery

PS: I love to hear from my readers and can be reached by e-mail at JeanneSavery@earthlink.net or by snail mail at P.O. Box 833, Greenacres, Washington, 99016. (Include a self-addressed stamped envelope for a reply, please.)